Love Finds You™
in
Glacier Bay
Alaska

DATE DUE

Love Finds You™
in
Glacier Bay
Alaska

Tricia Goyer
Ocieanna Fleiss

summerside
PRESS™

Summerside Press™
Minneapolis, MN 55378
www.summersidepress.com

Love Finds You in Glacier Bay, Alaska
© 2013 by Tricia Goyer and Ocieanna Fleiss

ISBN 978-1-60936-569-1

Scripture references are from the following sources: The Holy Bible, King James Version (KJV). The Holy Bible, New International Version®, NIV® Copyright © 1973, 1978, 1984 by Biblica, Inc.® Used by permission. All rights reserved worldwide.

The town depicted in this book is a real place. References to actual people or events are either coincidental or are used with permission.

Cover design by Koechel Peterson & Associates | www.koechelpeterson.com
Interior design by Müllerhaus Publishing Group | www.mullerhaus.net

Photos of Glacier Bay provided by the authors.

Author photos of Tricia Goyer and Ocieanna Fleiss © 2010 by Jessica McCollam | Jessica's Visions Photography.

Published in association with the Books & Such Literary Agency, Janet Kobobel Grant, 52 Mission Circle, Suite 122, PMB 170, Santa Rosa, CA 95409-5370, www.booksandsuch.biz.

Summerside Press™ is an inspirational publisher offering fresh, irresistible books to uplift the heart and engage the mind.

Printed in USA.

Dedication

....

To Lee and Linda Parker, the Gustavus Historical Archives and
Antiquities, and the wonderful people of Glacier Bay. The beauty
of the history is reflected in the open arms of the people.

Acknowledgments

....

This is the book I almost didn't get to write. During the writing journey, I was hit by an unforeseen crisis—I had a cardiac arrest. My heart stopped beating, twice, and my family didn't know if their wife and mom would ever come home. How fitting that the family in this book lost their mother, just like my family almost lost me. I have a heart full of thanks for all who helped me during that time, but here, it's most appropriate to thank Summerside Press, my agent, Janet Grant, and my coauthor and friend, Tricia, for their patience with my recovery as we researched and wrote this book.

I'd also like to thank my very special support team: my husband, Michael, and four children, who support me with their prayers, hugs, and love. I am also always most grateful for my McCritters, Annette Irby, Dawn Kinzer, and Veronica McCann for their support and critiques. My church and homeschooling families constantly bless me with their excitement and enthusiasm for each step I take as an author.

My deepest thanks go to the amazing staff at Summerside, including Jason Rovenstine and the best editor in the world, Rachel Meisel, for this awesome opportunity.

Most of all, I thank my Lord Jesus, the rock on which I stand.

—*Ocieanna Fleiss*

When I first heard about Ocieanna's cardiac arrest, two thoughts ran through my mind. First: *Lord, save her for her family.* Second: *Lord, I can't write* Glacier Bay *without her.* This is a story we dreamed up together. I knew it was one we had to write together. I'm so glad we could!

Thank you to Amy Lathrop and the Litfuse hens for being the best assistants anyone can have. Many people ask how I do it all. Thankfully, with you on my team, I don't have to do it all!

Like Ocieanna, I give kudos to the Summerside team. Rachel Meisel, you're the best, and Jason Rovenstine, you're one of the coolest guys on the planet. And thanks to all you who work behind the scenes—the managers, designers, copy editors, sales people, financial folks, and everyone else who makes a book possible!

I'm also thankful for my agent, Janet Grant. Your wisdom and guidance have made all the difference.

And I'm thankful for my family at home. John, I'm so thankful for a husband who believes in me and cheers me on. Cory, Katie, and Clayton—living far from you is hard, but I'm so proud of your family! Leslie, I love your heart for God and the way you like to share God's good news with others. Nathan, keep writing and trust God's plan for you. Alyssa, what a bundle of joy you are! Every day is brighter since God brought you into our lives! Grandma Dolores, I know not many people have the chance to spend so much time with their favorite grandparent. Thank you. And to the rest of my family, I appreciate each of you! I'm so thankful you're in my life. God gave me the gift of you!

—*Tricia Goyer*

God is our refuge and strength,

an ever-present help in trouble.

Therefore we will not fear, though the earth give way

and the mountains fall into the heart of the sea,

though its waters roar and foam

and the mountains quake with their surging.

PSALM 46:1–3 NIV

Glacier Bay, Alaska

THE STORY OF GUSTAVUS/STRAWBERRY POINT STARTED WITH THREE newlywed couples. They'd met an old steamship captain who told them about a beautiful land at the edge of an iceberg-laden bay surrounded by snow-covered mountains. Before they arrived, the native Tlingit people and others used the area for fishing, berry picking, and other similar uses.

The three couples arrived in June of 1914 and discovered wild strawberries growing across the flats. They journeyed across Icy Passage and up the Salmon River, where they found a nice spot to set up their tents. There were no roads, bridges, docks. There was only land and the wild animals that roamed it. The settlers worked hard and enjoyed each other's company. In 1917, more families arrived, including Abraham Lincoln Park, grandfather of Lee Parker. Lee and his wife, Linda, are an active part of the Gustavus Historical Archives and Antiquities.

In 1925, Strawberry Point was renamed Gustavus after a Glacier Bay landmark, Point Gustavus. This new post office served the seventeen settlers who called the place home. Thirteen of these families had patented their homestead before 1939. After that, President Roosevelt enlarged the Glacier Bay Monument boundaries and took possession of all unpatented Gustavus lands. This landlocked the pioneers and halted all development. Thanks to a letter-writing campaign led by Charles Parker, homesteading was restored in 1955, and nineteen thousand acres were released back to Gustavus. As a result, more settlers were allowed to homestead, and the area grew.

Canneries across Icy Strait provided an economic base for the settlers. Strawberries, root crops, and beef helped the residents to prosper. A sawmill was opened, and commercial mines started operation. In 1942 the threat of invasion by the Japanese provided the impetus for the US government to open a first-class airport. In 1956 the first road was built to Bartlett Cove to cover the "Gateway" to Glacier Bay, and tourists began to arrive.

Today, Gustavus is a remote destination getaway. The Glacier Bay Lodge is the hub of tourism, but there are also numerous inns. The only way to get to Gustavus is by plane or ferry. Those who live there are rugged and independent. Members of the community still get together and help each other. Today Gustavus has fewer than four hundred full-time residents, although thousands more visit every summer. Wild strawberries still grow, but residents have to fight the bears for them.

If you choose to vacation in Gustavus, you can get great coffee at the Fireweed Coffee and Tea House, delicious pizza at the Homeshore Café, and even rent a car from Bud. If you do, tell them that Tricia and Ocieanna sent you! Also, be sure to check out the amazing stories, photos, and facts at www.gustavushistory.org.

—Tricia Goyer and Ocieanna Fleiss

Chapter One

. . . .

Towering four-inch heels clicked on the marble floor as Ginny Marshall strode past mahogany pillars, gold-accented mirrors, and pristine white tablecloths toward music producer Danny Kingston, seated at a small table. Before him sat two objects: a yellow manila envelope and a small jewelry box. Danny never was one to beat around the bush.

An uneasy feeling danced around in Ginny's gut like the artificial twinkling lights that filled the art deco restaurant. Ever since she'd heard Danny's excited voice on her cell phone, she'd wanted to run—to escape the people, escape the traffic, escape the noise. But mostly to escape the scramble to the top.

The desire to run away made no sense. Wasn't this what she wanted—a big break in her recording career…and to be Danny Kingston's girlfriend?

Ginny touched manicured fingernails to the base of her neck, willing herself to swallow the emotion that attempted to surge upward. No, what she really wanted, a family—a place to belong—wouldn't be found in Danny's Mediterranean-style estate in Woodland Hills.

Audra, one of Ginny's foster sisters, had told her the type of home and family she wanted was a thing of fairy tales. If Ginny hadn't lived it, she would have believed Audra. Even worse than Ginny's nightmares were the sweet dreams of the simple, happy life she'd once had.

Don't ruin your night with what-ifs and a thousand prayers focused on what will never be. Ginny blew out a soft breath. On the phone he'd been adamant, so she'd done as Danny asked. She wore one of the gowns he'd had delivered to her apartment—a white, slinky halter dress she couldn't afford—and took a cab to the restaurant.

Danny rose. "Sweetheart." He stepped forward and wrapped his arms around her shoulders, kissing her forehead.

Ginny straightened her wrap, covering her bare shoulders, and stepped into his embrace. "Thank you for the dress. How did you know my size?" She softly kissed his cheek.

"I know more about you than you think, darlin'. You'd be surprised."

But not what really matters. The thought slipped in before she could stop it.

Danny didn't know that her birth mother had given her up, nor about the years she'd spent living with families who didn't love her. He didn't know about her last foster parents, Dale and Robyn, who had offered her the chance of a forever home. And he didn't know that they died when she was still a teenager, their deaths breaking her heart and robbing her of the family she'd always dreamed of and come so close to having.

He pulled back and held the chair as she sat, and then hurried around the table and did the same.

Forcing a smile, Ginny scooted in her chair.

His gaze moved from her plunging neckline to the long hair that tumbled over her shoulders. "You should have worn your hair up." Danny's hand lingered on her arm. "In fact, I can't remember you ever wearing it up."

She shrugged and forced a smile. "Didn't that reporter call the 'long beach waves' my signature style?"

He nodded, but she could tell his mind had already moved on to other things.

Two women at the next table eyed her, jealousy evident in their gazes. Months ago she wouldn't have believed she'd be here. Or that one of *People* magazine's bachelors of the year would be courting her. Or that top music studios would be doing the same.

Danny winked. "I have a little gift for you."

Norah Jones's velvety voice swirled in the air that smelled of fresh bread, basil, and bourbon. "Come away with me...." It was the song that had been playing the night Brett had proposed. Had it been three years already?

Come away with me....

Why did she think of him *now*?

They'd been sitting at the cove in La Jolla, watching the sea lions playing in the surf. Brett had pulled his iPod from his pocket and tucked the ear buds into her ears. He knew she loved the song. And she knew what he was asking.

Brett.

When she'd heard he'd flown back to Glacier Bay, Alaska, her heart had dropped like a pebble into a deep, dark pond. She couldn't blame him, though. It wasn't as if she'd given him any reason to stay. To have hope they could work things out.

Danny was saying something. She caught the end of it. "Seems as if you like it." His smile lightened her heart.

"Sorry. What were you asking?"

"You were staring off into space." He winked. "I guessed that maybe you like this song. This singer."

"Norah Jones? Yeah, she's one of my favorites." How could he not know that?

Danny reached across the table and took her hand, squeezing it. "Your voice is as beautiful as Norah's, you know."

"That's nice of you to say."

"Do you think I'm just saying it?" His grin showed a hint of dimple in his left cheek.

She tucked a strand of hair behind her ear. "Well, no." She looked down at the jewelry box, then at her bare left finger. She'd worn Brett's ring for months after he'd returned to Alaska. Finally, after her birthday had passed and he'd made no contact, she'd packed up the antique gold and diamond ring and mailed it back to him, Priority Mail.

Danny lifted the small box. *Tiffany & Co.* was emblazoned on the cover in gold script.

"A gift?" She brushed a strand of hair from her cheek. "My birthday isn't for months."

"It's to celebrate…but I'm getting ahead of myself. That's the second half of the surprise."

Danny placed the box on the palm of his hand, extending it. She took it with trembling fingers and opened it to find an exquisite necklace. A chain of small diamonds twisted in a knot, ending in two large stones. A soft gasp came from someone at the next table.

"It's…wow."

Danny leaned forward. "Do you like it?"

She trailed a finger over the chain that sparkled as if a hundred stars had been caught and linked together. "I've never seen anything so beautiful. It's amazing."

He motioned to the necklace. "Can I help you?"

Her cheeks heated. A camera flashed. In the morning, she'd see her picture on some celebrity gossip blog, with rumors circulating about Danny Kingston's new girl. He was Hollywood's ladies' man, and for this moment Ginny was glad to be that woman. Danny's woman. Or was she?

Ginny's chest grew heavy, as if the air she breathed was also filled with diamonds. The pain pinched, viselike. Her fingers tightened around the box. Norah's voice trailed off.

Their waitress pretended to rearrange a perfectly set table but was most likely gathering information to spill to the tabloids.

"It's beautiful, Danny, but I don't understand…."

If she accepted it, what would he expect? More than she wanted to offer? A man like Danny was used to getting what he wanted.

"Like I said, we're celebrating." He patted the envelope. "I was going to wait until dessert, but here I am spilling the news and we haven't even ordered." His laughter filled the air, and her tension eased. Being around Danny pushed the *what-ifs* and *what-nows* out of her mind.

He slid the envelope toward her.

"It's the new contract?"

Danny nodded. "Inside is something most artists only dream of. Your last contract was fine. Your last album sold well." He smiled. "But this label wants you, and they're putting all their resources behind it. Adele, move over. Colbie Caillat…well, she's about to be upstaged." Danny focused his eyes and leaned in closer. "People have heard about you, Ginny, but with this contract you'll be *known*."

His words filled a chasm in her heart that had been there as long as she could remember, giving her a lifeline of hope. At the same time, the necklace seemed like a lasso, ready to capture her, control her.

Ginny lifted the envelope, hefting its weight. *Promises.* Both the necklace and the contract. The only problem was that over the last few days all she'd been able to think about was Brett and the promise broken. About their hopes, which she'd dashed when success in LA glimmered like a jewel in a velvet box.

Danny straightened his silk tie, waiting for her response. "I've never seen you speechless."

She placed the envelope and the necklace on the table. "I'm sorry. It's all happening so fast. I need time to think."

"Of course, sweetheart." His hands reached for hers, holding them tight. "If you want me to explain the money, the terms…"

"It's not that." She pulled her hands away. Why had she come out in public wearing something so revealing? She readjusted her wrap and scooted her chair back, giving herself space to breathe. The restaurant pressed in, crowding her. What she wouldn't give for space.

"A while ago I, uh, promised a friend I'd visit Alaska. I need some fresh air. Time to breathe."

Danny's gaze narrowed. "Are you serious?"

She bit her lip and nodded.

"But I booked the studio for next week." His words came out forced, tight. "Do you know how hard it is to get a slot on such short notice? Publicity photos are scheduled for tomorrow, and a press release is prepped to go out. Ginny, this isn't your college choir. It's the real thing, babe."

"I know." She pressed her fingertips to her temple. "It's what I've always wanted—what you've been working so hard for, but if I sign this, I'll belong to them—to the studio."

And to you...

"And there's a problem?" His words were harsher now.

"I want to be a hit, to share my music. But first...I need space to think. And I need some closure in my old life." She leaned forward, placing her hand back in his. "Can you give me a week? One week?"

Danny's smile returned, but a wall now stood behind his gaze.

"Of course." His voice softened to a purr. He pulled her hand to his lips, kissing her fingertips. "Everything is happening fast. But take this contract. Look it over. Dream."

"Thank you." The words made barely a sound as they escaped her lips.

"And this." Danny stood, took the necklace from the box, and walked behind her chair.

Ginny pulled her wrap higher around her shoulders. Before she could protest, Danny brushed her hair aside and draped the necklace around her neck. It lay cool against her skin.

Danny cleared his throat. "This is to remind you what's waiting here for you. Who's waiting."

Chapter Two
....

Ginny walked down the departure steps of the commercial airplane and paused on the bottom metal step, peering out at the tarmac. She cocked an eyebrow as she glanced at the small building in front of her. It looked like a gas station without the pumps. Bicycles were lined up by the back door. Could this be the right airport? Surely it wasn't.

"Miss?" A man behind her cleared his throat.

"I'm sorry, sir." She cleared the last step and then moved to the side. A man in khakis and a faded blue knit sweater slung a gray duffel over his shoulder as he followed her gaze.

"I think I got off at the wrong stop," she muttered, glancing back up the steps and waving a hand to get the attention of the stewardess. "I'm going to Juneau. That's where I transfer."

"This is Juneau, miss." A businessman exited next, pointing. It was only then Ginny noticed the painted sign. WELCOME TO JUNEAU, ALASKA.

"But it's the capital city...." she said to no one in particular. "It looks more like a pit stop on the way to the North Pole."

"A pit stop?" The man in the sweater chuckled as he stepped away. "It's the most civilized place you'll see for hundreds of miles. Welcome to Alaska."

"Uh, thanks." The uncertainty that had trailed her all the way from LA now nipped at her heels. No time to worry about that now. She had only thirty minutes to get to her next plane.

She hurried into the building, carrying her guitar case in one hand

and her laptop bag in the other. Inside she looked around for an airport terminal map but discovered it wasn't needed. There was no way she'd get lost. She had friends with closets bigger than this place.

Two rows of plastic chairs and three vending machines welcomed her. Just ahead a young woman who looked as if she was still in high school waved.

"You Virginia?"

Ginny looked over her shoulder, but only the businessman stood behind her.

When she turned back, the young woman waved her forward. "Virginia Marshall, right? You're heading to Glacier Bay?"

She nodded slowly. "Yes, how did you know?" Ginny brushed a strand of long blond hair over her shoulder. "Did you see me on the *Today* show?"

Laughter spilled from the woman's mouth. "That's a good one. I've never heard that one before."

Ginny's smile dropped. Out of habit she peered around, scanning the area for paparazzi. When she was with Danny, she couldn't go anywhere without being photographed. Here, no one glanced her direction, let alone pointed a camera at her.

"To answer your question, you're the only female of the right age coming in from Seattle," the woman said. "And if you're looking for Fjord Air, we're right here." The agent patted the counter behind her. "I'll need to see your ID and weigh your things." She reached for the guitar.

Ginny's fingers tightened around the handle of her guitar case. "Oh, this isn't going into cargo."

An older man strode over from the vending machine wearing a khaki shirt and grease-stained jeans. "It'll be tucked away behind my cargo net. It's a small plane, you see." The man, whom she now realized was the pilot, winked. "I promise to keep it safe."

The pilot looked like Clint Eastwood in his younger years but walked with the swagger of John Wayne. A pain pinched Ginny's heart when she thought of the afternoons she'd spent shoulder-to-shoulder with her last foster dad, Dale, watching old Westerns. Not that the movies were that great. It was the closeness with her soon-to-be forever dad that she'd enjoyed the most. Something she'd never before felt.

"It's a small plane, but it gets the job done," the man continued.

Ginny turned her attention to the tarmac.

A small plane? That was an understatement. Except for the wings, the airplane was about the same size as her neighbor's Cadillac. "That? That's our plane?" she gasped. "How many people does that thing hold?"

"Ten…depending on how heavy everyone is." The wiry man wrinkled his forehead. "Just so you won't be surprised, she's going to ask for your weight next."

Ginny glanced at the counter agent, sure they were joking. That tin box couldn't be their plane. It looked like something that would take outfitters into the Alaskan tundra. Knots tightened in her stomach. *Where am I? What have I done?*

And was he serious about needing her weight? Numb, she leaned close and spoke so only the young woman would hear. Then she handed over her guitar and computer case and hurried to one of the plastic chairs. Her knees trembled as she sat, and the logical side of her brain begged her to march over to the larger Alaska Airlines ticket counter, buy a ticket back to LA, and start her future with both FLT Records and Danny. How could she even think of turning her back on something as wonderful as that?

She adjusted the collar on her shirt, then ran her fingers through her hair and pulled it over her shoulder, braiding it with quick motions. She hadn't heard from Brett in almost two years. The last time she saw him was in her rearview mirror as she drove away with all the things from her apartment, including a box of unsent wedding invitations.

On the drive to LA, she'd thought about her favorite movie growing up, *The Parent Trap 2.* Just when she'd thought there was no hope for the mom and dad in the movie to get together, and dreaded that Hallie and Annie would be living apart once again, Dad and Annie took a super-fast plane and beat the others back to London. The perfect ending.

On the drive to LA, Ginny had been sure Brett was going to do that. That he'd find a way to get there before she did and be waiting for her at the studio.

But she'd been wrong. Life would never be like the movies. Happily-ever-after didn't just happen. One had to work for it, strive for it, lest everything worth living for be snatched away.

After moving into her new apartment in Brentwood, she learned from a mutual friend that Brett hadn't lasted two days in Newport without her. He'd sold most of his things and headed back to Alaska. He never did come for her, and now…now she was the one pursuing him.

I'm a fool.

Yet her feet wouldn't move. She couldn't turn back now. She'd come this far. Something inside told her she had to look into Brett's face. She needed to talk to someone who knew her—really knew her—and ask if signing this contract was the right thing. She had no hopes their romance would be rekindled. It was too much to ask. Besides, she had Danny.

"Miss?"

Ginny glanced up.

The pilot pointed to the plane. "Ready for the ride?"

"Yes." She rose and followed him. Four others followed too, chatting easily among themselves.

"It's a beautiful day. There isn't a cloud in the sky," the pilot said as they exited. "That's an unusual thing in these parts. I even saw some orcas in the bay when I was flying in."

"Whales?" Her eyes widened.

The man nodded and led the way. Others were already climbing the five steps into the plane. She followed them, sat, and buckled her seat belt. When she was settled in and the side door was closed, the pilot turned in his seat, looking back at them. He launched into the safety speech, pointing out the life jackets, exits, and fire extinguisher.

"This your first time to Glacier Bay?" a woman who looked to be about Ginny's age asked. Her hair was long, like Ginny's, and braided down her back in a silky black braid.

"Yes, can you tell?"

"Well, since there are only about four hundred people in Gustavus, new folks sort of stick out. But it's a beautiful flight. We fly right through two mountain passes. I'm Karen, by the way."

Before Ginny had a chance to introduce herself, the plane started up with a shudder and a roar. They lifted off the ground. Bubbles bounced in Ginny's stomach, and she couldn't help but smile as the plane glided over a large bay. Huge houses lined the shore. If Danny were to see this, he'd already be on his phone talking to a Realtor and asking for showings. Danny collected houses like most people purchased shoes.

She pulled her camera out of her jacket pocket and couldn't snap photos quickly enough. The ocean stretched in all directions. Mountain peaks—bright green with pine trees—jutted into the blue sky. Like a small bumblebee passing between two green-horned rhinos, the plane buzzed between the peaks.

The man ahead of her pivoted in his seat. "Over there is where Alaska flight 1866 crashed in 1971."

"Did anyone get hurt?"

"All 111 people on board were killed. It's something folks around here won't forget."

She brought her fingers to her lips and leaned closer to the window to view the spot. It looked lush and green like the rest of the hillside. Not one scar gave evidence of the tragedy.

"That's unbelievable. So sad." She tried to think of the families of those lost, but even the sadness of the news couldn't quell her mood. There was a big difference between hearing of pain and walking through it. As much as she wanted to ache for those who lost loved ones, it was easier to appreciate the beautiful day and scenery. More than that, she'd soon be looking into the face of an old friend.

Ginny pressed her forehead against the glass and gazed down into the waters that stretched in every direction. Was it true she might actually see a whale? She jumped as she spotted motion but then saw that it was only the white crest of a wave rising and falling.

Ahead of them huge mountains spread across the horizon, white-peaked and pointed like a queen's crown. Excitement bubbled in her chest. How many times had Brett talked about the small community he'd come from?

"So what do you like most about Glacier Bay?" she dared to ask Karen.

The woman looked back over her shoulder and offered a wistful sigh. "Might be the only place in the country where the newspaper uses only first names in its reports and everyone still knows who they're talking about. I've lived in Juneau for six years now, and I miss that."

"Heading home to see your folks?" a gray-haired man seated in front of Ginny asked Karen from across the aisle.

"Yes. It's my parents' thirtieth anniversary. All the kids are coming back."

"Thirty years." Ginny leaned forward. "You don't hear much of that anymore."

TRICIA GOYER & OCIEANNA FLEISS

"Theirs is a great love story for sure. Dad came to Glacier Bay to work on the airstrip they were putting in. Mom was one of the local girls. They fell in love, and he never left."

Ginny put on a smile, but deep down her heart ached. "That's so sweet." Growing up, the ache had been more prominent than now. Or maybe she had learned to ignore it. What would it be like to have parents who'd been married for thirty years? She hadn't a clue.

Unwelcome memories came to mind of other mothers bringing cupcakes into school on birthdays. Of fathers milling around on Dads and Donuts Friday. She'd never liked Fridays. That stupid tradition of her school's was the reason why. The kids who had dads got to go to the cafeteria and eat donuts with their fathers. The others, like her—well, it was obvious they were the losers.

"So are you visiting someone in Glacier Bay or is it vacation?" Karen's words interrupted Ginny's thoughts.

"I'm, uh…" Ginny blew out a breath. "I'm visiting an old friend. Brett Miller."

"Brett!" The man ahead of her pivoted toward her. "So you know Brett? He's a great guy." He leaned forward, motioning to the pilot. "Did you hear that, Neil? This girl knows Brett."

"Brett? Really?" The pilot looked over his shoulder briefly. "I went to school with Brett."

"Everyone knows Brett." Karen fiddled with the ends of her braid. "He teaches adult Sunday school at Gustavus Community Church. I always enjoy going when I'm in town."

Ginny noticed the tinge of pink in the woman's cheeks.

She looked back at Ginny again, and her eyes narrowed. "Wait, what did you say your name was again?"

"I didn't, sorry. It's Ginny. Ginny Marshall."

The woman turned back toward the front of the airplane. Her jaw twitched and tightened. The others turned forward too, each gazing down at the ocean inlet as if they were seeing it for the first time.

Ginny's fingers wrapped around her seat belt, and her thumbnail clicked on the metal buckle. She should have figured this. If the town was small enough for the newspaper to print only first names, then of course they'd know about one of their own being dumped just before the wedding invitations were sent out.

Ginny sank lower in her seat. She hadn't set foot in the town, and she was already an outcast.

"What am I doing here?" she muttered under her breath, pretending to search the ocean waves for whales. *How could a girl like me be welcomed in a place like this?*

Some scars weren't visible, but the pain was the same. She should have remembered that. Remembered that when tragedy hit, the ripples went far, as each absorbed a small part into itself.

Maybe she didn't remember because for so long she'd carried her own pain alone. She'd shared it with only one person. Sometimes she wished she hadn't. Instead of allowing her to wallow in her grief and self-pity, Brett had encouraged her to take it to God, trust Him, ask Jesus to turn her mess into a message she could share with others. Easier said than done.

It was one of the reasons she'd gotten into that car and driven away from his love. From their future. She couldn't put on a mask in front of Brett. Maybe that was why she liked performing. She strode on stage a new woman—one people respected, applauded.

Ginny's hands gripped the armrest of the airplane seat, and she released a low breath. She thought she wanted the mask and a future that didn't hinge on her past. But if that was the case, what was she doing here? Why had she come to Glacier Bay?

Chapter Three

....

Brett's legs stretched out before him as he paddled the kayak toward Margerie Glacier, one of his favorite spots in Glacier Bay. Gliding over the waterline, he felt as comfortable here as he did waking up in his bed back home. The life vest captured the pounding of his heartbeat, which quickened as he approached the tidewater face of Margerie Glacier.

The brilliant blue reminded him of Ginny's eyes. That was the first thing he'd noticed when she'd glanced at him from across the table at the college Bible study. Both the brilliant blue and the sadness were hard to miss. Over the months and years that followed, he learned a lot about her painful childhood growing up in the foster care system. He had thought his love would be enough to unlock her heart and to help her chip away at the walls she'd built, brick by brick, pain by pain. He'd been wrong. It hadn't been enough. *He* hadn't been enough.

He rested his paddles and stared up at the blue ice towering over him like the spires on Cinderella's castle. Around him chunks of ice that had escaped the twenty-one-mile tidewater glacier bobbed in the water, crowding his kayak at times.

The sound of his partner's paddle grew louder, and Mitch slid up beside him.

"Ready to go back?"

"Not really." Brett blew out a foggy breath. Clouds gathered, and he guessed a light rain would greet them at their pickup spot. Brett spotted their ride, a boat from Glacier Bay Lodge, bobbing farther down the bay and heading their direction. It would arrive soon. It always excited the tourists when a kayaker hitchhiked back to the lodge with them.

The men and women on the small bay cruise—who paid to view the Alaskan wilderness from behind the glass of a heated boat while sipping clam chowder—always looked at him in awe. As did those on the nearby cruise ship. How many people watched his progress through the water from decks high above?

Brett turned slightly and glanced over his shoulder, taking in the sight of the cruise ship that filled most of the horizon. The ships were a constant presence near the glaciers; one or two at a time would pause to appreciate the views.

After living here all his life, Brett had learned that there were two types of people who visited Glacier Bay: those who took the beauty home with them in digital images, usually taken from the decks of ships, and those who walked along the shores, hiked among the pines, and glided close over the waters.

And there were two types of people who lived in Gustavus: those who had summer cottages and got their "fix" of the wilderness before heading back to the city, and those who didn't worry about having a fancy—or even a finished—house but who respected the land and water and learned to live in harmony with it, as the Tlingit Indians who'd come before them. After attending college in California for a while, Brett understood both types.

Overhead, a pair of kittiwakes rode on the air currents and called to each other with a dialect all their own. Near the far end of the glacier, a harbor seal rose and dipped, playing hide-and-seek with the visitors.

"Are you saying you're not heading back tonight?" There was no hint of surprise in Mitch's voice. Out in the wilderness, time didn't matter as it did back home, and Brett couldn't face the mounting responsibilities that waited. Was it selfish to want to stay out another day?

"I'm getting to the place where my mind is clearing of the clutter.

Seems like I've been hearing God's voice more in the past week than in years. Maybe because I'm finally taking time to listen."

Mitch nodded, pointing to a horned puffin swimming past. "When there are many voices, it's hard to tune in to the One you should focus on first."

"Ain't that the truth." Brett wiggled his feet against the pedals connected to the thin cables that controlled the rudder. When he pushed on the left pedal, the kayak went left. When he pushed on the right, it went that direction. Kayaking was easy; he knew how to maneuver to get where he wanted to go. *Wish life would work that way.*

He thought about his gear packed in plastic garbage bags and stuffed into compartments forward and aft. *Should have enough food to last another day.*

"Why don't you stay?" Mitch said. "Camp out for a few days. I have food I can leave with you."

A few days?

Brett shook his head. "My grandma needs me. I haven't been around much to check on things at the house. And some of the folks from church want me to make a run into Juneau for supplies."

Ice cracked around him, and even though the glacier appeared still, he knew it was in a constant state of motion. The little changes mattered enough to build up to a big shift. Nearly every time he was out, a chunk of ice broke free and slid into the clear blue water.

"There's food at the mercantile and Toshco. I can stop in on your grandma too." Mitch chuckled. "Glacier Bay survived without you for a few years when you were gone at that fancy college, buddy."

Come to Me. The words played through Brett's mind. Even though he'd played the guitar for years, he'd written only a few songs. One of them was a worship melody he'd penned with Ginny during their first month of dating.

Come to Me, and you will find rest. Find peace. Find hope. Find home.

She had been in his thoughts all day. This morning, as he stood on the shore of the bay looking out past the green islands and safe harbor, he sensed she was standing next to him. He'd even turned once, expecting to see her long blond hair blowing in the wind. Expecting to see her smile. How foolish. Last he'd heard from Lori the librarian—who kept up on all the entertainment news—Ginny had performed at George Clooney's birthday party. But that had been months ago.

"So you gonna take me up on the offer?" Mitch asked. "I'll float down, catch the tour boat, and tell them you'll be ready for pickup on Thursday."

"Today's Monday. If I wait until Thursday…"

Mitch raised an eyebrow.

Brett released a breath. "I suppose everyone around town can survive without me until then. With your extra food and the salmon heading up the creeks, I'll be good." He chuckled. "I might have to fight a bear to get some fish, but that's another story."

Brett tucked the food Mitch had given him down by his feet. He knew he was making the right decision, yet as he watched his friend's kayak glide farther away, defeat washed over him. He had to face the truth. He liked being needed.

Right now he needed to stay put, even though he didn't exactly know why. But he'd learned not to ignore these feelings.

Once before, when he'd been at college, he hadn't been able to get his grandpa off his mind. He'd told himself at least a dozen times to call him, but he hadn't. A week later he got the news that Grandpa had passed away in his sleep. Yet the feeling Brett was getting now wasn't that he needed to get back and call Ginny. It was the opposite. He needed to stay up here, where he felt closest to God, and pray. Really pray.

Chapter Four
....

The small plane landed on the airstrip, and the pilot ushered Ginny and the other passengers to the far side of a chain-link fence to wait for their things. He followed with her guitar and computer case and then hurried back to unload the rest of the items. The sun was bright but the air nippy. Summer was still in full force back in LA, but fall came early up here. With the gold on the trees and crispness in the air, autumn had already shoved its way in.

"You Ginny?" a man asked, striding up to her. He wore a gray shirt and hat that both read GLACIER BAY LODGE. Above the logo he wore a pin that read MIKE.

"Yes, that's me." She reached out and shook Mike's hand and then watched as he hurried to get the rest of her things. Heat rose to her cheeks when he snagged the two hot-pink suitcases. No need to ask which belonged to her.

The other passengers were greeted by family members. Some climbed into parked cars and drove away. She guessed she was the only one getting a shuttle to the lodge.

Ginny bit her lip. All of her clothes wore designer labels, and most of the shoes she'd brought cost more than the trucks in this parking lot. Why hadn't she thought about trying harder to fit in? Maybe she could find a store around here and get more casual clothes.

They loaded up, and Ginny climbed into the passenger's seat of the large white van. She started to put on her seat belt, but the driver's hand motioned her to stop. "You can wear that, but you really don't need to. The speed limit here is twenty-five miles an hour, and there's only ten miles of road."

She chuckled. "Oh yes, I forgot."

"So you've been here before?" Mike asked as he pulled out of the gravel parking lot.

"No, but I feel as if I have. I've heard so much about it from Brett." Ginny said his name so naturally that she surprised herself, as if being here erased all the pain of the last two years.

"Brett Miller?" The driver glanced her direction. "What a great guy. He helped me roof my garage. I'd been in town only two days, and he showed up with a ladder and hammer, ready to go. Won't find someone like him every day."

Ginny nodded. Wasn't that the truth. She looked around through the forests of pines on either side of the road, noticing the small houses tucked into the woods. "So does he live around here?"

"Well, back a ways. You turn right after the bridge. But his grandma lives just up a bit. You'll see her house about a half mile down on the right. We can stop there first, if you'd like. She could tell you if Brett is back."

"Back?"

"Didn't you know? He's out on a kayaking trip. From what I heard, him and Mitch should be heading home tonight."

"Do you always know the whereabouts of everyone in town?" She tucked her hands into the pockets of her fitted tweed jacket.

"Just about."

Laughter burst from her lips. His honesty surprised her.

"I drive back and forth from the lodge all day. I'm always stopping by Homeshore Café or Fireweed. Bound to talk to folks and find out who's up to what."

Ginny nodded and glanced out the window. What should she

do now? She hadn't considered Brett not being here. How foolish... to think he'd be sitting around waiting for her to show up.

Mike slowed the van. He glanced over at her, waiting for an answer.

Did she want to stop? She'd talked to his grandma a few times over the phone. What if he wasn't coming back today after all? What would she do then? One day was already lost getting here. How long would she wait around...for nothing?

"Well, it's hard to keep secrets, that's for sure." Mike filled in the silence as he slowed the van to a near stop. "I just heard someone at Toshco—our local warehouse store—saying that Brett was supposed to fly them to Juneau sometime in the next few days."

Ginny smiled. Brett had gotten his license to fly after all—something he'd always talked about. What else had changed? There was only one way to find out.

"Yes, I'd like to stop." She straightened in her seat. "Can you give me five minutes?"

"I can give you thirty if you'd like. I'm supposed to go back and pick up some guests from Homeshore Café. I'll swing back by on the way."

"Perfect." She fingered her guitar case. "But, uh...my things."

"Don't worry, just leave them in the van. I'll watch over them. There isn't much crime in these parts, miss. If something goes missing, we know who'd done it—and because of that, people tend to leave others' things alone."

"It's a different type of place," she said as they pulled onto a long dirt road.

"That's an understatement, but one thing's for sure. This place tends to get under your skin. I couldn't imagine not living here."

Ginny smiled, but her mind was focused on something else. What if Brett's grandma hated her too? After all, she'd hurt the woman's grandson. And she'd sent back the family ring, with its large diamond surrounded by little ones on a simple band, without so much as a note.

As the van pulled to a stop beside a small cottage that overlooked the sandy shore of the waterway, Ginny put her hand on the car door handle.

There was only one way to find out.

* * * * *

The van roared away before Ginny had mounted the front steps. The ocean breeze swirled around her and she breathed deeply, willing herself calm. After all, nothing about this place looked threatening.

The cottage was made of logs. White curtains framed the windows and the glass-paned front door. An old rocker sat near a wooden porch swing. Ginny smiled, imagining Brett and his grandma deep in conversation as they looked out onto the water.

She lifted a quivering hand and knocked. A shuffling could be heard inside. And then she saw the bobbing, white-topped head of an old woman walking to the door.

The woman glanced through the glass panes, and though curiosity filled her gaze, her smile didn't fade.

Ginny stepped back and allowed her to open the front screen door. "Hello…"

"Mrs. Miller?"

"Yes, that's me. Can I help you?"

"Ma'am." She folded her arms over her chest and lowered her chin. "I'm looking for Brett. I heard he's not here, but I was hoping—"

"Virginia!" Her name rang out, and color rose to the woman's cheeks. "Is that you? My girl, come in, come in! I've only seen photos, but I'd recognize you anywhere. Someone as beautiful as you with that lovely hair…and eyes. Oh yes, so blue."

Ginny raised her eyebrows in surprise, and her lips fell open. "Most people call me Ginny."

The older woman motioned her inside. "I'm Ethel. Most folks call me Ethel"—her eyes lit up, as if sparked by a fond memory—"but you can call me Grandma. Brett didn't tell me you were coming. Probably worried I'd tell Dove Fowler. News spouts from her lips like spray from a whale—not that you heard that from me."

"Yes, well, he doesn't know. I—"

"Come sit." Grandma Ethel plopped on the floral sofa and patted the cushion beside her. "Tell me what's happening with you. Lori from the library said you had the loveliest dress for that concert you did for those tornado victims. I hope you brought your guitar. I'd love to hear some of your newest songs."

Ginny stepped into the cabin, the old woman's words punctuating each step. She glanced around at the paneled walls and shiny wood floor. Lovely. So homey and welcoming.

To the right, the kitchen had white cabinets that looked homemade. A heart-shaped dish with cat food sat on the kitchen floor next to a silver water bowl. The cat was nowhere to be seen, but Ginny pictured it curled on the colorful rug in front of the wood stove.

A stack of red-and-white-checkered towels sat next to an old washtub, looking like a spread from Martha Stewart's magazine. The place was warm and inviting, and so was Grandma. Surely the woman didn't understand—*really* understand—what had happened between her and Brett.

"Ethel—I mean, Grandma." She rested her hand on the back of a curved-back dining room chair. "You know who I am, right? Brett and I used to be engaged?"

Grandma's lips pursed tight, and she adjusted her glasses on her nose. "Of course, dear. But I'm not surprised you're here. You see, I've been praying—praying you'd come. My friend Dove Fowler has been too. Prayers pour from her lips even more than gossip…and if you know Dove, that's saying something."

Chapter Five

. . . .

By the time Mike, the shuttle driver, showed up thirty minutes later, Grandma Ethel had already taken sheets and blankets from her linen closet and set them on her trunk by the couch.

"No use you paying good money for those old rooms at the lodge, dear. They haven't been upgraded in fifty years. I have to say my place is much more comfortable. Don't you like the view?" She waved a hand toward the waterway, and Ginny sucked in a breath as a bald eagle made slow circles over the water. Then she looked at Mike, who waited patiently by the door.

"It's a lovely spot"—Ginny nodded—"and I appreciate your invitation, but the website said my payment was nonrefundable."

"Posh." Grandma Ethel waved her hand in the air. "I went to elementary school with Dorothy, and her daughter manages the place. I'll call her up later and explain."

With a nod, Mike unloaded Ginny's things and headed off. As Ginny moved her suitcases to the corner of the room, excitement bubbled within her. She was really here, and Grandma welcomed her with open arms. Maybe things with Brett wouldn't be so bad. The women had been praying, right? A warm glow filled her.

For three hours, Grandma chattered on like a canary in the pet store, telling Ginny about everyone in Gustavus and where they lived. Not that it helped. Not knowing the people or the layout of the area made it impossible to keep track of what Grandma was saying.

And as evening faded into a long sunset, the sky glowing with Alaska's "midnight sun," Ginny's inner glow faded.

"Want something to eat, dear?" Grandma asked, suddenly realizing the time.

Grandma looked nervously out the window, eyeing the dirt road. Then in near silence they nibbled on bologna sandwiches for dinner.

"I don't understand it," Grandma Ethel said between bites. "Brett said he was going to be coming back today. That boy always keeps his word. More than anyone I know, when Brett says somethin', he means it."

Ginny nodded. She didn't need to be reminded. If Brett was anything, he was honest, trustworthy. How could she have forgotten that? Being in Glacier Bay and hearing everyone talk so highly of him reminded her of what she'd walked away from.

Ginny dabbed the corner of her lip with her napkin. "Maybe he's on his way." She tried to sound hopeful.

"Dear, that's kind of you to try to ease my worries, but it only takes ten minutes to drive from one end of Gustavus to the other. He—" Grandma Ethel's words were interrupted by the sound of a car engine. Ginny glanced out the window. Headlights moved down the driveway.

Her heart doubled and filled her throat, her mind flooding with a thousand things she wanted to say. Had he heard her music? Did he realize that she'd written most of her songs about him—even when she'd tried not to? She wanted to tell him she missed their long talks over coffee and that she hadn't had a good belly laugh since the last time they'd played Frisbee on the beach.

As the truck parked, her hands trembled—and her lower lip too.

"It's him." She stood and moved away from the window, hurrying toward the small woodstove, suddenly worried about how he'd respond when he saw her.

"No." Grandma shook her head. Her face clouded with disappointment. "That's the headlights of a Ford." The old woman rose and walked to the front door with quickened steps.

Grandma continued talking, but Ginny couldn't focus on her words. *What if something happened to Brett?*

"What if I came too late?" Her words escaped as a whisper and were drowned out by the sound of Grandma opening the front door and the growing roar of the engine as it shut off. The car door opened, and a short, stocky man stepped out. Reddish eyebrows complemented his pale skin.

"Everything all right, Mitch?" Grandma Ethel called from the doorway.

The man waved a hand. "Yes, Brett's fine. He's staying out there a couple more days. No need to worry, Ethel." He paused before her and waited to be asked in.

Grandma Ethel rubbed her forehead and then stepped to the side. He walked past her, then past Ginny as if she wasn't even there.

"A couple more days?" The old woman looked back over her shoulder and then shut the door. "There's some folks who need him to pick up an order in Juneau."

"He's aware of that." Mitch moved to the kitchen. He was older than Brett—in his midforties at least—but he walked with a quickness that surprised her. He sat at the kitchen table, grabbed a handful of chips from the bag, and then with his other hand pulled a stocking cap from his head.

"And why would he stay out?" Grandma's voice was sharper than Ginny expected. The sweet old lady was more of a pistol than Ginny had first thought.

As she watched, the man stroked down his hair. "Well, he had some thinking to do."

Grandma Ethel placed a hand on her hip. "Thinking?"

For the first time, the man dared to look at Ginny. His cheeks turned pink as he did. Then his eyes widened. "My guess is that Brett had to do some thinking about…her." He pointed.

Ginny sucked in a breath, unsure of what to do or say.

Mitch set his chips down on the tabletop, wiped his hand on his pants, and extended a hand. "Ginny, I'd assume?"

"Yes."

"Yeah, that's what I thought. Brett told me about you, but that was before."

"Before?"

"Before he came back to Glacier Bay. He hasn't said much since then."

"Oh, I see." She grabbed a handful of her hair and twisted it around her fingers. Then she leaned forward. "I came to talk to him. I should have called. I, uh, have some big life decisions to make and I thought he could help. But if he's not going to be back for days, I should probably head back to LA."

"Brett *is* a good listener." Mitch slowly ran his hands down the top of his jeans. "Isn't he, Gran—"

With a look of alarm on his face, he jumped up and rushed to the old woman standing by the sink. One of her hands was spread over her chest, and she struggled for breath.

Ginny hurried over, placing a hand on the woman's shoulder. "Are you okay? Come sit." Together they guided Grandma to the couch.

"Too much excitement, that's all." She offered a tired smile as she settled under her afghan. Ginny nestled next to her. "With you coming and the worries about Brett, it's quite a lot for a woman whose biggest excitement of the day is finishing a Sudoku puzzle. I just—"

A cat's meow interrupted the woman's words, and Mitch moved to the door to let in a black cat with short fur. It entered the house with the demeanor of a lion and glanced over at Ginny nonchalantly as if it had been expecting her.

"Maybe you should head to bed, Grandma. Rest," Mitch offered as he moseyed back to the kitchen. "I'm sure Ginny here would enjoy a quiet evening. Maybe get some reading done."

"Reading." Grandma Ethel's eyes brightened. "That's it!" She turned to Ginny and took her two hands in her own. "Maybe you're not only here to see Brett. Maybe you're here for the letters too. Yes, that *is* the case. I have a feeling, dear, there's something in them you need to understand. Something that will surprise you." Grandma clapped her hands together. "Oh my, I believe that's why Brett decided to stay out. God wooed him away for a reason. I'm sure of it."

Chapter Six

....

Before Ginny had even closed the bedroom door, she heard Grandma's breathing drift to soft snoring. "Good night, Grandma," she whispered. She plopped down on the old-fashioned floral couch and let out a breath. *When I left LA this morning, I sure didn't expect to be sleeping on an old woman's sofa tonight.*

She leaned back and gazed out the broad windows at the bay spreading before her. The clouds moved imperceptibly, opening gaps for blue sky, revealing the jagged snow-capped peaks bordering Glacier Bay. She closed her eyes, questioning the longing this beauty raised in her. *God, are You there?*

She hadn't asked that in a while. It almost seemed easier not to think about Him, not to wonder if her schemes were in line with God's plans.

Ginny released the clip from her hair, letting it fall to her shoulders, and slipped off her shoes. Grandma's cat immediately snuggled onto them.

Those are three-hundred-dollar shoes, she thought, but then that didn't seem to matter here. "Hi, kitty," she said instead and scratched behind its ears. The charm on the cat's collar read MIDNIGHT, and it purred as it rubbed against her legs. Beneath the coffee table, she spotted an old brown leather box. Lifting it to her lap, she opened it. On the inside lid was tacked a piece of thick, aged paper. On it was written "Our Story" in beautiful script. In the box were stacks of envelopes.

Midnight hopped to her side and nudged her nose against the book's cover.

"Are these what Grandma wanted me to read?"

The old woman had fallen asleep before she'd had time to explain what she'd meant about Ginny reading some letters. Ginny picked up the first one and moved her fingers over the aged paper and the indentations of the cursive writing. The return address read,

Ellie McKinley
1417 Baker Street
San Francisco, California 91002

Ginny imagined Ellie sitting at a glorious writing desk doing her "correspondence." Like Elizabeth Bennett in *Pride and Prejudice*. That was her favorite movie, one she'd watched with her last foster mom, Robyn, time and time again.

The letter was addressed to a Peter Barnett on Division Street, San Francisco.

"Hmm…a friend?" she spoke aloud, scratching Midnight's head. "Brother? Well, before we find out, I need background music and a cup of tea to set the mood."

She dropped the paper on the table and stood, but then she noticed the letter had shifted out of the envelope. The first words read:

May 2, 1928

Dear Grandfather,
    I have the most joyous news. James Standard and I are
engaged to be married! My wonderful beau proposed to me
yesterday. After our sad misfortune, I am the happiest girl in
all the world.

An aching lump filled Ginny's gut. "A love story?" She shoved the letter back into its envelope. "Sorry, Grandma. I don't think my heart can handle this tonight."

She flipped on her iPod and moved to the kitchen. The scent of fried eggs and coffee—most likely from the morning's breakfast—wafted to her as she filled the metal teakettle and placed it on the burner. Tacked to the side of the fridge was an old photo of a bride and groom gazing at each other in a sickening display of love. *It's everywhere.* She grabbed the photo and set it on top of the fridge where she couldn't see it.

From Ginny's iPod came the lyrics of a love song, something about being unable to fight love. Ginny hadn't remembered the lyrics and didn't need them mocking her now. She flipped it off. There couldn't ever be anyone like Brett, and maybe she liked things that way.

The ache in her stomach churned like the waves lapping the bay outside the window. It seemed so empty at this moment. No sea animals played on the surface, but she knew life pulsed underneath the whitecaps. A whole unseen world.

Could she allow herself to venture beneath the surface of her own heart? All the pain of her childhood, the loss of her beloved foster parents, her choice to push Brett away…

After her success in LA she'd never regretted driving away that day, at least not consciously. But at this moment, in his grandma's kitchen, she longed for something the music world couldn't give her.

She shook her head, casting away the thoughts. The teakettle whistled. As she poured hot water into a moose-decorated mug, she remembered the verse on a little plaque next to Grandma's bed: *For in the day of trouble he will keep me safe in his dwelling; he will hide me in the shelter of his tabernacle and set me high upon a rock. Psalm 27:5.*

The raspberry-flavored tea stained the steaming water dark pink, and Ginny tentatively caved in to the sofa. *Maybe a love story will be a good distraction after all. Better than being alone with my thoughts.* Midnight snuggled into her lap as she pulled the letter from the envelope and continued to read.

> *It was a simple proposal, delivered at the Davises' kitchen table. The servants had left; even Cook was taking advantage of the warm afternoon to tend her garden. With little Mercy and Ricky napping, James took advantage of the opportunity! He held my hand. "I love you, Elizabeth Sue McKinley."*
>
> *How I remember the days when James and I played from morning till suppertime. Even after bedtime, we'd light candles in our windows. If we worked it just right, we could spy each other's faces in the candlelight.*
>
> *Did you know of this? Don't scold. We were best of friends then. And later, of course, we fell in love.*
>
> *As for Mrs. Standard, I know you do not care for her, but she was always kind to me in her way. You must admit she taught me things—things about being a lady—that I would not have learned elsewhere, at least since my own dear mama's passing. James assures me his mother will come around.*
>
> *All this to say, I cannot wait to receive your congratulations in person. Early next week, I'll make my way to your lovely flat on the ocean. We'll drink tea and eat those scones you love.*
>
> *My dear grandfather, what a joy you are to me. With James and you in my life, I can honestly say I have found true happiness.*
>
> *Your Ellie Bell (Never stop calling me that. Promise?)*

"I have found true happiness." Ginny rolled her eyes as she spoke the words. "Is there such a thing?"

She placed the letter at the bottom of the stack, then noticed a newspaper article folded atop the next letter. It was dated July 1, 1927, almost a year earlier than Ellie's letter. The old type of the headline read: OIL TYCOON PETER BARNETT LOSES ALL IN REAL ESTATE DEAL GONE BAD.

"So that must be the 'sad misfortune' Ellie was talking about." The article went on to describe Mr. Barnett:

> *Throughout the course of his life, Mr. Barnett, who is now sixty-six, donated most of his great wealth to charitable causes. Even so, his skilled investments kept him and his only dependent, one Miss Elizabeth McKinley, quite comfortable— until last winter, when Mr. Barnett invested a great amount in the real estate firm belonging to his late niece's husband, Mr. Felix Cooney. The investment proved to be a poor one when Mr. Cooney was suspected of conducting an illegal property transaction. All moneys were seized by the Internal Revenue Service. No plans are being made to charge Mr. Barnett. Investigators refused to comment on Mr. Cooney's legal standing at this time.*

Ginny frowned. *So sad to lose everything*, she thought. *At least he had his granddaughter.* The last lines of the article quoted the older man:

> *"This earthly loss will only work in the Lord's hands for my good. I am happy to do whatever my heavenly Father desires."*

I count all things but loss.... A verse from Sunday school came to Ginny's mind. She'd attended Sunday school off and on as a child, depending on whom she lived with. The verse brought a measure of comfort, but knowing it wouldn't last, she shoved the feeling below the surface and sipped her tea.

The next piece of paper Ginny picked up was a newspaper clipping from *The Daily Alaskan Empire*. The headline read: MISSIONARY WOMAN LOST TO INFLUENZA IN STRAWBERRY POINT. MANY TLINGITS ALSO SICK. QUARANTINE IN EFFECT.

Underneath it was a letter in masculine script.

Sept. 17, 1927

Dear Brother Peter,

A letter has been sent to the missions board. Mail's slow here, as I expect you know. A few weeks back we had an influenza outbreak.

My precious wife was taken.

I don't know a better woman than Adelaide. She bore up under the Alaska bush, as I knew she would, with a heaping supply of determination. That woman feared nothing. Even shot a wolf one night.

My children—they're taking it hard. Linc, my fourteen-year-old nephew, has come to help. Don't know what good he is, but he tries. My sixteen-year-old son, Joseph, does what he can, but his heart's breaking too. In fact, I worry about him the most.

Pray for the little ones—Janey (although she doesn't think she's so little, nine's not grown by a long spell), Zach, and baby Penny. As heartbroken as we all are, we know our calling is here, and our Rock is the Lord.

Clay Parrish

Chapter Seven

. . . .

Ginny folded the letter and set it aside. Her heart ached. First for the Parrish children, who lost their mother, and also for this woman, Ellie, who struggled with her mother's passing. Ginny knew the hole both these families felt, knew how children without mothers never feel complete. How they struggle to feel the basic love only a mother can give. She couldn't remember a time when that emptiness wasn't in her own heart.

Ginny sipped the tea, now cold. How sad that this missionary, Clay Parrish, had come all the way out to Alaska only to lose his wife. Why would God allow something like that? *What a life for a woman.* She wondered what Grandma Ethel's life had been like when she was young, living in Alaska. Brett had told Ginny that the first settlers had come to Glacier Bay in 1914. If it was this primitive now, what would it have been like back then?

Also, where was Strawberry Point? Somewhere near Gustavus? Could the people in the letters be somehow related to Grandma Ethel? That would be cool.

Ginny flipped through the letters again. At least James stayed around for Ellie—that must be the love Grandma Ethel was talking about.

Love to stir my own romantic thoughts, no less.

Speaking of which…she'd promised Danny she'd call when she arrived. How could she have forgotten? She rushed to her purse and pulled out her cell phone. It was nearly dead, but she should be able to make a short call. Then she noticed the reception. There was none.

None.

Ginny blinked three times. *Where am I?*

Tomorrow she'd ask Grandma about a cell tower. Surely there had to be one. As a last resort she pulled out her laptop and checked for a wireless network. She wasn't surprised when she didn't pick anything up.

She thought about using Grandma Ethel's wall phone but changed her mind. Just because the sweet old woman welcomed her in didn't mean she could take over the house.

Ginny glanced over at the bedroom door and sent up a quick prayer that Grandma Ethel would feel better tomorrow. She hoped it was the excitement of the day that had gotten to her and nothing more serious.

Had Brett's grandma assumed Ginny was here to make up with Brett, rekindle things? Guilt over getting the old woman's hopes up trickled like rivulets down Ginny's back and neck, but she ignored it. She'd gotten used to ignoring such things.

Ginny couldn't pinpoint exactly when things went wrong between her and Brett. A growing numbness about the dreams she and Brett had made had collided with a growing excitement about her rising fame. It had been easy to follow the praise, the comfort, the money. Yet why did she feel emptier today than she had in a long time?

Ginny shook her head and turned her attention back to the letters. She picked up the next in the pile, one with no address, just the words "To James, from Ellie." *Most likely some kind of love letter.*

Ginny wondered how Ellie delivered it. The two soul mates probably had a secret place where they left letters for the other to find. *How romantic.* She wrinkled her nose and removed the note from the envelope, disappointed to find only one line written in dark, black ink.

James—Grandfather has suffered a stroke. I will not see you tonight. Please pray!

Ginny stared at the paper as it ruffled in the breeze, but when she looked around, she realized there was no movement of air, no window that had been left open. Rather, her own hands were trembling.

Life wasn't fair. Growing up in foster care wasn't fair. Losing the only true family she'd ever had…

"Have you heard about Ginny?" people had whispered. "How sad."

A lump grew in her throat, and she snuggled into the couch on her side. She remembered the moment when she decided to focus more on people's praise than their pity. She had been in college, and a few of her friends had talked her into singing a solo for their Uganda mission trip fundraiser. Though music had always been special to her, she'd never really shared it with others. But that night, as she poured out her heart, performing for the first time a song she had written herself, the awe of the crowd fueled her. They'd jumped to their feet in a standing ovation and wouldn't sit until she agreed to sing another song.

Ginny closed her eyes. Everything changed that night with her music. It was also the night she met Brett.

She wondered if what Mitch had said was true—that Brett still thought of her, just as she thought of him. Wondered if their story was written on his heart, just as James and Ellie's story was written in those letters.

Ginny yawned and rubbed her eyes. She needed some rest. She'd have to get up early and figure out how to return to LA. It was the only obvious choice. She couldn't sit around Grandma Ethel's house for three more days waiting for Brett to return—not when Danny was chomping at the bit to get going on her new contract.

She glanced over at her paisley computer bag. Should she pull out the paperwork he'd sent with her and look over the legalities? No, she'd rather read another letter from Ellie. But even as she pulled out a slip of thin, discolored paper, she wondered if all this was a sign—Brett being away, these letters from a woman in the distant past. Maybe it was a sign to tell her the last page was closed with Brett and she should focus on what lay ahead. Things could be worse… like they were for Ellie. Maybe she should cling to what was right and good in her life.

With another yawn, she glanced down at the script.

Let's hope for a happy ending…whatever that means.

Park Emergency Hospital

May 21, 1928

Dear Miss McKinley,

We have been informed by one Mr. Felix Cooney that your grandfather is unable to pay his medical bills. Mr. Cooney has offered to pay the first bill, but since you are legally the next of kin, we must obtain your written permission. Please come to the hospital's billing office to fill out the necessary paperwork.

All bills must be paid in a timely manner in order for the patient to remain under the care of Park Emergency Hospital.

Sincerely,

Robert H. Longman

Collections Facilitator

Ginny swallowed hard, feeling like she was reading news about one of her own friends rather than a stranger who lived nearly a century ago. How in the world would Ellie pay for her grandfather's medical bills now that they'd lost everything? Ginny balled her fists at the thought of Felix. Of course he'd help…and where would that leave Ellie? Dependent on him, on his mercies. A thousand ants crawled up her spine, remembering the shame of being so helpless, so dependent. At least Ellie had James. He would help her.

Next was a letter with no address that read "To Ellie." A man's handwriting. *Must be from James.* Ginny blew out a slow, even breath. She had a feeling deep down that James wouldn't disappoint.

May 21, 1928

Dear Ellie,

How sorry I was to hear about your grandfather's stroke. I admire his strength and business savvy. I know he means a great deal to you. I am thankful recovery seems near.

Ellie, the joyous memories we share make this letter difficult to write.

It is in my heart to marry you. It is. But your absence this week has provided me a chance to objectively consider our future. I have questions and, to be honest, doubts about our compatibility. I wonder if our rush to marry was based not on true affection but rather on familiarity and friendship. Mother is against it, as you know, because she believes you wish to marry me for my money. But her threats have not influenced me. It is because of my own doubts that I must break our engagement.

James

The guilt and frustration rooted in Ginny's heart made good soil for the anger that sprouted as she read the man's words.

"How dare you, James," she mumbled under her breath. "Of course she doesn't want to marry you for your money! How could you think so? Even I can see that."

Ginny resisted the urge to rip up the letter. She blew out a breath. This letter was from a man in the past. This James guy was long dead.

"Good thing." She put the letter back into the envelope. "Or I would have done you in myself."

Not with her hands. She was much too meek to raise a hand. No, she'd write a song about someone who didn't trust the heart of another—didn't believe her intentions could be true.

You doubt my motives, but look into my eyes. Don't see love? You're looking through shadowed glass. Sunshine's on the other side of the lens. If you'd only trust in the beauty of my delight.

The words came unexpectedly. Most of Ginny's songs happened that way. She'd tried to work with others in brainstorming sessions, as Danny suggested, but the pressure sucked the creativity out of her. Instead, words came when she least expected them. When her emotions built, they found release in melody and chorus.

Ginny put down the letters and hurried to her purse for her digital recorder, singing the words that played through her mind. There were only five lines, but it was a start.

Take that, James. As if it were her own fiancé who had sent the note, not a stranger.

Ginny looked at the recorder in her hand, wondering if this, too, was a sign. She was made for music. It was a part of her. She couldn't walk away from it.

She'd been a fool to even think she could.

Chapter Eight
....

As morning sunlight danced on the waves outside the window, Ginny dressed in designer jeans, silk blouse, and cashmere sweater. The sweater had been one of the things she'd bought with her first big paycheck. She still remembered stepping through the door of a boutique on Rodeo Drive and picking out the things she liked without any concern for their cost. She ran her hand up the soft sleeve. She hadn't worn the sweater more than a dozen times. What was she thinking, buying an item like that in sunny LA, where the average temperature was seventy degrees?

A memory filtered into her mind. She'd been in the fifth grade, and unlike most years, a pile of presents had been waiting for her under the tree on Christmas morning. She'd felt like she'd had a visit from Cinderella's godmother when she returned to school after winter break wearing her new jeans, a cute red sweater, and shiny white tennis shoes. Fellow students had eyed her new clothes with interest, and for the first time, she had felt like she fit in.

Ginny hadn't been too surprised when Kaitlin Kennedy motioned her to the lunch table where all the popular kids sat. Yet before Ginny could join them, Kaitlin raised her voice above the din of the lunchroom.

"How do you like your new outfit, Virginia? I had a fun time picking it out with my mom. Every year we go shopping for a needy kid. If I'd known it was you I would have picked out a blue sweater, though." Kaitlin smirked. "It would have gone better with your eyes."

Ginny had rushed out of the lunchroom with the snickers of the other students trailing behind her. When she got home, she gave the clothes to one of her foster sisters without explanation. Her foster parents hadn't noticed. They rarely noticed anything.

Ginny shook her head, tossing the memory out of her mind. She wished she could toss the ache out of her soul that easily. She didn't need to worry about that now. She had enough money to get what she wanted, when she wanted. And if she signed the recording contract, she'd never have to worry about money again. She wouldn't have to worry about anything—except this nagging, unsettled feeling in her heart.

As she started the coffeepot, she heard Grandma getting ready in the bathroom. Ginny released a breath. How would she break it to this sweet old woman that she'd be heading home as soon as she could call Fjord Air? She had to book a flight back to Juneau. She couldn't just sit here—cut off from life—when all her dreams were waiting to come true as soon as she returned to LA. She hadn't had a chance to talk to Brett, but maybe that wasn't the point. Maybe she was supposed to read these letters and be reminded to never be at the mercy of others again.

The bathroom door opened, and Grandma Ethel shuffled out, her hands braided in a worn fur shawl.

"Good morning, dear. Did you see the orcas in the bay this morning? There were two out there having their breakfast."

"No. Really?" Ginny hurried to the window.

"They're gone now, but they might come back." Grandma Ethel smiled, but her face still looked weary.

"I was watching the bay—the boats going out. I don't know how I missed them."

Grandma Ethel patted her shoulder. "Sometimes you simply need to know what to look for, dear." She pulled out a kitchen chair and sat down slowly, pointing to the bay out the window. "A few stragglers are always fun to watch, but you should have seen the whales this summer. They'd come into Icy Passage in a group of twenty at least. They worked together, dipping and circling in a feeding pattern known only to them. In all my years I've never seen anything like it. I believe my mother told me about it once...."

The chiming of the clock on the wall caught Ginny's attention. When Grandma Ethel drew a breath, Ginny found the opportunity to jump in.

"Grandma, I'm sorry to interrupt, but do you mind if I use your telephone?" Ginny pulled her cell phone from her jeans pocket. "I'm afraid my cell isn't working."

"Oh no, that won't work here. The only place it works is by Four Corners."

"Four Corners?"

"Yes. Didn't you see it coming in? There was the gas station, the pizza place, the coffee shop—"

"Oh, I remember that." Ginny forced a smile. "Then again, I think it was the only gas station we passed."

"Yes, dear, and did you see the old pumps? They're antiques that have been refurbished, and if you get a chance, you need to go inside. Dick—the owner—has created a museum of sorts. He's quite the collector."

Ginny nodded as Grandma Ethel went on about how some of the museum items were brought over on the ferry that travels to Gustavus. Tension tightened Ginny's chest, but a few more minutes of paying attention to this sweet old woman wouldn't hurt anything.

As Grandma Ethel continued on about the price of the ferry and her last trip to Juneau, she got to her feet, poured Ginny a cup of coffee, and then placed creamer on the table, motioning her to sit. Instead,

Ginny added a little cream and sugar to the cup and moved closer to the counter where the rotary phone sat.

She glanced up at the sheet of paper that was taped to the cupboard. Fjord Air's number was there. Trying not to let her impatience show too much, she tapped the pointed toe of her boot on the linoleum floor that had seen better days.

"Some folks don't understand how so many of us can survive here all year long. Well, we take care of each other, that's how. It's how community is supposed to be, loving your neighbor. I heard that in some parts of the country, people don't even know their neighbors! I can't imagine."

Ginny leaned against the countertop, lifting an eyebrow as Grandma Ethel continued on, seemingly without taking a breath. Things were that way in LA. She knew two people from her apartment complex. The rest were familiar faces, if that.

Finally, when the older woman took a sip of her coffee, Ginny found her moment.

"There are so many things to know about this area. I'd love to get a chance to look around, but I really need to use the phone...."

Grandma Ethel pursed her lips, a flash of disappointment in her gaze. "Oh yes. I forgot. Go right ahead."

As Ginny dialed, Grandma rose and moved to the cabinet. She pulled out a couple of chipped plates and placed cake doughnuts on them. She lifted them toward Ginny with a smile, then settled at the kitchen table.

"Fine time for my grandson to decide to get all introspective," Grandma Ethel mumbled loud enough for Ginny to hear. "Always told him that wilderness would get him into trouble one of these days."

A silent plea laced the old woman's spoken complaints. *Please stay. My grandson will come around. Don't head back already.*

He'd come back, but when? And what would she lose in those days? Danny's enthusiasm. The recording studio's time and attention.

She pushed all hesitation out of her mind and dialed the number to the airline. The phone rang three times, and then an answering machine picked up. "Fjord Air, Trish here. You want to fly? Leave a message and we'll get right back."

Ginny scanned the phone list, looking for Grandma Ethel's number. It was there, right under Brett's. Ginny's heart leapt when she read his name, but she didn't have time to chide herself. Instead she left a message, stating she'd like a ticket back to Juneau for sometime today. Since her cell wasn't working, she left Grandma Ethel's number.

They ate a simple breakfast of scrambled eggs and toast with grape jam. Apparently the doughnut was a snack. When the phone rang, Ginny jumped, but it wasn't Fjord Air. It was a woman named Dove, and from the half of the conversation she could hear, Ginny gathered that Dove was telling Grandma Ethel about an ankle injury.

Ginny scanned a week-old newspaper and read about a recent field trip by the second, third, and fourth graders. During their cruise up Glacier Bay, their ferry hit a whale. Thankfully no one—including the whale—was injured in the incident.

"I'm so glad the weather was good enough for Brett to fly you into Juneau to get that checked out." Grandma Ethel clicked her tongue into the phone. "Yes, he is a sweet boy. So helpful, you're right." Ginny glanced up to see Grandma Ethel's eyes fixed on hers. "I know, Dove. You've been so faithful with your prayers. I know God has the *perfect* young woman chosen for my grandson. He's good in that way."

Ginny smiled, but guilt weighed down on her as if that whale sat on her chest. *Poor woman. I shouldn't have come here. I shouldn't have gotten her hopes up like this.*

Grandma probably believed Ginny had come to confess her love to

Brett—maybe that's why she'd offered the letters. *One good love story deserves hearing about another.* Not that Ellie found love with James. Not that Ginny had found it with Brett.

After she finished eating, Ginny loaded her dishes into the dishwasher and then hurried to the living room. Tension tightened her shoulders. *Stupid, stupid, stupid.*

Not only was she stupid for coming here but also for not trying to find a way to Four Corners where she could use her own phone. If Grandma stayed on that phone much longer, Ginny would miss a call from the airline and her chance to be on the next flight out. There couldn't be too many flights out of Gustavus every day.

Ginny checked her cell phone again, as if by some miracle she'd suddenly have service, but she still didn't have a single bar.

She picked up the box, telling herself that Ellie's letters could occupy her mind for fifteen minutes. After that she'd have to interrupt and politely ask Grandma if she could again use the phone. Or if that didn't work, she'd go on a walk and try to pick up a cell phone signal. It couldn't be more than a couple of miles to Four Corners, could it?

May 29, 1928

Dear James,

 Please, my love. My hands are shaking, my eyes blurred with tears. Please don't do this. Can't you see how desperate I am to prove myself to you? To win you back? You will see. I will somehow regain our good name and fortune. Your mother will approve, and then I will forgive you, for the sake of our childhood memories and my ever-loyal love. I will forgive you and we will be together again.

 Ellie

Ginny paused. There was only silence coming from the kitchen. After a moment she recognized Grandma's soft humming. The phone was free, and Ginny told herself she'd call the airline again. But first she needed to find out James's response. She'd call—she would. After one more letter.

June 5, 1928

Dear Grandfather,

So much has happened since I saw you last week. I wish I could be with you now, sitting by your bed, reading the next chapter of Pilgrim's Progress *(don't you know it by heart yet?).*

I hesitate to even tell you in your condition, but with whom else can I talk? And I must tell someone. Oh, Grandfather, James has broken my heart. He called off the engagement and doesn't want to see me again. Every hope of my future included him. My dreams, goals... And he holds my past as well. I can't remember a time when he wasn't my friend.

But then—it's so odd—my misery sneaks away and another feeling boils up—anger. How could he hurt me this way? Why did he stop loving me? How could his mother say I only considered his money when I've loved him from nearly my first memory? How could he listen to that?

Yet, despite my pain, I forgive him, wholeheartedly. I am determined to win my James back. He is blinded by his mother's poison. I must provide the antidote—my continued love and devotion. I will prove myself to him. If he can't marry a poor governess, I will become the woman he can marry. There must be some way we can climb back to the position we were in before we lost everything.

Oh, Grandfather, the ironic thing is I'm perfectly content as a simple governess, as long as I have you and James. But for James's sake, I will try. I refuse to be dependent upon that dreadful Felix Cooney for anything.

I haven't the foggiest idea how I will do this. But I will figure it out.

I suppose this is enough of my sad story. I love you, Grandfather. I will check on you soon.

Ellie

Chapter Nine

· ·

Ellie's letter was troubling, but not as troubling as the news Ginny received from the airline when she finally got ahold of them. "Sorry, miss. The visibility's so bad, we can't see the end of the runway. Looks like we won't be goin' anywhere soon."

"But…surely there's another alternative. Is there a ferry? A, uh, boat I could hire to take me back to Juneau?"

"Your next chance to take the ferry out would be Sunday."

Ginny glanced over at Grandma Ethel, who was hard at work whipping up egg salad. Was that a hint of a grin on her lips?

"Sunday? Well, can I buy a plane ticket for tomorrow?"

"Sorry. There's a reunion group going out, but I have a friend who's flying in to Juneau. He might have an open seat. I can check with him and call you back."

"Yes, I'd love that. Thank you."

Grandma Ethel's smile was bigger now.

Ginny had barely sat down when the phone rang. She cocked an eyebrow.

"Go ahead and answer it, dear. It's probably for you."

"Hello?"

"Ginny?" The man's voice caught her by surprise. She recognized it immediately, but she couldn't connect Danny's voice with Grandma Ethel's house.

"Danny?"

"Sweetie, finally. Are you okay?"

"Okay? Yes, of course. Why wouldn't I be?"

"Are you kidding? I've been calling and texting for two days. I called the lodge at least a dozen times. Finally I got someone at the front desk who knew you were staying with Grandma Ethel—whoever that is. She gave me the number." Worry and frustration filled his voice.

"I'm so sorry. I should have called."

"Yes, you should have. There are a few things I need to talk to you about. In fact, you need to come back to LA as soon as possible."

The inflection in Danny's voice reminded her of one of her foster fathers, Clem. He spoke in demands and demands only. There was no such thing as a conversation.

"But I told you I'd be gone for a week…." The urgency of her desire to return dissipated like fog over the bay.

"I know that, sweetheart." She heard the shuffling of papers on his desk. She couldn't think of a time when Danny wasn't multitasking. "You said a week, but I thought you'd change your mind. It's not every day a girl's invited to perform at the Grammys."

"What? The Grammys?" The words caught in her throat. Danny had to be joking. "I'm certain I didn't hear you right."

"The Grammys. You need to get down here right away. The producer wants to see you. We need to pick a song, your dress. Too many details."

"They're held in the spring—months away."

"Do you think these things happen overnight? It takes awhile to plan."

Ginny glanced out at the bay and noticed small white birds swirling and dancing in circles, a perfect picture of delight. Her heart felt like that. After all those lonely years. After all the questions of why she'd been born and if she even mattered. "But I tried to book a flight. There aren't any."

"None? I'm sure my assistant can find something. Let me get her on it. Seriously, Ginny, next time you run off to find yourself, pick a place that's not off the end of the earth."

She wanted to retort. For some reason she felt like she should stand up for the place—for the people—even though she'd been here for fewer than twenty-four hours.

"I can probably get a flight home tomorrow. Surely that'll be good enough."

"No, today. Even if I have to hire a private jet to come up to get you."

Ginny chuckled. Mostly because she'd like to see that happen. She tried to imagine John Travolta's jet—which Danny borrowed on occasion—landing on the small airstrip at Gustavus. "Okay, well, I really don't have any place to go. Call me when you have it all figured out."

"Sure, sweetheart. Love ya."

She said a quick good-bye, frustrated. The excitement of being part of the Grammys was diminished by Danny's attitude. Her stomach clenched, and she felt as if she was going to lose her breakfast. Was this why she'd run off to Glacier Bay? She hadn't even signed the contract yet, and Danny already wanted to control her every move.

She strode to the window and crossed her arms over her chest. Was there any way to get a message to Brett? *Just to have someone to talk to.* Someone who would actually listen to her before offering an opinion. Or barking a demand. Could she leave without seeing him, without getting the advice she longed for?

But how should she find him? Could she hire someone? Would they even know where to look?

"Ginny?" She turned toward Grandma's voice. The old woman staggered toward the living room. Her face was pale and her hands shaky. She placed a hand over her heart and slumped onto the couch.

"Grandma Ethel." Ginny rushed to her side. "Are you okay?"

"My heart...pal–pitations." Grandma's head tilted forward. Her eyes fluttered closed.

I've killed her. It's all the drama. I've been here less than one day and I've killed Brett's grandmother!

Ginny situated her on the couch, laying the fur shawl over her, then rushed to the phone. She needed to call someone—anyone—for help.

What did people do for emergencies around here? She scanned the phone list. There. The number for a medical clinic. Her hand trembled as she dialed the number.

From the living room, Grandma moaned. That was a good sign, wasn't it? At least it meant she was breathing. Ginny scanned her memory, trying to remember CPR from a babysitting class she took in junior high. She could perform it if she had to.

Let's hope I don't have to.

The phone rang and rang. Finally on the sixth ring an answering machine picked up. "Hello, this is the Gustavus Medical Clinic. We are open the second Tuesday of every month. Please call back at that time." The machine hung up. The second Tuesday wasn't until next week. What did people do if there was an emergency the other twenty-nine days of the month?

911?

"Do they even have 911 here?" she cried out to the phone, as if it could answer.

"Ginny," Grandma's raspy voice called to her. Ginny rushed to her side. "Two houses down...Jared used to be..." She clutched her chest again. "EMT."

"Two houses down. Got it." Ginny looked at her high-heeled boots. She'd packed so foolishly. Where had she thought she was going? Black rubber boots sat by the front door. She took hers off and slipped them on. They were a little tight, but they'd work. She rushed outside. Had Grandma meant two houses to the left or to the right? The house to the left was closer, so she hurried that direction. The first house was a small log cabin that looked empty. At the second house, a dog's bark split the air.

"Please don't bite me," she mumbled under her breath as she rushed up to the gate. The dog stayed on the porch and continued barking. There was no movement from inside. She took a deep breath, gathering up the nerve to bravely move past the dog and knock on the door, when it opened. A barefoot, very pregnant young woman took a step out. A dark-haired toddler peeked around her.

"Is Jared here?" Ginny called to her. "I need his help. It's an emergency."

The woman cocked an eyebrow and looked at her warily. "He's still sleeping. Worked late last night."

"Can you wake him? It's Ethel—two houses down—she's having chest pains. I don't know where to go for help."

"Ethel?" Shock registered on the woman's face. "He'll be right there."

Ginny nodded and then hurried down the muddy road. Her rubber boots stuck in the mud with each step. An ache of worry filled her chest. She glanced out at the bay and the mountains that stretched toward the horizon. *Brett, where are you? I need you.* Then, for the first time since she'd arrived, she thought of someone else who could help.

"God, I know I've been doing my own thing lately—and I'm sorry about that," she spoke into the fresh, crisp air that smelled of pine trees and ocean breeze as she ran back to the house. "But if You could help, even a little, I could use it here. Please let this not be serious with Grandma Ethel, please, oh please."

Ginny rushed up the porch steps, taking only a few seconds to kick off the boots. She darted into the living room. Grandma Ethel still lay slumped on the couch, but now a bit of pink tinged her pale cheeks. Her breathing seemed more regular.

Ginny rushed over and sank to her knees, grabbing up Grandma Ethel's hand. "Grandma?"

The older woman's eyes flew open. She squinted slightly as if the room was too bright.

"How are you feeling?"

"Better some. I thought for sure my Maker was callin'. I—"

The front door opened, and a young guy—Jared, she assumed—rushed into the room. He was tall, with broad shoulders, and he looked like one of the wrestlers her foster brother used to watch on TV.

Ginny quickly scooted out of the way. Jared carried a small medical bag with him. He checked Grandma Ethel's pulse and blood pressure, looked at her pupils, and then sat back.

"Her pulse is okay now, but my guess is that she had an episode."

"An episode?"

"It happened about six months ago too. Brett flew her to Juneau, and after two days of testing, they guessed that she had a minor heart attack. They told her to eat right and rest. And they adjusted her blood pressure pills, but there wasn't anything more they could do."

"Do you think that's what this is?"

He shrugged. "I'm not sure, but all they did was send her home on bed rest, making sure someone was there to watch over her twenty-four-seven. Brett stayed for the most part. They didn't even want her up fixing her own meals." He focused on Ginny, as if realizing for the first time that he didn't recognize her. "Speaking of Brett, where is he?"

"Out kayaking, camping. He should be back soon. I'm not really sure—"

"Sometimes those guys stay out later than they say they will. It's hard to come back to civilization after being in beauty like that. Could be a few days. Could be a week."

Ginny's brow furrowed. Didn't Grandma say just yesterday that Brett kept his word and was always back when he said he would be?

Yes, but he was supposed to be back yesterday, and that didn't happen.

Grandma Ethel reached over and took Ginny's hand. "I need you to stay with me. Please. I'm afraid of you going." Her lower lip quivered. Tears rimmed her red eyes. Grandma Ethel tightened her grip.

"Yes, of course." Ginny nodded. "Of course I'll stay." How could she not? Grandma needed her. If she left and anything happened to this sweet old woman, she'd never forgive herself.

Brett would never forgive her, either.

Chapter Ten

....

Brett sat at the edge of the shore watching a black oystercatcher on the beach, where it was nestled between two rocks. It was Brett's favorite bird, with its shiny black feathers, bright straw-like bill, and orange eyes. The bird stirred slightly, and to Brett's amazement, two hatchlings popped out from underneath. Their fluffy feathers were gray- and black-speckled like the rocky shore, and their beaks were still gray. The mother oystercatcher's partner drilled his long beak into the sand of the shore, pulling up mussels and carrying them to his family. When lunch was done, the mother oystercatcher bathed herself in the water of the bay. Her chicks copied her, dipping their heads and tossing the water over their backs.

Brett blew out a contented sigh and broke off another piece of granola bar. That was what he liked most about being out here—seeing the simple events in God's creation that happened all day, every day, while people went about their busy lives, unaware. Sometimes he'd thought about that when he'd been stuck in a Southern California traffic jam. There could be smog, noise, and taillights for as far as he could see, but he'd think about an oystercatcher nesting, a rock where barking walrus lounged, or a brown bear fishing for salmon, and everything would seem right in the world again.

The family of oystercatchers moved down the shore, and Brett's eyes regularly scanned the water's edge. The creek was a mile up the shoreline. He was far enough from the salmon running upstream that he hoped the bears wouldn't bother him. Sometimes they got a little curious and came sniffing around. He had to trust that God kept him out here for a reason. One that didn't involve being mauled.

He looked down at his supplies, which he had already repacked, and the campsite he'd set up perfectly. He chuckled. It looked as if he was planning on staying a month rather than just overnight.

Brett lit the small campfire he'd prepared and added a few more sticks as it grew. The fire danced before him, but his mind wasn't on that. Instead, a to-do list trailed through his thoughts. There were folks back home who needed his help, counted on him. There were roofs to patch, flights to Juneau to provide, and mostly his grandma to keep an eye on. A heaviness pressed on his shoulders every time he left her, and he wished she'd take up his parents' offer to stay at their guest cottage in Seattle. At least she'd have someone close at all times, especially after the recent scare with her heart.

Yet he wasn't doing any of those things. He was here, waiting. Exactly what he was supposed to be doing. Still, he didn't understand why. He'd read his pocket Bible, and the Scriptures had stirred his heart, but he'd expected more—maybe an audible voice to explain God's plan for his future. That would make sense. Sitting, just sitting and waiting, didn't.

Keeping himself busy came naturally to him. Helping those in his community did too. Sitting made him nervous, and it had gotten worse over the last couple of years. Maybe it was because it was during the still, quiet moments that Ginny entered his thoughts. He didn't want to think of her, but he couldn't help it. An invisible tether connected them over the miles.

He scooted closer to the fire, stirring it with his stick. He guessed that his memories had been stronger recently after recognizing Ginny's voice playing over the radio in the Fireweed Coffee Shop.

Over the satellite radio, Ginny had sung about dancing in the ocean waves and being afraid to plunge deep. Brett didn't have to listen to all the words to understand Ginny wasn't talking about the water but rather her soul. Listening to Ginny's songs was like reading her journal. She pretended to write about other people, with pains and joys all their own, but he knew her too well to believe that. Every word of her songs came from a reservoir deep within. Deep waters he'd barely dipped his toes into before she ran away.

Lord, be with her.

What bothered him most was not understanding what had gone wrong. Within six months of their first meeting, they had both known they wanted something more than friendship. On a mission trip to Uganda, they had found themselves in pace with each other. They were drawn to the street children who danced around them, hanging on their arms and kissing their hands.

Tears had filled Ginny's eyes their second night there, and when they returned to the mission compound, passion filled her face. He knew the words that were going to come next—longed for her to say them. "Wouldn't it be a wonderful thing to move here? To care for these kids?"

Brett had fallen in love with Ginny at that moment. They'd returned home, and he'd known two things: that he was going to marry her, and that they'd dedicate their lives to the street children, giving up everything to serve the least fortunate.

And now? What had happened to those dreams?

He glanced at the gentle waves lapping the shore, thinking about his proposal. He smiled and lowered his head, thinking of the moment she'd said yes.

Ginny had embraced the idea—their marriage, their future— but as their wedding day had loomed closer, things had changed. She started going to more auditions. She worked with a guy at their college who had a small studio in his garage and recorded some songs. Brett encouraged her efforts—knew God had given her that talent for a reason—but he didn't understand the new dreams she was forming that didn't include him.

The day after they got their wedding invitations, she came to him, moving with confident strides across campus, and told him she was dropping her classes because she had gotten a regular singing gig in LA. It wasn't a recording contract, and it wouldn't make her famous overnight, but it was a start. Even now his stomach ached like he'd been sucker punched.

The more he'd tried to talk to Ginny about her plans, the more she'd pulled away, until one day she packed up everything and headed for LA. At that moment he'd no longer been concerned about caring for needy children in Uganda. He had to escape to mend his broken heart. He returned to Glacier Bay.

Brett rose and walked along the shore, then headed up the hillside. Over the top of the ridge he could see the Fairweather mountain range. He needed this. Needed to be reminded of God's creative order. Needed to realize that if God cared enough to create such beauty in this distant place where few experienced it, maybe He would create something beautiful out of Brett's life too.

Brett quickened his steps, as if the answer was on the other side of the ridge. A loud rumbling caused him to stop in his tracks. He knew that sound—a bear lumbering up the hill. He reached for the Mora knife on his side, but he knew that if the bear chose to attack, he had no hope.

The noise grew louder. The bear had to be fewer than twenty feet away over the top of the hill.

The wind blew against his face. He closed his eyes, praying it would stay away. Praying the breeze wouldn't shift and alert the bear.

His heart pounded. Everything became clear—what he wanted most. He couldn't die without talking to Ginny again, without letting her know that he hadn't forgotten their love.

He'd never forget.

His eyes popped open.

Go.

The voice filled his thoughts, but it didn't stem from fear. He had a sensing the bear would stay on its part of the ridge, away from him.

Instead, Brett knew the command to go was a release. He could return to Gustavus. And from there...maybe, just maybe, he'd get up the nerve to follow the next directive scrolling through his mind.

Find Ginny.

For some reason, he needed to tell her that sometimes the hardest things in life make us strong. And that love—true love—would always be there, even if she chose to run.

* * * * *

June 15, 1928

Dear Ellie,

I know our conversation last night hurt you. You have been a wonderful governess for our children, and if it were up to me, we would keep you under our employ for years to come. This would be the children's wishes as well. But Mrs. Standard carries our mortgage, and if she wishes for you to go, even though it breaks my heart, Mr. Davis says I must submit.

I am enclosing your final paycheck along with a little extra to help. With your skills, experience, and kind heart, I am sure you will find another situation quickly. Please use me as a reference.

Mrs. Joan Davis

Ginny had decided to grab a few minutes to read while Grandma rested. Poor Ellie. Couldn't catch a break. The loss of her wealth, her grandfather's health, her true love, and now...her job? Ellie's struggles gave Ginny courage to face her own—especially when she told Danny that she needed to stay a little longer after all.

June 19, 1928

Ellie Bell,

Our friend Nurse Schroeder—that most gracious German woman with the arms of steel—is writing this for me. Praise the Lord she can understand my rickety old speech. She does say it's getting better every day, and I believe her!

(Nurse S.: Don't know why he call me gracious. I am meanest, strictest, most efficient nurse here.)

It is always a joy to see you, even when your green eyes are darkened with concern. Yet you're no longer my little Ellie Bell who needs a mere tickle to replace rain clouds with sunshine. A broken heart does not heal so easily. Nor does the fear of an unknown future. But if I may, let me share an old man's wisdom.

I've seen much in my day. My arms that used to lift you over rushing rivers now hang weakly. (The one barely moves at all, wicked thing.) Yet, in all my experiences, my Lord Jesus never failed me. He's with me now just the same as He was when I headed the company among men who would gladly watch me fall. He never left me when your mama and papa died, Ellie, though I thought He had. No, He was ever my rock, though I couldn't always see Him.

Now, I must tell you about the half stone I gave you the other day. You're probably thinking I lost my marbles, giving you a broken piece of rock. Not to worry—I have my reasons. I'll never forget the glorious November morning when your mother plucked that stone from the Merced River that flows through Yosemite. El Capitan seemed to smile down at us from its post over the grass and trees.

Your mother, Millie, was about five. I'd say she spent an hour dipping her hands into the icy cold water searching for the right stone. Then, suddenly, she found it. After wiping it on her skirt, towheaded little Millie placed the cool, smooth rock in my hand with all the solemnity she could muster.

"Your name means rock, so I found you a 'Peter,'" she said simply. Her green eyes smiled, and her lips puckered, sort of like yours do when you're extra proud of yourself.

I rubbed it between my thumb and forefinger. "This is a fine 'Peter,' Mill, very fine."

As I moved it toward my pocket, your uncle Elliot splashed water, and the carefully chosen rock slipped from my hand and broke in half on another sharp stone. Your mama gave Elliot a strong whack on the arm.

But then I told her, "Now we have two. One for me and one for you." Holding them both in my palm, I reached out and let her choose.

She smiled and picked the big one.

After that, I carried the stone in my pocket, and the thought of my darling girl brought a smile. When she died, the two stones came together again. Both residing in my pocket. What a treasure they became. When I touched them, I'd see Millie's sweet face, trusting that I'd always love her, take care of her.

But as much as I loved her, I couldn't always protect her.

I couldn't keep that runaway trolley from crashing into her and your father. I wasn't a strong enough "Peter."

Like the rock, Bell, I break. My body is breaking even now. I will let you down, my dear heart. I have failed you many times, even though you don't want to admit it.

Others are bound to fail you too. There is no hope in a new career, a fiancé, or even in me (especially in me!). You must place all your hope in the One who is forever faithful. The Bridegroom who will never leave you, the Master who will never dismiss you, the Father whose strength will not fail.

Hold on to the rock I gave you. Let it remind you of me and your beautiful mother, but mostly touch its smooth surface and remember your solid rock, Jesus. Stand on Him, my sweet Ellie, and no matter what storms come, He will hold you. Amen and amen!

So to honor our German friend, I say alvederzane *to you for now. Write soon.*

Grandfather

Chapter Eleven

....

Ginny folded up the letter and placed it in the thin envelope with faded writing. Her stomach growled. She was thankful she'd gotten Grandma Ethel to eat some chicken noodle soup. Even though Grandma's problem was far more serious than a cold, it made Ginny feel better that she ate something.

Jared had left with a promise to be back later that evening to check on Grandma. The nurse would arrive on Tuesday, and he suggested they not do anything rash but rather wait to see her.

Ginny made herself a peanut butter and jelly sandwich and moved to the front porch looking out on the bay. "Brett, where are you?" Her heart was heavy. How could she find answers here? Waiting…playing nursemaid. She'd have to think about what staying meant to her career, but she'd do it later. Her worries about Grandma were her greatest concern now. She hoped Jared would be available again if she needed him. She didn't want to think of the alternative.

She crossed her arms over her chest, shielding herself from the cool breeze off the bay. Her blond hair tossed around her, and she was sure it looked a mess, but that didn't matter. Who around here did she have to impress? No one, that's who.

She also felt a sadness over Ellie's letter. Who was this Ellie? Ginny had been planning on asking Grandma about her, and she would— after Grandma had time to rest. After she knew Grandma was going to be okay. That was the most important thing now.

Ginny settled onto the porch swing and took a big bite of her sandwich. In LA she would never eat a sandwich like this, but here—carbs and calories didn't matter. Fitting in a designer's sample dress was the furthest thing from her mind.

In the distance, boats moored in the bay rocked gently with the movement of the waves. It looked like a photograph. Something that could hang in a trendy café. An image that would convey ten seconds of peace to a harried customer as she waited for her coffee—if she dared to glance up from her smartphone long enough to look at it.

How many times had Ginny forgotten to stop, to pause, to enjoy?

The cat, Midnight, leaped onto the wooden swing next to her, causing it to sway, and curled up beside her. Ginny stroked his back and scratched behind his ear. An uneasiness stirred inside that even the tranquil scene before her couldn't ease. Grandfather's words—written to Ellie to provide a sense of peace—troubled Ginny. She ran a hand down her tightening throat, willing the emotion away. As she'd read the old man's words, she'd felt as if the letter had been written to her. Even now the words replayed in her mind.

Others are bound to fail you.... There is no hope in a new career, a fiancé.... You must place all your hope in the One who is forever faithful, the Bridegroom who will never leave you, the Master who will never dismiss you, the Father whose strength will not fail.

The last sentence made her heart twinge. She thought again of Dale and Robyn, the only foster parents who had ever come to her with smiles on their faces, saying they wanted to adopt her—her of all people—and make her one of their own.

They were the family she'd prayed for. They had lived out their faith in every part of their lives. Watching them had made it easy to believe in God, in love, in hope and a future. But after their deaths in that horrific car accident…her faith had died too. Slowly. Painfully. She'd tried to hang on.

Ginny balled up her napkin, rose, took it back into the kitchen, and tossed it into the trash. She was about to peek in on Grandma again when the phone rang. She hurried over to answer it.

"Hello?"

"Miss Marshall?"

"Yes."

"This is Chucky from Fjord Air. We, uh, worked some things out. There's a seat for you at six thirty tonight."

"Let me guess. Did someone named Danny call you?"

"Yes, ma'am." He paused. She waited but didn't say more than that. Was it money or persuading that had found her a seat? Neither would surprise her. Ginny had long ago stopped asking how Danny always got what he wanted.

"Do you need me to give you a ride to the airstrip?" Chucky asked. "I'll be going right past. You're at Ethel's, aren't you?"

"Yes, I'm at Ethel's. You just called me at Ethel's." She spoke through tight lips. Usually Danny's ability to open doors for her was charming, but for some reason, today it grated on her nerves. "But I won't need the flight. I'm staying."

"Till tomorrow?" he asked. "I might have a seat."

She thought of the Grammys. Danny wouldn't be happy. But she wasn't going to leave Grandma Ethel alone.

"No. I'm sorry. Not tomorrow either. I'll have to call you when I'm ready. But thank you. I appreciate your help."

"Yes, ma'am." He hung up, and energy surged through her that she hadn't felt in a while. She was here, and she'd make the best of it. She was in a beautiful place, with someone who needed her, and she had space to think. She'd also have time to read more of Ellie's letters as she sat by Grandma's side. And time to think about what to say to Brett when she saw him.

She scanned the phone list again, finding the number for Bud's Rental Car. Grandma Ethel didn't have a car that she could see, and she needed to get a few things. Some good, healthy food in this place, for one. And she needed to go someplace where she could get cell service to download her e-mail and to text Danny that she wouldn't be coming home anytime soon.

Ginny spoke briefly with Bud, who told her he'd drop off the rental car. That was good, since she hadn't considered how she'd get to the rental car office.

The sunshine outside beckoned her again, but before she could make herself head out to the front porch to wait for Bud, Ginny pulled out another letter. It was only when she was lost in Ellie's life that she didn't worry about Grandma, Brett, or Danny. The letters took her mind off her problems—and she was grateful for that.

Chapter Twelve

....

July 22, 1928

Ellie Bell,

I'm afraid I had to burden my friend Nurse Schroeder once again, for last night, while choking down the deplorable chicken-fried steak provided by my friends in the hospital kitchen, an idea struck me.

I have found the solution we've been looking for this past month. It is a good one, but you must be the open-minded girl I know you are. Promise not to reject the idea offhand, but pray and know I have only your best interests at heart. Promise?

As you have heard, my friend Clay lost his wife ten months ago. Terrible sadness. Those poor children. You know how they feel, don't you? Well, he is alone in a faraway place with five children, one a mere babe. I tell you, he can't continue the work of the gospel and raise those little ones.

We old curmudgeons on the missions board don't want to call Brother Clay back from the field when the work is just beginning.

So, what is the only other solution, Ellie? Do you see it?

Now, you promised not to reject my proposal without giving it serious consideration and prayer. It's the perfect solution.

Have I not taught you to love adventure? Did we not seek

it in every way possible when you were a child? Now is your chance! You must decide quickly, for the need is great.

Nurse S. is tapping her foot and scolding me with her eyes.

All my love,

Grandfather

July 24, 1928

Dear Grandfather,

I received both your letters on the same day. I haven't much time to respond. I'm so touched by the stone you gave me. It's safely resting in its new home in my pocket and will always remind me of Mama and you.

I'm not sure what you're asking, Grandfather. It almost seems as if you want me to leave you, go to the Territory of Alaska, and marry a man I've never met in order to raise his five children.

I read that sentence over again. That must NOT be what you're asking. It's preposterous! How could I leave the only family I have? You are not well, Grandfather. I simply won't leave you.

Besides, I have plans. I've posted applications at many respectable homes around nice neighborhoods like Atherton. I also applied at Barney's and the Emporium. That might be a way into the fashion designing industry. Grandfather, I've been thinking—if Coco Chanel can create her own way in fashion designing, why can't I? Perhaps it could be the way we regain our status.

I love you dearly.

Ellie Bell

"No, dear, that's not what he's thinking." Ginny rose, shook her head, and then chuckled at herself for talking to the woman who wrote these letters over eighty years ago.

But she was sure she was right. Ellie's grandfather couldn't have been thinking of *marriage*. Ginny was sure he'd been thinking she'd make a great governess to those little dears. Maybe the missions board was even willing to pay her.

Ginny checked on Grandma Ethel, who was sitting up in bed, reading her Bible. Not wanting to interrupt, she settled down to read a few more letters.

> *Park Emergency Hospital*
> *July 25, 1928*
>
> *Dear Miss McKinley,*
>   *We regret to inform you that your bill is now two weeks overdue. Unless payment is made by August 31, 1928, your grandfather will no longer be permitted to receive care or inhabit our facilities.*
>   *Sincerely,*
>   *Robert H. Longman*
>   *Collections Facilitator*

Ginny unfolded the next letter to find a stack of four notes folded together. Each one was a rejection letter from someone Ellie had applied to. Each mentioned Mrs. Standard's name.

That lady's trying to run poor Ellie out of town. What an evil witch! Doesn't she know Ellie's grandfather is sick? Ginny was surprised how much she was starting to care about these folks.

She heard a car outside and looked out the window. A van was pulling into the driveway. She assumed it must be one of Grandma Ethel's friends, or maybe a concerned neighbor, until she noticed the yellow plastic license plate that read BUD'S RENTAL CAR. Ginny's jaw dropped. *That?*

It was an older blue Ford van that had rust spots in places. She walked out as an older gentleman climbed out of the van.

"Bud?"

"You got that right." He nodded and stretched out his hand. "You a friend of Ethel's?"

"Yes." Ginny smiled. They were new friends, but friends all the same.

Bud ran a hand through his graying hair and glanced around. "Brett's not in town?" He cocked his head, eyeing her.

Ginny placed a hand to her neck. How should she answer that? Should she dare let a stranger know that two women were alone in the house with no one checking in on them?

She brushed her hair back from her forehead. "Why would you say that?"

He shrugged. "Seems silly that you'd be renting my car when you can drive his truck. Only thing I could think of is that Brett's out of town and Ethel doesn't have a set of keys to wherever his truck is parked. Although Kelly at the coffee shop might have a set. Have you thought of that?"

"Um, no. Why would Kelly at the coffee shop have keys to Brett's car?"

"Most people 'round here leave their cars unlocked and their keys inside, just in case someone needs to borrow it. They also leave an extra set of keys with Kelly. She's in that shop mornin' till night, trying to make a living for herself and her son."

Ginny nodded, unsure of who Kelly was or why she needed to know all this information, although her ears did perk up at the words "coffee shop." Grandma's Maxwell House coffee was fine, but her heartbeat quickened slightly at the thought of a chai latte. She'd add that to her list of things to do once she got the keys to the van.

He wrote down the information for her credit card, and she tried to ignore the sand and gravel that littered the worn carpet inside the van. Ginny forced a smile as she filled out the paperwork.

She handed him the completed form and then glanced down at her mud-caked rubber boots. At least she didn't have to worry about tracking dirt into the vehicle.

"Actually, I have to ask, do you have other cars? A smaller car, maybe? I mean, it's just me. I don't really need a, uh, van."

"Sorry, miss. It's my only one. In fact, I need a ride home. That's not a problem, is it? It's only a few miles away."

Ginny tried to hide her shock. "Of course I can give you a ride. Can you give me a minute to tell Grandma where I'm going?"

"No problem. Don't mind waiting one bit."

She ran inside and found Grandma Ethel writing something down in a notebook. The woman looked tired but better than before.

"Grandma." She sat and took the older woman's hand in hers, noticing how paper-thin the skin on the back of her hand was. "I rented Bud's van, and I'm going to drop him off. I might stop by the store too, if that's okay."

Grandma Ethel looked at her with watery blue eyes. "Of course, dear. I'm fine. I'll be a good patient and rest here until you return. Take your time."

Ginny nodded but told herself she'd take as little time as possible. Some nurse she'd be if she spent the whole afternoon gone.

With a soft kiss on Grandma Ethel's cheek, Ginny moved to the living room to get her purse—even though it really didn't matter. It wasn't as if there were any cops to pull her over and ask for her driver's license.

As she picked up her purse, the next letter in the pile slipped to the floor. It was short, and she couldn't help but read the few lines.

July 29, 1928

Dear Ellie,

I am grateful you have signed the paperwork granting me the privilege of taking care of our grandfather's medical expenses. It is unfortunate we both lost so much in the ill-fated real estate deal, but I am happy to state that I have fully recovered, due to some quick thinking on my lawyer's part.

You are never in my debt.

Cousin Felix

"Never in your debt?" Ginny hurried out the door. "Of course she's in your debt, Felix, and that's exactly where you want her!" Ginny shook her head. "It's criminal."

And then she paused and smiled, realizing she'd again spoken out loud. Only this time Bud heard and was gazing at her curiously.

Should she explain? Bud's knowing look told her that talking to oneself wasn't so unusual around these parts—she'd fit in just fine.

Chapter Thirteen

....

Brett rowed his kayak to the side of the catamaran. He grinned up at the dozens of tourists who stood around the two levels of decks of the day boat from Bartlett Cove, snapping photos. Smiles filled their faces, and he recognized languages other than English being spoken as he climbed on board. All eyes were on him, and he could almost read their thoughts: *a real Alaskan wilderness man.* One of the lodge employees, Willie, rushed to his side and helped him haul the kayak onto the deck.

"Amy and I had a bet," Willie said. "I said the storm was coming in and that you'd be at the pickup spot. She worried you'd tough it out and she wouldn't be able to say good-bye." Willie wiped away an invisible tear.

A young teenager stepped closer to take Brett's photo. He smiled for the camera then turned back to Willie. "I'm really a wimp."

More tourists took photos, and they weren't shy about it. Brett understood for a moment what movie stars must feel like when they walked the red carpet. The difference was, he hadn't showered or shaved in a week. He ran a hand down his scruffy face. Maybe it added to the allure—that and the body odor.

"Excuse me." A man in a red stocking cap strode up to him. "Were you out there…alone?"

"Alone, no." Brett pulled off his gloves and tucked them into his jacket pocket. "I heard some bears rummaging around last night." He didn't mention the one that he nearly ran into that morning.

The man's eyes widened. "No joke?"

"No joke." Brett smiled.

The two interior levels of the catamaran were heated. The top deck was open to the elements. Most people stayed inside where it was warm. Brett wouldn't mind getting warmed up himself.

Inside, Amy was busy serving up cups of chowder. She was a college-aged intern who spent her summer working the galley. Every weekday she traveled up and down the bay, serving cookies and clam chowder to the tourists who paid to get a glimpse of Alaska from within the heated cabin.

Brett found an empty table, pulled off his jacket, and slipped into the booth, scooting close to the window. A couple sat at the table next to him, snuggled side-by-side. Brett tried to ignore them and focused instead on the whirr of the catamaran's motors as it glided home.

He felt movement beside him, and a manicured hand presented him with a mug of steaming chowder. Brett's stomach growled, and he took the offering.

Amy's light brown ponytail flipped from side to side as she sat. "Tomorrow's my last day, then I'm heading into Juneau to buy some Eskimo dolls and fake fur slippers and shot glasses. I'll be like one of the cruisers taking home trinkets that fail miserably at relating the wonder of this place."

Brett nodded and stirred his chowder, watching the steam rise. He took a bite and warmed from the inside. "Alaska is like your first kiss. It's not what you thought, more wonderful than you realized, and it fills you with more emotion and longing than you can explain." He chuckled. "And that no fake fur slippers can ever express."

Amy patted his hand and then rose to head back to the galley. Even though her lips turned up in a smile, tears rimmed her eyes. In a few weeks she'd be back at college, hauling around a backpack filled with books and dreaming about puffins gliding through the water.

Brett had taken Amy on a few dates, but in the end, they'd decided they were only friend material. Partly because his heart was stuck on someone else, and partly because he knew Amy would soon be gone.

Is that how Ginny feels about everyone in her life? His stomach dropped, puddling in his gut. She'd been through a dozen foster homes during her growing-up years. And then she lost the one family she loved most. It was no wonder she had a hard time letting anyone get close.

Brett rubbed his forehead and lowered his head. He had to find her. He also knew what to pray—something he hadn't thought about praying until now.

Lord, when I find her, help me see Ginny for who she is. Not who I hope her to be. And help me to find a way to be there for her...in a way she's never known, Lord. In a way she's never known.

* * * * *

Ginny found the next letter wrinkled, as if it had been crumpled and straightened again.

> *August 4, 1928*
>
> *Mr. Cooney,*
>
> *I have no desire to be in your debt; however, circumstances being what they are, I must. I accept your offer to pay Grandfather's bills, but only as a loan. I will personally repay every penny, even though it was your own treacherous deeds that sent us to ruination in the first place.*
>
> *Elizabeth McKinley*

The next letter—revised, from Ellie to Felix:

August 4, 1928

Mr. Cooney,

Thank you for your gracious offer to pay Grandfather's medical bills. I promise to repay every penny.

Elizabeth McKinley

Ginny smiled and looped a stray hair behind her ear. *Wise girl. Wiser than me. I would've sent the first one.*

She'd taken Bud home, then returned and made Grandma Ethel a small bowl of soup, watching to make sure she ate every bite. Grandma had pointed to the letters, and Ginny had read the note to Felix aloud. She'd thought about asking Grandma who Ellie was but then changed her mind. Ginny was never one to read the end of a novel first, and Ellie's letters had become a fanciful tale to her. She wanted the story to unfold and had noticed Grandma Ethel's nod and smile as if she knew a secret that would be revealed in time.

She glanced over to find that the sweet old woman had drifted off to sleep in the La-Z-Boy chair. Ginny put away the notes to Felix and pulled out a newspaper article.

Women Entrepreneurs in the Territory of Alaska

The call to a great Alaskan adventure has issued forth to select women peppered around the United States and Canada. It is not the gold hunger that spurs these young ladies. No, it is a good old business opportunity. Women are scarce in the gold fields, forcing men to take on the "women's work" themselves. One sourdough put it this way, "I ain't fer washin' clothes and cookin' vittles. An' when my socks got holes, heck if I know how to darn them dang things. When I heard tell of womenfolk up here willing to do some mending and fixin' vittles and all, I thought that to be a joyful thing."

It certainly seems to be a "joyful thing" for Miss Dorene Simms, who has earned four times the living she made as a seamstress in San Francisco in only six months. "Plus, I found myself a bit of gold as well," added the professor's daughter.

Ginny leaned back as she skimmed the rest of the article. It quoted more women who made livings in Alaska, not by prospecting but by selling services like sewing, cooking, and knitting. She imagined what ideas spun through Ellie's mind, and then hurried to read the next letter.

August 11, 1928

Dear Grandfather,

I'm sitting at our spot by the bay. It's sunset. The lavender sky falls against the horizon.

I have five letters in my shaking hands. Collections, rejections from prospective employers, and your letter, offering me the opportunity to go to the Territory of Alaska. I don't want to go, Grandfather. I don't want to leave you.

A minute ago a man and woman strolled by, happily holding hands with their little girl bobbing between them. It's the perfect picture—except for the little girl's grandfather. He should be there too.

Yesterday I left the home of my employers, the Davises, on the very street where I grew up. It's difficult to let it go, but I must. I'm content here in this tiny flat next to the hospital, but of course, my limited funds won't sustain me for long.

My legs want to run—run to your hospital room and hide

in your arms forever. But I can't. I must leave this life behind and go to a faraway land of cold and darkness.

Yes, I will go to Alaska and help Mr. Parrish with his children. Perhaps the adventure will distract me from this gloom. I'm trying to keep wearing my smile, Grandfather. I know you'd want me to.

Please do not ask me to marry him. It is beyond my poor heart's ability. I will serve as a governess. I will try to make money sewing and mending as well. I will do my best, because I love you.

Elizabeth

August 19, 1928

Dear Brother Peter,

I am mighty grateful for your concern. Despite our spotty mail service, I received the two photos with biographies the missions board sent me. I imagine they're wanting me to choose between the women. Now, I'm sure they are both fine young ladies, but truth is I don't see myself driving down the road to matrimony again. Marriage is a wonderful institution, but I've got good reason not to partake.

First, I expect being single will allow me, like the apostle Paul, to serve my congregation well.

Second, I figure I can tend my kids well enough myself. Don't need any help.

Third, I owe it to Adelaide's memory. She was about the best wife a man could ask for. Tethering my heart to another— well, that would say someone else held a candle to her, and that just isn't the case.

Fourth, my children need my full attention. A wife would only serve to distract me.

And finally, I sure don't intend to care for a woman only to suffer another loss.

In sum, I don't require a wife, now or ever.

Please forward my wishes to the Missions Board, and I'll consider the whole issue settled.

With my kindest regards,

Clay

Ginny pulled out an odd-looking letter next. It looked like Clay's handwriting, but it was a little shakier, as if he'd written it on a boat. It was addressed to Ellie's grandfather.

August 24, 1928

Dear Brother Peter,

Changed my mind. I do want a good wife after all. Please send the pretty one.

Yours truly,

Reverend Claiborne Parrish and his children, especially my dear daughter Janey, who wants me to be happy again

August 25, 1928

Dear Ellie,

I am so glad you agreed to go. The missions board and Reverend Martin in Hoonah are pleased as well. We all want the Lord's best for Brother Clay. I received a letter confirming my friend Clay's desire and need for a wife.

(Nurse S. here: He means governess. I tell him you don't want to marry some strange Alaska man. Alaska's a wild country. Only swindlers and crooks go there.)

I am sorry you must give up your dreams of becoming a

fashion designer. The Lord's plans are better than ours. You will see in time, although it's difficult now.

I'm enclosing your ferry ticket to Seattle, with a transfer to Juneau. You will have to find your own way from Juneau across the inlet to Glacier Bay. I am told there are those who will give you a ride. Be careful. I know God's hand of providence will guide you. Amen and amen!

The Missions Board was kind enough to include money for food and whatever you may need on your journey.

Grandfather

Thursday, Sept. 1

Grandfather,

What a ship! I love my room. It's small, with a bunk bed and a little sink, but it's clean, and I'm basking in the simplicity of it. I may never want a world full of things again.

It was as if the sun's rays, like arms, enfolded me as I stood on the deck, watching San Francisco become smaller. And, oh, Grandfather, the ocean! I've always loved the crashing waves, but it's different out here. The calm, the waves lapping against the hull like a gentle drumbeat. I admit my sense of adventure is stirring—you knew it would. Maybe I should be a boat captain instead of a seamstress.

Friday, Sept. 2

Grandfather,

Oh, Grandfather! You won't believe what happened. I found a letter, hidden away in a fold of my coat pocket, from James! The day I moved from the Davises', I'd left my coat on the seat of the taxi. He must've slipped it in while I was saying good-bye. I thought I saw him hovering around that day.

I'll copy the letter for you!

Ellie,

I heard you plan to travel to the Territory of Alaska to marry a reverend you have never met. I know it is too late to renew our plans, but Ellie, before you take this step, perhaps we should try to patch things up between us. I am sorry I failed to support you when your grandfather was sick. I know your kind and compassionate nature will cause you to forgive me.

I hope you will write and keep me from wallowing in loneliness for you.

James

Isn't that amazing? I'm all the more determined to come home as soon as I make our fortunes.

Good night, dear Grandfather.

All my love,

Ellie Bell

Chapter Fourteen

....

The blue van creaked and rocked as it lumbered over the potholes in the dirt road, and Ginny almost wished Danny could see her now. What would he think? He'd insist she leave this nowhere place, but as Ginny drove toward Four Corners, the small, rumble-tumble houses, unique businesses, and picturesque inns were growing on her. And the fact that everybody waved. She'd never been in a place like this. She passed two cyclists, folks in their yards, and a few women out on a stroll, and they all waved as if she was their best friend and they'd been waiting all day to see her.

Did Ellie come here? What would it have been like in 1928? No paved roads. Fewer houses. Then again, it wasn't as though this place kept up with the rest of the world even today. There were no strip malls. No fast-food drive-throughs. No Starbucks. No chance to hide from your neighbors.

No chance to run away without putting some thought into it.

Ginny bit her lip. She couldn't just get in the car and run from Brett, as she had done in California. No matter the tension that knotted her stomach like a ball of tangled yarn, she had to stay. She had to face him.

As Four Corners approached, Ginny realized she'd missed the mercantile. She'd just flipped her turn signal to turn around when a sign on the left caught her attention: FIREWEED COFFEE AND TEA HOUSE.

She slammed on the brakes, turned the wheel, and pulled into the gravel parking lot. Thankfully no one was behind her. Then again, she didn't think she had seen anyone behind her the whole drive.

She parked the car, glancing at the pine trees, the sky, the clouds. She opened the door and climbed out—skirting around a mud puddle—and wondered again about Ellie. Surely she had to be related to Grandma Ethel, or at least a dear friend. Ginny tried to remember what Brett had told her. Had Grandma Ethel grown up in Glacier Bay? Had she known Ellie?

Ginny stepped onto the small boardwalk that led up to the coffee shop, and the ringing of her cell phone caused her to jump. It had been days since she'd heard it ring. She pulled it from her pocket, and it wasn't until she answered that she realized she hadn't checked to see who was calling. Too late. She hoped it wasn't Danny. She didn't want to explain why she wasn't on a flight home.

She bit her lip. "Hello?"

"Ginny. Wow, you answered."

She recognized her older brother's voice immediately…and then her heart sank, remembering she could not officially call him that. Drew wasn't really her brother. She was never adopted into the family. No court in the country could prove she belonged to them.

Drew treated her like any of his other siblings, but each time she was around his family, she felt like a traitor. She felt even worse that he'd given her so much—paid for her college—and she'd walked away to follow her music dream.

She blew out a deep breath. "Drew, yeah, it's me. Sorry I've missed a few of your calls lately."

He laughed, and it reminded her of his dad's laugh. Pain tightened her throat, but a sad smile touched her lips. She was thankful for the days she did have with them.

"Well, it's so good to get you," Drew continued. "We were wondering if you wanted to come up for the weekend. It's Cooper's birthday."

"Really? Is he four?"

"Six."

"Six already?"

"Years pass quickly, don't they? It's hard to believe it's been five years since—"

"I wish I could come," she interrupted, knowing where he was going with the conversation and not wanting to go there. "But I won't be able to make it. I'm not in Los Angeles. I'm actually in Alaska."

"Alaska? Are you up there to film a music video or something?" Excitement tinged Drew's voice.

"No, uh, I've come to talk to an old friend."

"Wasn't that guy you dated from Alaska? Was his name Brian? He was a nice guy. Whatever happened to him?"

"Brett." She pressed her lips together, and she had a strong urge to take her phone and chuck it under the tires of the large truck that had just pulled up.

She'd tried to explain to Drew before why things had ended between her and Brett. The problem was, no one accepted what she had to say. She repeated the rehearsed words again. "Brett and I were heading two different directions. I took a leap of faith and followed my dream. Everyone has a dream, right?"

"Of course." His voice sounded more distant than it had a few minutes ago. "So is that why you went up there…to see him?" Drew wasn't going to let her off easy.

"Yeah, I did, but he's off in the outback somewhere. I need some advice about a recording contract, that's all."

"Hmm…"

She imagined her brother stroking his chin and nodding like he always did when he was deep in thought.

"That should tell you something," he finally said.

"About what?"

"That you're running again, but this time, it's in the right direction. Last time you ran to your dream, but when your fears arose about this contract, you ran to where you felt safe. When we're afraid, we always run to who we feel safe with."

"Mm-hmm." Ginny nodded, but she wasn't convinced he was right. She was about to tell Drew that she'd made the right choice in going to LA when the coffee shop door opened and an older couple walked out with paper cups in hand.

"I better go," she hurriedly said, before he had a chance to repeat the lecture of how irresponsible she'd been to leave college midsemester, especially since she'd been doing so well in all of her classes. "Tell Cooper I'll try to call on his birthday, okay?"

"Sure. Tell Brett hi too. Love you, sis." Drew hung up the phone.

"Love you," she whispered, even though the call had already been dropped. She did love him and the rest of his family—that was the problem. Being around him reminded her what she could have had. What she'd never have again.

Ginny blew out a long, slow breath. Should she call Danny? With cell phone service, she had no excuse but…

She glanced at the time on the clock. He was probably out playing tennis, like he did every afternoon. That was enough of a reason to justify sending a text.

Danny. Miss you lots. Bad cell service here. Hope you're enjoying your game. A sweet old lady I know had a heart episode. I needed to stay. Be down there soon. xoxo Ginny

Ginny sent the message. *Why am I putting off talking to Danny?*

He cared for her. He had her best interests at heart. He was a good man. He'd already taken her places she never dreamed she'd go.

But…if she talked to him, he would persuade her with his charm, his influence. He'd figure out a caretaker for Grandma Ethel, send a huge bouquet of flowers, and whisk Ginny back to LA.

She wasn't ready to go back. Not yet.

A bulletin board filled with ads was posted on the exterior of the coffee shop. She read one about a "Gustavus-style" car for sale. It had no headlights and no brakes. She supposed with a twenty-five-mile-an-hour speed limit and not too many roads, neither were needed. She tried to imagine a for-sale ad like that in Beverly Hills, and a chuckle bubbled up. This place was refreshing. It couldn't be more different from LA—where body parts, names, and biographies were more fictional than real.

Another handmade note on pink paper drew her attention. *Baby Shower at Gina's. Saturday at 2:00.* Ginny grinned, shaking her head in disbelief. Evidently everyone knew Gina, where she lived, and what Saturday.

If Ginny lived here, everyone would know her, but would they like her? Maybe if she allowed herself to be as real and unpretentious as everything else around here.

She blew out a breath, and tension released from her shoulders. Was the God-loving girl whom Brett once loved still in there somewhere?

Chapter Fifteen
. . . .

Ginny strode into the Fireweed, her high-heeled boots clicking on the wooden floor, and her heartbeat nearly doubled as she noticed the professional espresso machine.

"Real coffee, yes!" She didn't realize she'd said the words out loud until she heard laughter from behind the counter. A young woman rose and smiled, tucking her hands into the back pocket of her jeans. She had short-cropped dark hair. She looked like a young Winona Ryder, only cuter.

"What would you like, ma'am?" The question didn't come from the woman. It came instead from a younger voice. As Ginny stepped forward, she noticed a boy who appeared to be about five peeking over the counter.

"Hey there." She peered down at him. "Are you going to help me today?"

He nodded, displaying a gap-toothed grin. "Yes, ma'am. I'm helping, aren't I, Mama?"

"Yes, Jace. You're the best helper."

Ginny glanced to the young woman and immediately noticed the resemblance. They had the same wide green eyes and smattering of freckles across their noses.

"Well, sir." Ginny tapped her chin with her fingernail. "How about a tall, skinny white chocolate mocha."

"Skinny?" He glanced at his mom.

She chuckled. "That means nonfat milk. It's in the blue carton. Can you get it for me?"

"Okay!" He hurried to the fridge. "Can I do the whipped cweam, too?"

The woman glanced over at Ginny as she measured coffee into the coffee press. "Do you want whip?"

"Of course. How can I say no?" *Not so skinny, but oh well.*

He pulled the carton from the fridge and brought it to his mom.

Ginny smiled. "You have some good help there."

"Yes, Jace can run this place as well as I can. I bought this shop when he was a baby. I used to set up a high chair right over there." The woman pointed to the corner by the counter. "And Jace's first word was 'coffee'!"

Ginny laughed.

"I'm Kelly, by the way."

Ginny waved a hand. "Nice to meet you. I'm Ginny."

The woman nodded. "Yeah, I like your songs."

Ginny cocked an eyebrow. On one hand, it was a compliment that someone all the way up in these parts would appreciate her music. On the other, she'd enjoyed being just Ginny.

Kelly instructed Jace on how much white chocolate syrup to put in the cup, and Ginny eyed the sketches, wildlife photos, and paintings that hung on the walls of the adjoining gallery. One of her favorites was a photo of an old truck parked in a field of wildflowers. The photographer had made the print look antique yet colorful, as if it was an image from a dream.

"Wow, you have some cool things in here. Are you an artist?" she called back to Kelly.

"Yes, but these aren't all my pieces. Just those two, uh, sketches over there."

Ginny stepped forward and glanced at the two pencil drawings. One was of a sea lion bathing on the rock. The detail was intricate, amazing. "If I didn't know better, I'd think it was a black-and-white photograph."

"Thanks. I—" Kelly continued, but her voice was drowned out by the noise of the frothing machine.

The other drawing depicted a father and son sitting on a dock with fishing poles in hand. The boy was a toddler, but it was obviously Jace. And the man...was that Jace's father?

She looked closer and then caught her breath as she recognized the strong jaw, the broad shoulders, the smile. Goose bumps rose on her arms, and she shifted her weight from side to side.

Hurried footsteps approached as the young boy ran to her side. "That's me and Bwett. We caught a big salmon that day, didn't we, Mama?"

Kelly approached, handing Ginny her coffee. "Yes, you sure did."

As Ginny took the paper cup, her fingers trembled. She nodded but didn't respond.

It's been two years. Plenty of time for Brett to connect with this beautiful woman and her son.

She wanted to cry. She wanted to leave, but she couldn't do either. Her feet felt like they were glued to the floorboards.

Instead she eyed the sketch. Where would she be—they be—if things had worked out between her and Brett? Would they have children together—a son?

"Those are like two peas in a pod. I swear Brett is Jace's favorite person."

"It seems like he's everyone's favorite person around here," Ginny mumbled under her breath.

"How can he not be? He's done more for this community than anyone I know. Done more for me." Kelly brushed her long bangs back from her eyes, and Ginny noticed their sparkle. Did Kelly have feelings for Brett? Had he returned them in any way?

Ginny took a sip of coffee and forced a smile. "Brett's that type of guy. Always thinking of others and caring with his whole heart." She glanced over at another framed photograph hanging on the wall of a kayak skimming over the water with a glacier looming in the background.

"Was that photo taken around here?" Ginny asked.

Kelly nodded but didn't elaborate. Jace's eyes were still fixed on the drawing of him and Brett.

"We love Bwett, don't we, Mama?" Jace pointed to the drawing and then rushed back behind the counter to retrieve his toy car that he'd left sitting next to the milk.

"Of course we do." Kelly cocked an eyebrow and then moved back behind the counter. Ginny followed, paying for the coffee and tucking a couple extra dollars into the tip jar. She was trying to think of what to say—how to say it—when the door opened and a tall man stepped through.

"Hey, Hank. Your usual?"

Hank was thin with reddish hair and a big smile. He wore some type of uniform, and Ginny guessed he worked for the park service. She'd almost forgotten Glacier Bay National Park was right here. She thought of the lodge—her reservations. The beautiful park was nine miles down the road. Would she ever get there?

"Of course the usual. Why change now?" His smile was broad, but it faded when he noticed Ginny standing there.

Ginny stepped forward. "Just admiring Kelly's artwork," she said, as if needing to explain.

"She's a fine artist. I'm surprised she can keep any artwork in the place. The tourists gobble it up. Speaking of which…" He cocked an eyebrow.

Ginny extended her hand. "I'm—"

"That's Ginny. She's visiting these parts for a few days, isn't that right?" Kelly pulled two tea bags from a glass jar on the counter.

"Oh, so you're the one with Bud's van?"

She took another sip of coffee and then nodded. "Yes, and speaking of which, I should get going. I have a few more errands to run."

"Come back again!" Kelly called after her. "It was great meeting you."

"Bye-bye," Jace echoed, returning the milk carton to the fridge.

Ginny strode out into the cool air, feeling a faint tightness in her stomach. Kelly seemed nice, but there was something in those green eyes she wasn't saying.

Ginny sighed and hurried toward the old blue van. A cold, brisk wind blew in off the bay, and storm clouds gathered in the horizon. Would Brett stay out there in this type of weather?

Maybe it was easier this way—him being gone. Maybe she wouldn't see him after all, especially if Grandma continued to improve.

Ginny took another sip of her coffee. It blew Starbucks out of the water.

It figured the prettiest, sweetest woman in Gustavus could also make a perfect latte.

She pulled the van keys from her pocket and unlocked the door, noting that she needn't worry about locking up next time. Like Bud said, most people left their cars unlocked with the key inside. Even if the van did get stolen, it wasn't as if the thief had any place to hide. Glacier Bay wasn't big enough for that. And the only way it could get someplace else was by ferry. More than that, everyone knew Bud's van. It was hard to remain incognito.

She thought about heading on to the mercantile as she had planned, but the heaviness of meeting Kelly weighed her down. She could shop tomorrow. Besides, she didn't want to leave Brett's grandmother for too long.

She'd only made it three steps into Grandma Ethel's living room when the old woman's voice caused her to jump.

"You didn't catch the death of cold, did you?" Grandma Ethel asked.

Ginny rubbed her hands together. "I am a bit chilled."

"I thought so. Your face is pale. I should have insisted you stay in."

Grandma Ethel reached out her hands. The woman still appeared weak. Ginny approached and returned the gesture. Grandma gripped her arms affectionately. "Can you do me a favor?"

"Yes, of course." Ginny sat down beside her.

"Can you make me a cup of tea?"

"Tea? I'd love to." Ginny rose and moved to the kitchen. "Did you have a chance to rest?"

"Rest? It's all I seem to do." She placed a hand on her chest. "It's not easy getting old." Grandma Ethel let out a long sigh.

It took only a few minutes for Ginny to prepare the tea and bring it to Grandma.

"Can you place it on the end table please?"

"Of course." Ginny did as she was asked.

Grandma Ethel patted the sofa beside her and Ginny sat.

"Get a chance to look around some?" Grandma dotted the corner of her watery eyes with her Kleenex.

"Just the coffee shop. Met Kelly and Jace. Nice family."

Grandma nodded, but Ginny could tell the older woman's mind was on something else.

Grandma cleared her throat. "I appreciate you changing your plans. Staying. I know you didn't come all this way for me."

"No, but you're an unexpected gift. I've enjoyed getting to know you. I wish you were feeling better."

"Yes, well, I've learned at my age you can't take anything for granted. This morning was more serious than I wish it would have been, but I'm glad it wasn't worse…which leads me to what I really want to say."

Ginny nodded, waiting. "Okay."

"Virginia, I've had a good life—an awfully good life. God has given

me more than I deserve, namely His Son, and if something happens...
well, just know that I'm prepared. I have no fear of meeting my Maker.
In fact, I've been looking forward to that for many years."

Ginny gasped and placed a hand over her heart. "Grandma Ethel,
don't say that. Nothing's going to happen."

Grandma cocked her head and narrowed her gaze. "Really, darling
girl, are you sure of that? Do you know the future?"

"Well, no. But I don't like that thought." Ginny's chin trembled,
and she hoped she wouldn't break down. Not here. Not now.

"It's a fact of life, sweet one. It's the one thing guaranteed for each
of us. A certainty of certainties, yet we humans walk around life as
if we'll live forever." She reached over and took Ginny's hand, giving
it a gentle squeeze. "It's a disclaimer that I've already given to all my
friends who live here in Glacier Bay. In fact, it's one thing all of us older
folks around here understand. There's not the medical care here available to most in the lower states, and I understand that. I also want you
to know that nothing you do or don't do will change the fact that my
Lord knew the moment of my first breath and the moment of my last
one before the creation of the universe. Imagine that."

Ginny nodded again, feeling a chill travel down her arms. She considered making her own cup of tea but felt too weary to move. This talk
of death in such a light manner—well, it just wasn't normal. She hoped
that Grandma Ethel wasn't feeling worse than she was letting on, that
this wasn't her way of preparing Ginny. A shiver ran down her spine.

Midnight sauntered into the room, watching the storm building
outside the window and letting out a long meow. Ginny followed the
cat's gaze, amazed by how quickly the storm came up. Brett was out
there somewhere. Did he have a tent? Was there a cabin?

She hadn't asked him too many questions, and she tried to
remember what he told her years ago when he explained the coves, the

mountains, the glaciers he explored. She was pretty sure he packed light and went into places most people didn't dare venture, which worried her. Especially with Grandma Ethel's casual talk of death.

"There's another thing too." Grandma interrupted Ginny's thoughts. "If something happens—anything happens—and you don't get to finish the letters while you're here, I want you to take them with you. I want you to read them all…do you understand?"

"What? No. I can't. They're a treasure. I wouldn't dare think of hauling something so priceless away."

Grandma pointed a shriveled finger her direction. "No arguing, you hear?" She frowned as she glanced back at the mountain storm. Was she worried about Brett too?

Then she turned and focused again on Ginny's eyes. "We meet people, live with folks, build friendships our whole lives, and there are those few tenderhearted souls who stand out. These letters highlight such people, but it's more than that." Grandma Ethel yawned and settled deeper back into the couch. "As we go through life, it's hard to see the big picture. Things happen that seem random. We question why God allows hard things to happen to good people. And while those letters aren't always easy to read, they give a glimpse of a bigger picture." Grandma Ethel offered a soft smile. "It's not often you get to see how one life can impact many, but it's something I have a feeling God wants you to know. Promise me."

"Yes, of course. I'd be honored."

"Good." Grandma Ethel rose. "Even though it seems I just woke up, it's my nap time again." She patted the box on the coffee table. "And you have some reading to do."

"But your tea…" Ginny pointed to the steaming cup on the end table.

"Oh, that's for you, dear." Grandma Ethel smiled. "I always like something warm to sip while I read. Don't you?"

Chapter Sixteen

....

September 7, 1928

Dear Brother Peter,

I expect this story may interest you. Tuesday last, I ventured in my small fishing rig to Juneau for supplies. Early afternoon, Joseph, Linc, and I were loading up for the trip back. It was one of those clear Juneau days that can turn on a person. The waterfowl acted nervous, darting around. They know when a storm's coming. So we hastened to beat it.

We were ready to set off when a young lady clomped across the dock toward our vessel, tugging a huge blue trunk behind her. A sewing machine—electric—was roped to the top of the trunk. Of all things.

The dock swayed some, and the way the young woman rocked, I thought she'd fall right in. Now the water underneath the dock sinks down to a darkness that looks as if it could swallow a person up. I sent Linc to help her, and she clung to his shoulder. Near drew blood. You should've seen the fright in her eyes.

Well, she made it, but as she came to our vessel, her feet slipped out from under her (those fancy boots didn't help). She fell right down on her backside. A sad sight. Felt sorry for her, but I admit the three of us choked back chuckles. This fancy lady tossed down on her backside, fluttering and fussing. Not the nicest behavior on our part.

I helped her up, asked her what she was wanting.

Still tottering, she gripped my arm and brushed herself off with the other. Didn't want to fall again, I'm guessing. Then she smiled and even laughed a bit.

"I've always been clumsy."

At first she seemed a decent young woman, but then she asked the most irrational question.

"I need a ride to Strawberry Point. Will you take me? I can pay."

This woman was in no way prepared to go to Strawberry Point. I said no and bid her good day.

Did she turn and go? No. Instead, she asked me to refer another ride.

Well, if she wanted to be unreasonable… I pointed toward a canoe. A Tlingit family was almost ready to push off. "That should serve well enough. Good people. Don't know if that trunk of yours will fit."

Her eyes shrank to the size of pebbles. Seemed to feel a mite irksome.

"Fine, sir. If I must, I'll go with them." With a royal spin, she stomped toward them, tugging her trunk behind her. The boys and I waited and watched.

A few minutes later, she marched back. "They don't speak English, as I'm sure you know. Would you please ask them for me?" Her tone showed no politeness.

"Look, miss. I don't know why you want to take a little visit to Strawberry Point, but you can find a bargeful of other fine places to tour. Have you seen Juneau? The Mendenhall Glacier? It's like a piece of heaven come down—if you watch out for bears. So, I'd appreciate it if you'd stop taking our time.

A storm's coming, and we aim to beat it." I nodded with as much kindness as I could muster. "Boys, time to head out."

As I turned my back, her girlish hand gripped my shoulder. I didn't know how she reached it, me being at least a foot above her. When I faced her again, I saw she was standing on her trunk. Oh good heavens, I never saw a proper lady so fired up.

"Listen to me, Mr. Whoever-you-are!" She stabbed my chest with her finger. "I must go to Strawberry Point today. I've left everything I own, all the people I love, and my whole life to live there. Not just to 'take a little visit.' To stay."

The whites in her eyes reddened, which shook me a bit, and then the tears came. Womenfolk cry when they're angry sometimes. Adelaide did that. It only made her more angry too.

"You have to take me. You must. If you have a shred of decency..."

Just then, I'm sorry to say, a wave rocked the dock hard. Her trunk slid from under her feet and she fell into me. Worse, that big old chest scooted right across the dock, straight to the edge. It tipped a moment, like it might stop. She shrieked, pushed away from me, and tried to grasp it. But another wave shook the dock and that trunk slid into the Alaskan depths. The sewing machine too.

She leaned over the edge, grasping for it. Finally I hauled her back up. My anger turned to pity. Her shoulders quivered.

"We better go!" Joseph, his blond hair flapping in the wind, called to me. He was right.

"I'm so sorry, miss," I said. She was still staring at the bleak spot where her chest and sewing machine had sunk. "That machine wouldn't have worked anyway. There's no electricity at Strawberry Point."

Linc added his great offer to jigger something up for her. He said he'd heard of someone hooking a sewing machine up to a bike to generate the electricity. The lady pedaled while she mended. I wanted to elbow him in the ribs, because it didn't matter now. Not with that machine at the bottom of the bay.

Linc's mighty smart with mechanical how-to, but such trouble in the mouth.

At Linc's words, she looked like she was going to crumble into a sobbing fit. Mercy, I'm not skilled at dealing with a sobbing woman.

She grabbed me again. This time my arm. "Please, sir. Please." She didn't sound angry now. More desperate, like a fearful child. "I've come this far. I can't be turned away. I promised to make this work. I have to at least try."

Something about her sad face. The green eyes. Well, I let her onboard—against my better judgment.

As we boarded, Linc called to me. "All is ready, Uncle Clay."

Suddenly, the woman halted. "Your name is Clay?" Before I answered, an odd look came over her face. "You're not a reverend, are you?"

I nodded.

She glanced at her hands and then sized me up, from my scraggly hair and scruffy beard down to my dungarees, bowie knife, and mud-crusted boots. Then she really sobbed.

That's when she told me.

"I'm Ellie. Elizabeth."

I admit, I still didn't know what she was talking about. You see, Brother Peter, I wasn't expecting your young lady. I had put the matter out of mind—seeing as I told you "thank you, but no thank you" in my letter.

"Elizabeth McKinley."

Then it hit me like a lampoon in a whale's gut. This woman was your granddaughter.

Clay

September 9, 1928

Grandfather,

I can't even put into words. I lost my sewing machine. And everything else. All my plans for earning enough money to pay the medical bills, to prove myself to James. Gone. I found out there's barely anyone living here to sell things to anyway, plus no electricity. I don't know how I'll ever pay Felix Cooney back.

Much more to tell. The man hates me. Why am I here?

Ellie

Dear Mr. Barnett,

I'm sorry. I fibbed when I wrote you. I mean the letter was a big fib, but I didn't fib that Papa needs a wife and I like the pretty one. But I was wrong to break the commandment and I'm sorry.

Janey

P.S. My dad made me write this. I'm not that sorry because I like Miss Ellie.

Dear Janey,

It is very wrong to lie. God is truth, and He wants His children to tell the truth. But I'm glad you like Miss Ellie. Do you think your papa likes her too? I'll count on you to keep me informed, all right?

Your friend,

Mr. Barnett

So Ellie did end up in Strawberry Point. Ginny pulled her cell phone from her purse and turned it over in her hand. If she had service she could open a browser, type in a query, and find out exactly where that was. In Alaska somewhere—or whatever this place was called before it became part of the United States. The Last Frontier, yes. The letters mentioned Juneau and traveling there by boat. Maybe it was somewhere near here.

Ginny let out a long sigh, imagining herself in Ellie's situation. She felt out of place, and *she* still had a full suitcase and money in her bank account. With one phone call she could book a flight back to LA. How did that poor woman do it?

Ginny was picking up another letter, eager to discover how sweet Ellie handled everything, when she heard a stirring from the bedroom. Grandma Ethel was heading to the bathroom, perhaps?

As she rose to see if Grandma needed any help, a vehicle outside caught her eye. A white truck, extended cab, with a kayak in back, pulled in and parked next to her van—Bud's van. Rain poured from the sky, but even through the raindrops, she could see who it was. Her heartbeat quickened, her knees softened, and in a strange way she felt herself relax. Seeing Brett was like seeing home after a long journey.

Chapter Seventeen

....

Ginny set the letters aside, and all worries about Ellie and Clay dissipated at the sight of Brett's handsome face. He jumped out of the truck, glanced at Bud's van, then looked toward the cottage, concern evident in his gaze. Hurrying to the front porch, he pulled off his rain jacket and laid it over the back of the rocking chair. He opened the door and stepped into the house.

He froze when he saw her standing there in front of the couch.

"Ginny?" His voice caught in his throat, lips parted. Joy filled his eyes, then a tenderness that she wished she could bottle up and keep forever.

Why had she run? His love was evident in his gaze. It felt like it had been only two weeks rather than two years since she last saw him. And nothing in that time apart seemed half as important as being with him now.

"You're here. How…how did you find me? How did you track down my grandma?"

Ginny toe-tapped as she resisted the urge to hurry toward him. Didn't her heart know he was no longer hers? She cleared her throat. "It's Gustavus. It wasn't that hard."

He laughed, his whole face brightening. "I suppose you're right about that. Everyone knows Grandma—"

"And you." Her chest felt so warm, so full, she was sure her feet would leave the ground. "You're the talk of the town—if you can call this place a town."

He ran a hand down the stubble on his face. "I wish I would have cleaned up first."

"You look great." She took a step forward. "It's wonderful to see you."

Should she give him a hug? Before she had to decide, he approached and wrapped his arms around her. The flannel of his shirt was soft against her cheek. His chest was warm. Brett smelled of the outdoors, of the land and sea and rain. She was afraid to wrap her arms around him. She thought of Danny. What would he think if he knew she'd come to see the man she once loved…the man she was realizing she still cared for? She gripped the sides of his shirt, holding tight.

"Wow. After all this time, here you are." His voice was a husky whisper.

Tears sprang to her cheeks. Tears of joy? Tears of missing him— his smile? A bit of both.

Raindrops from his hair brushed her cheek. She pulled back slightly and wiped them away.

"Are you crying?" He gazed at her curiously, his hazel eyes wide.

"Not yet. It was the rain." She pointed to his hair.

"Not yet?"

"I don't know why I said that." A quivering hand touched her lips. "I'm happy to see you. I came up here—hunted you down—because I need advice. There's so much happening with my life, my music. I wanted to talk to someone who knew me."

Brett nodded. He brushed the raindrops from his hair and smiled sadly. "I used to think I knew you better than anyone—and that you knew me—but it's been two years, Ginny. Can you believe it's been two years?"

Gazing up at him, Ginny felt her heart swell and grow. She'd forgotten how handsome he was. She placed a hand over her chest, resisting the urge to wrap her arms around his neck and hold on— to never let go.

She blew out a sigh, telling herself that she wasn't the same girl who'd driven away and that he had most likely changed too. They couldn't just pick up where they'd left off.

A mixture of joy and confusion filled his gaze. "So what do you need to talk about? Are you all right? Nothing bad happened, did it? I hope not. I mean, it's great to see you. In fact, I was just thinking about you. Wow."

"I'm okay, I'm good." Ginny smiled. She heard the shuffling of feet coming from the bedroom and remembered. "I'm okay, but your grandma, she...she had a—well, something happened with her heart. She's resting—"

A crash sounded from the bedroom. Ginny jumped. Without hesitation, Brett rushed past her. "Grandma!" His voice echoed through the house. "Grandma, are you okay?"

They rushed into the room, and Ginny stopped in her tracks as she saw the old woman crumpled on the floor. Grandma Ethel's face was distorted. Her eyes were wide, her lips pressed tightly shut. Ginny rushed to her side. Brett dropped to his knees beside her.

"Grandma? Grandma, are you okay?"

Her lips opened, and Ginny waited for the cry of pain to come. Instead, laughter spilled out.

"I—I—" The older woman patted her pale cheek and sucked in a deep breath. "This ol' heart. Won't let me get away with nothing." She looked at Brett. "I heard you come home. Was trying to eavesdrop. Leaned too far near the open door and got light-headed."

Ginny took Grandma Ethel's hand. "Does anything hurt? Do you need me to go get Jared?"

"You know Jared?" Brett eyed Ginny. "How long have you been here? I've only been gone a week."

"Two days. But I wasn't here long when I had to go get him. Your grandma, she—"

Grandma Ethel waved a hand in the air. "I had an episode, that's all. Not as bad as last time. I'm fine, fine." She lifted her arms as if waiting for Brett to help her to her feet. He did, holding her, steadying her.

Ginny stepped closer. "You sure you don't have a pain somewhere?" She tried to keep her tone light even though she was worried. "You didn't break a hip, did you?"

"Nah, I held on to the nightstand as I was going down. I'm good as gold." Grandma Ethel took tentative steps forward, and it was obvious she was still a little shaky. She walked to the living room, paused, and looked from Ginny to Brett and back to Ginny again.

"Of course, maybe I should have Ginny stay a little longer. It's good to have someone around—another woman." She reached out and patted Ginny's arm. "I know you came to see Brett, my dear, but having you here has been a gift to me. Oh, what a gift."

"I'm not sure if I can stay. I need to get back. There's a record deal. And Danny said—" She glanced at Brett as she said Danny's name and couldn't help but notice the hurt in his gaze.

He turned his attention back to his grandmother. "If you need me to stay instead…"

"Ginny, dear." Grandma Ethel paused and turned to her. "I know what you're saying. But I also know you didn't come all this way just to leave again. Give yourself a few days to connect with God. To talk to Brett. To finish the letters…" Her voice trailed off.

"The letters? Ellie's letters?" Brett's jaw dropped.

"Yeah, why?"

"Oh nothing…" He looked at his grandma, his brow furrowing. But the old woman paid him no mind and continued on toward the sofa.

When she sat, Brett turned to Ginny. He looked at the letters, then at Ginny, clearing his throat. "I know things didn't work out with you wanting to surprise me and all." He chuckled. "I mean, I was surprised, but…if I had known…" Brett leaned forward. "What I'm trying to say is, it sounds like my grandma would like you to stay. But even more than that, I would too."

A flood of warmth grew in Ginny's chest, spreading until it flowed to every part of her body. "Really?"

"Really. I would like that very much. In fact, I"—he looked at his grandmother and smiled, then back at Ginny—"I'll have to tell you about why I stayed out longer."

Ginny nodded, brushing her hair back over her shoulder.

"But later." He rose and turned toward the front door. "Right now I'm going to grab my things and get a shower. If I wasn't so happy to see you, I'd be embarrassed by how I look. Then again, who knew I'd need a shower and a shave when I left the wilderness today?"

She watched as he walked out and grabbed a backpack from the front seat of his truck. The rain had slowed some, and he was only slightly damp when he reentered.

Ginny approached him. She was unsure why, maybe to make it more real to her that he was really here, but she raised a hand and tousled his dark hair. "I'm not sure I've ever seen your hair this long."

His eyelids slid closed for a brief moment and then he leaned down, his mouth close to her ear. "You always told me to let it grow out. That you wanted to see my curls."

"You did it for me? You still thought of me?" She didn't move, didn't put space between them, even though she knew she should.

Brett placed a hand on her shoulder, and only then did she dare lift her head to meet his gaze.

"Ginny, how could I ever forget?"

The phone rang, jarring Ginny back to reality.

"I'll let the machine pick it up," Grandma Ethel called. "Some timing this is…." she mumbled.

Ginny glanced toward the kitchen as the phone rang a second time and noticed her paper coffee cup sitting on the counter. She remembered Kelly, too, and the obvious affection in the woman's eyes when she talked about Brett.

She offered him a sad smile. "You haven't changed, you know that? You still say the sweetest things."

"I'm not just saying that, Ginny." He stroked her cheek.

"I know, and that's what worries me. You'd better go shower..." She pinched her nose as if bothered by his odor and then shrugged, trying to pretend his words hadn't buoyed her heart.

As he walked away, Ginny sighed. "I thought I knew why I came, Brett. But standing here, seeing you...I suddenly have no idea."

Chapter Eighteen

....

September 12, 1928

Dear Grandfather,

Since winter's on its way, you won't be receiving many letters from me, I'm afraid. The mail goes out very sparingly in the winter, but I'll keep writing you anyway. It'll be like the adventure stories I used to scribble when I was a kid, only this time, they will be true adventures! Plus, writing has always been a comfort in struggles. In this place, I guarantee I'll need that comfort.

The trip over in the reverend's fishing boat was the most harrowing experience of my life. Because of my little incident on the dock, we didn't get out early enough and ended up facing the storm. The way the boat tipped and swayed, I actually fell into the water—plunged all the way under. If the reverend hadn't pulled me back in—well, I don't want to think about it. He's a firm man, not gentle, kind, or compassionate, but I'm grateful he saved my life.

On the boat, I did not have a chance to talk much to the reverend or the boys—except when they hollered at me to do something. But one thing I learned: they had not been expecting me.

After we docked, we began our muddy, two-mile walk to their cabin. The rain had cleared, but the sky was still gloomy and foreboding as in a scary motion picture. The reverend and Joseph matched the murkiness with their own foul moods, but Linc smiled and chatted with me.

His sweet fourteen-year-old grin made the tightness in my shoulders relax. He told me about his ma and pa back on a ranch in California. His mother was Adelaide's sister. When she died, Linc's mother suggested he come on up to help with the children and chores. Linc was happy to come. His eyes lit up when he told me about his adventures since he arrived, and I spotted a sweet affection when he mentioned the little ones. He talked almost nonstop, in fact, but I welcomed his conversation—until Reverend Parrish asked him to be quiet. After that, we strode in awkward silence.

That was until I made my first blunder. Everything had suddenly grown even quieter. The reverend put a finger to his lips, but I had no idea why. Then he reached behind him and grabbed a rifle strapped to his back. Joseph did the same. My hands began to sweat. My chest tightened. Guns! I had never seen one up close before. Out of the bushes, an antler appeared. Then the whole moose clomped out with a little one next to it.

It was huge, and it stood so close to us! Plus, it had startled me. So I screamed like a madwoman. The moose jerked its head and charged Joseph. Scared the dickens out of me. Joseph scrambled up a tree, and the reverend tried to shoot the moose, but she and her calf got away. I'm glad. You can't shoot the mother and leave the little one alone.

The reverend was very unhappy with me. "You don't scream when a man's hunting. Could get a person killed." He shook his head in disgust.

I wanted to sob, but I lifted my chin instead and told him that since I'm not accustomed to enormous moose, guns, or rude ministers, perhaps he could've warned me. I was rather proud of that retort.

His jaw clenched, but I could not tell if he was sorry or simply restraining himself from further hostility. That's when the rain began to fall. He wrapped his coat around my shoulders, a thick, fur-lined one, then stomped ahead.

Poor Joseph's face still looked pale as this paper when he got down from the tree. He eyed me with a look that said, "You don't belong here," before joining his father.

I thought the same thing, but I had to overcome the doubt for the sake of this family. I could already tell they needed me—especially Joseph. It was evident he'd been raised well. I could see he was loved, taught, and given attention. But his eyes betrayed a deep pain. It reminded me of my grief after Mama and Papa died.

"Ginny dear, I'm sorry to interrupt your reading, but I don't want you to worry about dinner…." The voice filtered through her mind. Grandma Ethel was talking to her.

She blew out a breath, prying her eyes from the page. "Did you say something?" Her heart pattered like the rain on the roof. She hadn't realized how tense she was until she lowered the paper, but if she was honest, she would admit that Ellie's troubles contributed only a fraction to Ginny's heightened emotions.

"It's just that it's dinnertime. I've hardly eaten a thing all day. I don't want you to have to worry about cooking, so I was thinking of sending Brett for pizza at the Homeshore Café. The pizza there is truly delicious…."

Grandma continued talking, but Ginny's mind stuck on Brett. The bathroom shower still ran, and the minutes seemed like hours as she waited to see him again, to be with him. Why had he seemed so concerned that she was reading Ellie's letters? More than that, what would happen when the shock of seeing her wore off and the pain of what she'd done to him resurfaced?

She turned her eyes back to the older woman. "The Homeshore... did you want us to go pick up some pizza?"

Grandma Ethel offered a patient smile. "Weren't you listening, dear? Can you call and see if they are still open? They close early at times—for family birthdays and other special occasions. It's always better to check."

"Yes, of course." Ginny put down the letter and hurried to the phone. She quickly dialed the number she found on Grandma's list above the phone.

"Homeshore Café," a young woman's friendly voice answered.

"Yes, I'd like to order a large pizza."

"And this is…"

"Ginny."

"Do I know you, Ginny?"

"I'm staying with Grandma Ethel."

"Oh yes! Did Brett make it back?" the young woman's voice bubbled.

Ginny shook her head. This place still managed to surprise her. "Yes, he did. Got in this afternoon. He's taking a shower now…you know how it is, getting cleaned up."

"Sure do. So do they want their favorite pie?"

"Of course." She found herself smiling. "What else?"

The woman gave the total, and Ginny chuckled as she hung up, realizing she had no idea what Brett and Grandma Ethel's favorite pizza was.

Like Ellie, she'd been plunged into deep waters too. She was drowning—in friendliness, in community—and she was starting to think she didn't want to get pulled out.

But Ellie, poor Ellie. She hurried back to the letter.

Having no hat, my head was drenched by the time we reached the cabin. You know my hair, Grandfather. When it's wet, it curls up into tiny kinks. How I must've looked!

As soon as we stepped inside, the three children rushed to their father. A big smile filled his face as he knelt down to receive them into his arms. Then Janey spotted me. She's nine and has become my best friend here. Her beautiful eyes brightened as she drew close to me. With a big grin, she whispered, "You're not Miss Ellie McKinley, are you?"

When I said yes, she grasped my hand and whispered into my ear, "I've been praying you'd come soon. I'm the one who wrote the missions board. I copied his handwriting."

Oh, Grandfather, my heart sank to my frozen toes. She wrote the missions board? Not Reverend Parrish? No wonder he was surprised when he found out who I was. Before I could respond to Janey, four-year-old Zach marched up. His blond hair sagged across his forehead as he peeked up at me. "Who are you?"

I knelt down and told him my name.

"I'm Zach!" He scooted over and hugged his father's leg, then shot me with a wooden popgun. I pretended to be wounded, to which he smiled shyly and repeated his attacks.

When I straightened, I laid eyes on the sweetest little girl in the world. Baby Penny. The reverend had picked her up, and she rested her head on his shoulder. One of her tight blond curls stuck to her face. I fingered it free, and she smiled, then sucked her thumb.

I was so tired, and cold, and wet. My heart overflowed with melancholy. I missed you and our life, the comforts of San Francisco, our home. But, Grandfather, I wasn't hopeless. Meeting the children, seeing their loving home, made me think I could be a blessing here.

But then the reverend pulled me aside. "No offense, miss, but we've got no need for a governess here. I'm sorry you've come all this way. We'll keep you here till the next boat, but then you'll have to go."

"Reverend, please reconsider. Perhaps I could help your children..."

But as soon as I said that, he crossed his arms and frowned. He made it very clear I'm not to help them in any way. He's their father, and he will be the one to help them. And Grandfather, if I can't serve here, I may as well go home. The reverend's right about that.

I'll be seeing you sooner than we thought.

All my love,

Ellie Bell

Chapter Nineteen

....

Brett emerged from the bathroom sporting a pair of jeans, a wrinkled T-shirt, and damp, rumpled hair. He'd shaved, and his cheeks were pink. His smile was soft, inviting. His eyes locked with Ginny's from the moment he exited the bathroom door.

Her stomach did a flip. She offered a whistle. "Rodeo Drive would double their profits if they had models like you strolling the street."

She meant it as a joke, but the smile slipped from his lips. "I'm not going to LA."

"I didn't mean—" She put Ellie's letter back in the box. "It was just a compliment, that's all."

He nodded, but she wasn't sure he believed her. Was that what he thought, that she'd come all this way to lure him back to California?

"Listen, I really just came as someone needing a friend. I'm sorry I showed up unannounced. You know how impulsive I can be at times."

He nodded but didn't answer.

"I had Ginny order a pizza. It should be ready soon," Grandma called from the kitchen. "After we eat I'll head to bed so you two can talk."

Sweet Grandma. Did all grandmas think that every problem in the world could be solved with carbs and conversation?

Ginny moved to her pink suitcase next to the couch and pulled out her jacket.

"You're coming with me to pick up the pizza?" Brett's eyes widened.

She slid on the tweed blazer and then planted a hand on her hip. "Of course. I have to discover one of Gustavus's fine dining establishments."

He chuckled. "You mean Gustavus's only dining establishment, unless you count the Inn—but if you want to have dinner there, you need to call ahead of time so Judy can make enough."

Ginny's stomach filled with bubbles just hearing him talk. "Well, I definitely don't want to miss the only dining establishment then."

It took only three minutes to get to the Homeshore Café, which was housed in the same building as the Fireweed. The place was packed. Every table had a cluster of people around it, and they all looked up when Brett and Ginny entered. Many of them waved. At the table closest to the door, a very pregnant woman nibbled on the last piece of crust.

Ginny placed a hand on Brett's arm and leaned close to his ear. "That must be Gina," she said.

His head whipped around. "How did you know?"

She couldn't help but laugh. It felt good to laugh, cleansing. Ginny shrugged. "In a place like this, everybody knows everybody, right?"

Their pizza was waiting, but instead of picking up the box, Brett took her hand and led her around the room, introducing her. There were Lee and Linda Parker, Lori the librarian with her family, Gina, Susan, and Stephanie, who were enjoying a dinner away from their husbands and kids. They all welcomed Ginny to Gustavus, told her they hoped tomorrow would be better weather, and asked how Grandma Ethel was feeling.

"She's better. Perky, ever since Brett's been home."

Ginny chatted with Linda Parker as if she'd known her all her life. If anyone knew she was a recording artist, they didn't seem to care. Instead, Stephanie asked Ginny what size curling iron barrel she used to create soft waves, and Lee warned Brett about a bear he saw outside his back door.

"The salmon are spawning and the bears are enjoying the sushi." Lee chuckled. "Watch yourself on walks though." Lee looked at Ginny as he spoke. "They always seem to find the fresh meat."

"Lee, leave the girl alone." Linda playfully slugged his shoulder.

"They all wanted to ask why you're here and how long you're going to stay," Brett commented as they got back in the truck.

"I'm not sure." She shut her door. "I haven't decided."

And from the look in Brett's eyes that shone in the fading sunlight, it was clear he realized the one statement answered both questions.

When they got back home, Brett set the pizza on the table, and Ginny made a decision. She wasn't going to think about the past or about leaving. She wasn't going to worry about LA, the Grammys, or her boyfriend—if she could call Danny that. She'd just sit down and enjoy her pizza with an old friend.

As the pizza warmed in the oven, Brett went into Grandma's room to fix a leaky faucet, and Ginny eased onto the couch. She figured she'd have just enough time for one letter.

September 23, 1928

Dear Grandfather,

I've been here for two weeks now. The weather's getting worse, so there may not be a boat till spring. Otherwise, I'd already be gone. The reverend hasn't backed down from his determination to send me home.

Nevertheless, I'm doing my best for these children. I cannot just ignore them. They're joyful, obedient dears, but each one hides a sadness, a hole nothing but their mother can fill. I know that feeling. I still have it. I can't take the pain away, but perhaps I can ease it some. Bringing a loving touch to these lonely ones gives me some purpose.

It's not easy. That man hinders me at every turn. He won't accept my help, even in the smallest things. I try to make dinner and he says, "Let Janey do that." She's nine! I try to chop wood, and he says, "Let Joseph do that." I've made mistakes, but if he'd give me a chance, I could learn. His words are so cold. His disdain pains me, makes me feel even more alone than I already do. If he could just be a friend to me.

I confess I wanted to go home. Despite the sweet children, I could not imagine having to endure such an insufferable human being for another day. Before I knew the boats weren't running, I agreed to take the first ride back to Juneau.

But then, beautiful little Janey changed my mind. Her white hands curled beneath mine as she climbed onto my cot one evening while I was reading. She has the same big brown eyes as her father. Her bobbed brown hair flopped in her eyes, and she blew it away. Without a word she handed me three ripped pages from the reverend's journal. I know I shouldn't have read them, but I did.

And I want to stay.

Ellie

"Pizza!" Grandma called. Ginny put away the letter and joined Grandma and Brett at the table. Ellie wanted to stay with Clay. Did she see something under that tough exterior? As she looked across the table at Brett, she could understand.

"Now, tomorrow I don't want you two to stay around here all day." Grandma Ethel used a fork and a knife to cut her barbecued chicken pizza into small pieces. She pushed it around on her plate, and Ginny tried to pretend she didn't notice that Grandma had only taken a few bites.

"If you want something fun to do, there's a golf course right over yonder." Grandma tipped up her head in pride. "I have some clubs you can borrow…if I can find them. I believe they're in one of the storage sheds out back."

Ginny forced a smile. "Or I could rent some." She took another big bite of pizza. It was as good as any she could get in LA. Better even.

"There's no place to rent clubs. It's actually just a nice turf that Morgan keeps tended. There's a coffee can where you leave your fee."

Ginny paused with the pizza halfway to her mouth. "But what if someone takes the money?"

"Why would they want to do that?" Grandma Ethel clucked her tongue.

Grandma went on to tell her how Morgan created the golf course out of a field. After a few minutes, it was clear the older woman was getting tired.

"Grandma, would you like me to help you get ready for bed?" Ginny asked.

She offered a slight nod. "Would you? I'm afraid I'm sorer from my fall than I thought."

Ginny tucked her arm under Grandma Ethel's and helped her to stand. Then she turned back to Brett. "I'll be right back."

His eyes were on her, and his lips were parted slightly. He didn't say anything but he nodded. She could see appreciation in his gaze.

Ginny helped Grandma dress in her pajamas, noticing a large bruise on her side. "Are you sure you're all right? That looks like it hurts."

Grandma Ethel waved a hand in the air. "I've had worse; just smarts a little. I need a good night's sleep, that's all."

Ginny nodded and then tucked her in. As she prepared to turn out the lamp on Grandma's nightstand, she noticed tears in Grandma Ethel's eyes.

"Are you okay?" Ginny leaned in closer.

"You remind me of someone, that's all." Her voice wasn't much more than a whisper. Ginny followed Grandma Ethel's gaze to the side table. On it sat a black-and-white photo of a woman with sweet features and a contented smile on her face. She pointed. "Her?"

Grandma Ethel shrugged. "Maybe, maybe not. I'll tell you more later…"

"Later?"

"After you finish the letters."

"Then you assume I'm going to stick around until I do?"

"I won't assume nothing, dear." Grandma Ethel yawned, and Midnight jumped up onto the bed, curling up next to Grandma Ethel's feet. "But I can tell from the look in your eye that you want to. After all, the letters and my grandson are sitting in that living room out there. So why don't you let this old women get some sleep while you dive into the past…and maybe talk about the future?"

* * * * *

Brett sat on the floral sofa, leaning forward with his elbows on his knees. His fingers were knotted through his hair, and Ginny figured he was deep in thought. It was only as she sat in the chair next to him that she realized he was praying.

Her cheeks warmed; she felt as though she was intruding. Prayer was such an intimate thing, and for the first time in a long time Ginny wondered why she didn't pray more often.

After a minute he lifted his head. "I can't tell you how good it is to see you."

"Thanks." She curled up her legs and tucked them under her. "I'm glad I didn't leave. I would have regretted it if we never had that chance to talk."

"So what is it, Ginny? Why have you come?"

It was the open door she needed, and for the next ten minutes she told him about the recording contract, the concert tours, the cameras that followed her everywhere she went, and even the invitation to the Grammys. The only thing she didn't tell him about was Danny.

Brett nodded as he listened, but he had a strange look in his eye, as if he were expecting something else.

Finally she paused. "You know what? I'm being completely selfish. You're tired. I would be if I slept on the ground last night. I should probably let you go. You don't need to listen to this now." She looked out the window. "Maybe we can go golfing tomorrow. Or you can show me around this place. I'm sure there's much to see in Gustavus beyond your grandmother's living room."

"I'm not tired. I'm okay. It's just…" He let his voice trail off.

"What?"

"I thought you'd maybe start with an apology first."

"Apology?" Her brow furrowed. "I'm the one who came up here and found you."

"You're the one who left." He leaned back on the couch, crossing his arms over his chest. "It's been two years, Ginny."

"It's been two years because you didn't come after me."

"Come after you?" He stood and strode toward the wood fire. "You left, Ginny. Did I need to follow so you could turn your back on me again? I'm sorry if once wasn't good enough for you."

She cocked her head and stared, unsure of what to say. What to do. What a fool she was to think Brett wouldn't bring that up. Wouldn't be hurt. She expected a happy reaction from him—like the one she saw earlier.

Brett paced the room, going back and forth between the woodstove and the front door. Then he paused, turned to her, and shook his head.

When he focused on her, hurt radiated from his gaze. It was like a knife to the gut. He wasn't only mad that she'd left, he was wounded. And here she was explaining all her success—success she achieved only by walking away from him. *What a fool.*

Ginny stood and moved toward him, stretching out a hand. "Brett—"

He held up a palm, blocking her advance. "Listen, Ginny. I'm glad you're here, and I want to talk to you. I really do. But…well, the truth is, I've been praying for you, thinking about you a lot lately, and I'm still trying to wrap my mind around you being here. If it's all right, I'd like to talk tomorrow. There's too much going on in my mind tonight." He placed a hand over his heart. "It takes my breath away just being in the same room with you—and I mean that in a good way. But I need to think. Pray."

Part of her ached. He'd been thinking about her? Praying for her? Could that be the reason she was here?

"Yes, of course." Ginny stepped forward, clasping her hands in front of her. "I'm looking forward to seeing you then." She smiled, feeling her chin quiver. It had been easy to forget how much she'd hurt him when she was so far away. But here, looking into his eyes… She struggled to suck in a breath.

Without another word, he turned and strode out the door. He didn't say when he'd be back. He didn't tell her to look after Grandma. Thirty seconds later, his truck backed out, leaving Bud's van looking lonely in the driveway.

Ginny locked the door, but was that even necessary? Then she turned and pressed her back against it.

So much for not thinking of the past. So much for trying to get advice. She'd gotten a peek into Brett's heart, and it was obvious she'd left some holes by leaving. Ginny rubbed the back of her neck as it hit her—really hit her as it never had before.

She'd been sad her whole life.

Ginny barely remembered her mother, and she wished she could forget some of the foster homes she'd lived in. *What did I do to deserve Mother's leaving?*

"Opened the front door and dropped Ginny off without looking back," she'd heard one of her foster mothers whisper to a friend.

How could it be that the pain of abandonment she'd carried all these years hadn't stopped her from doing the same to Brett?

Love lost. Loneliness. Maybe she should get used to it. Who was she to think she could ever give her whole heart to anyone—even a guy like Brett—without causing more pain than joy?

She returned to the box of letters, discovering pages with ripped edges underneath the letter she'd just read. They must be the pages from Clay's journal. Ginny sat down to read them, knowing that at least Ellie's story could take her mind off her own sad tale for a while.

Chapter Twenty

....

September 30, 1927

This day, the thirtieth since Adelaide's death, no sun shines on the bay. Summer's gone. Winter's in the air. Chopping wood's been a kindness to me. My hands protest with their blisters and calluses, but my damaged heart finds solace in the excursion. I have fished, as I am doing now, for hours each day in hopes of stocking our cellar with smoked salmon. The children clam from what seems like morning till night, with Joseph leading. My boy's got a temper on him—like his Scottish mama—but he also shines all manner of tenderness and joy. Adelaide's.

We managed to salt and smoke the fish, can the clams. We made an attempt to can the strawberries. May not have as many this year, or rutabagas.

A Stellar's Jay—that irksome blue bird—squawks from the bush across the river, intruding on my calm. My hands are still wet from the first salmon I caught. They smell, I suppose, but I don't notice. Don't feel much at all.

Little Zach collects wildflowers—forget-me-nots—and creates a wreath on Adelaide's side of our bed each day. One handful at a time, he lays them down and mouths, "God bless Mama."

Yesterday, after he set out the blue flowers on Adelaide's patchwork quilt, I pulled him to my knee to ascertain what his little mind was figuring.

*"When my mama comes home, she will like it. I don't
want her to think I forgot her."*

*Zach went to her funeral at the schoolhouse. Heard
"Amazing Grace" sung by our ragtag congregation whilst Edith
Parker played the pump organ. Zach watched his mama's coffin
get lowered into the ground, disappearing under handfuls of
black soil. He listened as we gave thanks for my priceless wife—
better than rubies. He heard the prayers of the reverend—me. A
husband ought not have to perform his own wife's funeral.*

*Then I hugged him. "Mama would surely think it a kind
gift." And he ran off to dig clams with his brothers and sister.*

*Each day by nightfall the flowers wilt; the circle wreath
wrenches apart. So I throw the petals away. He does it again
the next day.*

Tears rolled down Ginny's cheeks. Midnight approached, meow-
ing. She wiped her nose with her sleeve and continued, turning to the
next page.

October 5, 1927

*I'm sitting beneath this hemlock. I scouted along the banks
of our Salmon River about two miles for a fishing hole, but I
could've stopped anywhere. The river glows orange-red with
salmon. But I couldn't pick a spot. Every nook reminds me of
her. Her smile, her laughter floats with the brook's music.*

*I passed a landing where we picnicked. Our friend
Patricia took care of the baby so we could make our escape.
Thank God for her.*

*My wife giggled as we crossed the river, hopping from log
to log. Then my foot slipped into the water, soaking my boot.*

*She mocked me relentlessly. But then she lost her balance and
soaked her skirt. The words that spewed from those candy-
sweet lips! I told her she lost her salvation for sure, spouting
such language, but then she reminded me I'm Presbyterian.*

*So we sat by the campfire, keeping each other warm, eating
the smoked salmon she packed, before we wandered on home.*

*Like a salmon upstream, a smile fights to reach my face when
remembering her, but how can I smile? How can I? Ever again?*

October 1, 1928

Dear Grandfather,

This is surely a strange place. We have frequent visitors to our
garden. Remember the moose and her calf that terrified me on my
first day here? Well, they've found their way to our garden. The
children tolerate them, but since "Mama Moose" (that's what they've
named her) charged Joseph, I have a hysterical fit when I see her.

Linc tried to help me by rigging a chair to a rope from
the house to the outhouse. He thought I could just sail above
the moose, but what a disaster that was. The reverend has no
endurance for my outbursts. He's still hard on me, but all I can
think of are those journal entries. I try to be patient.

All my love,
Ellie Bell

October 5, 1928

Dear Brother Peter,

I'm grateful for your desire to help my family and me by
sending your granddaughter here, but I'm afraid she's not
suited either to the rough Alaska life or governing a quiver of
children. Not only is she terribly afraid of wildlife—coyotes,

marmots, porcupines, and especially moose—but she allowed
my nephew to rig up a foolhardy invention that sent the
outhouse into the river.

And she doesn't know how to shoot. Now I don't blame
her for that, but she's not even willing to learn. Won't go near
a gun of any kind.

She's not a bad girl. Just not cut out for this place or my
family or me. I've half a mind to send her to the Parkers' for
the winter, but seeing as Janey's taking a liking to her, I'll let
her stay. Just until spring.

Clay

October 20, 1928

Dear Brother Peter,

I fear for the nutritional needs of my children.

Last night when we got home, we found the house nearly
burned down. Smoke billowed out the door.

Rushing inside, we found Ellie covered in corn flour, on her
hands and knees in the kitchen. When she heard us, she jerked up
with sheer terror as if a bear family had moseyed through the door.

I yelled a bit, I'm sorry to say. I don't know why she tried
to cook in the first place. I never expected her to, but she
assured me she could.

This girl's causing me more trouble than help. I'm sorry,
Brother Peter. It's just the truth.

Heard her crying last night, not loud wails, but soft pleading
sobs. And she said a name, James. A love lost, perhaps? Is that
why she came? It will be best for all when she goes on home in
the spring.

Clay Parrish

Nov. 2, 1928

Dear Grandfather,

Life is difficult here, as you've probably garnered from my letters, but I'm starting to see how these folks get by. They depend on each other. We have some very nice neighbors. The Curtises live close by—meaning five miles downriver. They have a teen boy, and a Tlingit girl also lives with them. It's good for Joseph to have friends.

I'm also eternally grateful for the Parkers. Some of the first homesteaders here, they have a good-sized farmhouse and even bigger hearts. Edith Parker and her daughter, May White (with her six children!), came by today and brought me a basket of cakes and treats. They even brought clothes fit for life on "the flats" (that's what they call this area because of the acres of grassy fields). They gifted me sturdy men's boots—like the ones they wore. What James's mother would think of me in these!

Edith Parker shared stories from her early days, some funny, sad, harrowing. And that was enough. Knowing another soul traveled this path before me—and survived—gave me hope.

You know, Grandfather, maybe that's all I have to offer Joseph. I lost my mother too. I pray I'll have an opportunity to share those memories with him—and that his heart will be open. I know you'll pray too.

Later

I could deal with this strange way of life—the skunks, moose, even bears (a real nasty one's been killing the homesteaders' cattle)—but it's particularly difficult to handle a man who seems to hate me. Just yesterday morning, he snapped at me for giving the children maple syrup on their oats. I didn't know they only used it for special occasions. And then later in the afternoon, I asked if we could eat some of the smoked salmon in the basement for lunch. You'd think I'd asked for Cornish game hens. Apparently, I have "no common sense about how to survive a winter."

The worst of it, Grandfather, is when he ignores me. It makes me feel worthless, unfit not only for this place but for even his meager attention. I don't know why he won't even be cordial to me. Maybe he thinks that if he accepts another woman's care of his home, he'll be disrespecting Adelaide. It's her sugar, her salmon, her kitchen, her family I've invaded.

Janey just came in and pulled a chair next to mine. We like to work on quilts together when we have the chance. As she stitched, she again asked me not to give up on her papa. "He's a good man, kind and funny. The best papa in the world. Please, don't leave him—and us." The reverend called her from outside, and she scampered away.

A few minutes later, the reverend appeared in the doorway. I don't know what Janey said, but I think she influenced him somehow. She's a very influential girl.

"Come on out. We're playing with those rings Linc and Joseph made. Seeing which one rolls fastest."

So I did. And it was fun.

Love, Ellie

Dec. 1, 1928

Dear Grandfather,

Folks around here love to throw a shindig. This one couple especially, Ruth and Fred Matson. Every Saturday night (and often other nights too) they invite everyone to their large home.

There are only about thirty of us on the flats during the winter months. So Mrs. Parker, her daughter Mrs. White, the other ladies, and I relish time together. I've made friends, Grandfather. I'm falling in love with this community. I can't help it.

Well, when we first went, the reverend avoided dancing with me, but maybe because it seemed rude to avoid me, he finally asked me to dance. He's asked me every time we've been back.

Last night, we headed downstream to the Martins' homestead. When we arrived, the house was all lit up with kerosene lamps and the party had already started, with Mr. Parker playing the guitar and Ruth Matson pumping on the organ.

Joseph, Linc, and Janey jumped right in with the musicians. May White's girls hoisted Zach and Penny from us, and Clay and I were left alone in the little entryway. I took off my gloves and was headed to the parlor when he stopped me. At these dances, he looks so different from the scruffy man I first met. When he combs his hair and wears clean clothes, he's almost handsome. Actually, he is handsome. I have a hard time not staring at his dark eyes. But you don't want to hear that, do you, Grandfather?

Anyway, in the entryway, he stood crooked in front of me, one shoulder lower than the other, his hands in his belt loops.

"Ellie, I was hard on you today, and I'm sorry."

I blinked. First, because it was the first time he'd called me Ellie and not Miss Ellie. And second, because he'd been hard on me every day since I came. I couldn't fathom what made today different. Seems he's either scolding me or ignoring me (except when we're dancing).

"It's all right." I offered a smile.

He smiled back. He has a nice smile. Then he unstrapped his guitar from his back, tugged me to a sofa in a nook in the

kitchen, and told me to wait. A minute later he came back
with another guitar.

"We like music up here. Time you learned."

He offered me the instrument. My throat tightened at his
gesture. I slowly received it, awestruck.

"Does this mean we can be friends?" I asked as he sat down.

He grinned. "I didn't say that."

I chuckled. He showed me how to hold it. And until my fingers
got too sore, he patiently sat with me, showing me basic chords.

Later, as we weaved and sashayed the quick country
dances, I felt a closeness to him. It was a nice feeling.

I may grow to like him after all.

Love,

Ellie Bell

Ginny stretched, her feet hanging off the floral couch, and felt pressure on her chest. She glanced at her guitar case leaning against the wall near the window. She hadn't opened it since she came, hadn't thought about music, but she liked reading about how it gave Ellie a connection with Clay. She wondered if Ellie kept it up. No matter what happened—whether she was a recording artist or simply Ginny— music would always be a part of her life. That she knew for sure. She propped herself up and continued reading.

December 2, 1928

Dear Grandfather,

I want to tell you about something that happened that
needs your prayers.

On the nights we don't live it up at the Matsons' for music
and dancing, we spend our evenings around the fire. Mostly

we play games. You would love it. All different sorts. Cooties is the most popular—it's fun! You roll dice and, depending on the number, draw a body part. Whoever builds a whole body first yells "Cootie!" I'll have to teach it to you sometime.

Before the fun begins each night, we have family worship. It's not so different from how you and I spent our evenings when I was growing up. Clay reads the catechism and a passage from the Bible, and we sing a hymn as he plays guitar. He seems gratified that I know my catechism. We're on "What are God's works of providence?" Janey's always the first to answer: "God's works of providence are His most holy, wise, and powerful preserving and governing all His creatures, and all their actions."

One time, the always-direct Linc asked why, if God preserves and governs everything, did his aunt Adelaide die? The reverend swallowed, but in the fireplace's glow, I saw his brown eyes soften.

I wanted to hear his answer, but Joseph jumped in. "You shouldn't ask that."

"What do you mean?" Linc asked. "Don't you ever wonder?"

"Nope." Joseph's lip pinched as if he were forcing it still. The tight lines on his forehead returned.

Clay shook his head. "It's all right, Joseph. Your cousin asked a fair question. We don't always know why the good Lord chooses certain things for us, and there was a long time after Mama died that I was angry."

"At God?" Janey gaped up from where she rested her head against his knee.

"God seemed to have abandoned me up here. I wouldn't trust Him. And that was wrong. If anyone can be trusted, *it's the Savior. He's always true, always faithful, loving, kind, right. I couldn't see that then.*

"But, you know, I've been through a fair share of painful times. Not complaining, just telling. My mama passed, my sister, even Aunt Penelope. He never left me then, but stayed firm and strong, like a rock. I learned—even though it's tough sometimes—my Father knows best."

Joseph interrupted by slamming his fist against the wood-planked floor. "That's a load of bull! God could've saved her and He didn't. I'm sick of hearing about how good He is." He stomped through the room toward the door.

Ever ready to help, little Zach ran after him and grabbed his leg. "Don't leave, Joseph!"

"Let go." Joseph's voice softened a touch toward his little brother. "I need to get out of here."

"Where?" Clay asked.

"To the Curtises'. They don't talk about God all the time."

"You go ahead." Clay stood and patted Joseph's shoulder. "Be back for breakfast."

Without a word, Joseph stalked out the door into the dark night.

Zach started to cry and clung to me. I held him on my lap, and he buried his head in my chest. "I miss Mama."

"Joseph misses Mama too." Janey nuzzled into Clay's side.

I stood, carrying Zach, and patted Janey's shoulder. I caught Clay's eye and tried to express compassion.

He touched my hand, and his eyes looked almost grateful. That's when I knew I loved him.

Love, Ellie

Chapter Twenty-One

....

Ginny forced an eye open and noticed Midnight, curled up and sleeping next to her on the couch, content not to move.

She tried to open her eyes all the way, but they felt sticky and heavy as if they'd been stuck together with superglue. Then she remembered—the tears. They'd come as she finished Ellie's letter.

She picked it up and reread the spot where she'd stopped:

He touched my hand, and his eyes looked almost grateful. That's when I knew I loved him.

There were more letters, but the emotion had stopped Ginny from reading on.

Reading Ellie's words had cut through all *her* excuses for coming. Ginny had said she wanted advice, but maybe it wasn't advice she'd come for after all. Maybe a nudging deep in her heart told her there was something—someone—more important than what fame and money could bring.

But what did that mean now? How could she fly home knowing this? Worse, how would Brett feel if he knew? He'd moved on—settled in. What would he think about her disrupting his happy little world?

She stretched again, and Midnight got the hint. Ginny rose and slipped her silk robe over her pajamas and then glanced at the clock. She didn't want to get up too early and wake Grandma Ethel.

She reached for the letters, her heart full of longing, aching. Had Ellie felt the same?

Ellie had lived in the same home as Clay, cared for his children. How did she love without letting him know? And how did she handle his missing Adelaide? Ginny's heart ached even more thinking about it.

Ginny picked up the next letter, in a strange way feeling as if an invisible string had tied her heart to this sweet woman from the past.

December 10, 1928

Dear Mr. Barnett,

Your granddaughter, Miss Ellie, is so pretty! I like her brown, curly hair. I'm learning to read better. She brought the Aesop's Fables, *and we do our numbers. I like it when she makes dinner because she gives us meat from the basement. I think it's naughty, though. The boys don't tell her that meat's supposed to be used sparingly.*

I think she likes Papa. She's got big eyes when he's around. I don't know why since he's not that nice to her. He should be nicer. It's making her not as happy here and I'm afraid she might go stateside.

My papa likes her too. At first I thought he hated her, because he's so mean sometimes. But then I remembered what my brother Joseph told me when the Curtis boy used to call me "buckteeth." Joseph said he was mean because he liked me but didn't want to admit it. I think that's what's going on with my papa. Plus, his eyes are soft when he looks at her and she doesn't notice.

Do you think Mama would mind Papa being in love with Miss Ellie? I wouldn't want to hurt Mama's feelings. Joseph said he doesn't think it'd be right. He doesn't like Miss Ellie. When Papa was real nice to her one night, Joseph got mad and left.

What can you do to help us? Will you come visit?

Janey

December 20, 1928

Dear Grandfather,

It must be obvious to you by now how this life wears on me at times—not only the perils of moose and wolves, but also the day-to-day, backbreaking chores. I try to stay positive. In fact, I'm finding satisfaction in my callused hands and muscled arms. Not many women master the ways of the Alaskan wild, but I'm learning (though I definitely haven't mastered it yet!).

Just when I think I'm doing better, I'll pull off another terrible blunder. I'm afraid I've done something to cause even more frustration for poor Clay. I offended some of his parishioners.

It was a gray day; the icy mist never burned off, even by noon. My muscles ached from splitting wood, and the little ones whined and fussed, refusing to take their naps. Penny's getting big enough to climb out of her crib, and when after the fourth time she tumbled onto the floor, I lost my patience. "Penny!" I blurted. "You are so naughty!"

In that moment, a troop of Tlingit women, including Patricia—the one Clay has told me about several times—emerged from the misty afternoon into the middle of our parlor. They didn't even knock, just marched up the front steps and traipsed on in.

I've only heard the most favorable reports about Patricia from Clay and the Parkers as well—how much she helped after Adelaide passed, how the children love her, and so on. Linc even told me she's why Clay turned down your offer to provide a wife—Patricia took care of everything. (Her Tlingit name isn't Patricia, by the way. We can't pronounce their sounds, so they kindly take on names we can say.)

Well, she and the other women barged in and started cleaning and putting the house in order. I don't even know them. They hung the quilts, gave Penny and Zach baths with a sap-smelling soup, swept the floor, washed the dishes, and even cleaned the new outhouse. I tried to help, but they worked so fast, and I couldn't understand their language. They laughed at how I folded a sheet and took it out of my hand to do it for me.

When the Indian women finally finished cleaning, they cooked. Warm scents of salmon, clams, and wheat cakes breathed life into the musty cabin. There were rutabagas too. Everyone's favorite (except mine)!

As I opened the door, I heard Patricia say in English (apparently she knows both), "I can see why Reverend needed us to clean. Poor girl." She must've heard me coming because she stopped and smiled sympathetically.

My heart plunged.

Then they served me rutabaga pudding, and I hate to say, but I was not able to keep it down. I was forced to spit it out again in my cloth. Oh, Grandfather, it turns my stomach to even think of that horrid stuff!

Couldn't the women see their presence proved what a failure I've been at this? I thought I was doing better, but obviously Clay doesn't think so, or he wouldn't have had them come.

I asked them to leave. I wasn't very nice or thankful. Rude, you could call me. I wanted my little Alaskan world back to normal. My normal. Not the way Patricia or anyone else wanted it.

But what was I thinking? This is not my world. I have no say if the reverend wants a cleaning crew to do my work.

I'm not important here. And as far as Clay is concerned I'm leaving at the first sign of spring.

Ellie

December 21, 1928

Dear Brother Peter,

I'm afraid much of my work with the Tlingits in the outskirts has been compromised. Reverend Martin sent a note with a courier, letting me know his concern.

The women from his parish, led by that saint Patricia, came all the way from Hoonah to help Ellie with the cleaning yesterday. To be clear—and Ellie doesn't believe this—I did not ask them to come. They wanted to help, and I said it would be fine. It was their idea.

Honestly, I thought it might serve as a respite for Ellie. I think she was overwhelmed by all the work. With the snowfall and the short days, a person can get depressed. I wanted to help her.

Fact is, I don't need help from her or anyone. I let the Tlingit ladies come only because they seem to like it. I want to parent my children and shepherd my flock. That's it. I don't need or want to get married again.

Anyway, the reason for my letter is to tell you the Tlingits and Reverend Martin have requested I come to Hoonah, taking Ellie with me, to discuss how to soothe the offended women.

We leave as soon as the weather clears.

Clay

Chapter Twenty-Two

....

Ginny's hair was still damp when she exited the bathroom. She paused in her steps to hear Grandma Ethel humming in the kitchen.

Grandma stopped stirring something in a bowl and turned. "There you are."

Ginny hurried forward and planted a kiss on the woman's soft cheek. She smelled like Olay. Ginny knew that smell. It was the same face cream Robyn used to wear. "Good morning, Grandma."

"Brett called. He should be here in thirty minutes. He had some errands to do this morning but has a special surprise for you."

"Really, what?"

Grandma Ethel clicked her tongue. "If I told you, it wouldn't be a surprise, now would it?"

Ginny placed a hand on her hip. "My, aren't you full of vinegar this morning." She chuckled. "It looks as if you're feeling better."

"Yes, I prayed to the good Lord that He'd let me stick around a little longer. I'm eager to finish the story."

Ginny cocked an eyebrow. "The story? Are you in the middle of a novel? Wow, I bet that novelist would be excited to know his or her book captured you that much."

Grandma tossed her gray curls from side to side. "No, nothing like that. I want to be around to discover God's good plan for sending you up here. That's more exciting than any novel."

Grabbing a mug and pouring herself a cup of coffee, Ginny

smiled. Did she believe that? That God was writing a story with her as the main character?

"You have time to read one more letter before he gets here." Grandma Ethel's voice interrupted her thoughts.

Ginny placed two pieces of bread in the toaster. "But don't you need help?"

"I'm feeling better. Thank you, though." She pulled out a butter dish from her small refrigerator. "Besides, I can see what letter you have next. I think you'll like it." The old woman wrinkled her nose and smiled.

"You know which letters are which?"

"Oh yes. I've read them many times. In fact, whenever I need a bit of hope I reread them all again."

February 20, 1929

Dear Brother Peter,

We've had storms. Storm after storm. Even stormed on Christmas, but we all managed to huddle in the Matsons' parlor and gobble down yuletide fare. The kids acted out the Christmas story. Such a joy to see them learning about Jesus. And we sang carols.

The storms finally let up, and all signs point to a spell of clear weather. We can finally make that trip to Hoonah tomorrow. Tonight, I spoke to Ellie about it. The children all settled, she went to fetch water, and I joined her. It was a beautiful night, clear and cold. As we walked, we talked. She's easy to talk to, I'm finding. And we laughed out loud together. I confess to a certain comfort in those moments, laughing with her.

I had a notion to tell her how good she's been with the children. When I mentioned I appreciated her gentle touch with them, well, if her eyes didn't gleam a bit, teary like. And then she hugged me. My arms wrapped around her, and I didn't want to let go.

And there you have it. This isn't working, Brother Peter. Any pretty and kind woman living in close proximity would stir up feelings in a man, even me. But we've been hurt too much to risk another loss.

I pushed back then and told her to be ready with Penny at daybreak. We walked back in silence.

But before we retired to our separate rooms, her soft hand touched mine. Said she was sorry. I thought she meant for the hug, but she went on, saying she was sorry about my wife's passing. She said, "I pray every day I can shower love on the children." Then she let go of my hand and looked in my eyes. "And on you." That's what she said! She covered her mouth and stepped back. "Help you, I mean. Be a help to you."

Now I fear she'll get hurt too. All due respect, Brother Peter, this is all your fault.

Clay

Chapter Twenty-Three

....

Ginny climbed into Brett's truck, remembering their first date. He'd won free passes to Knott's Berry Farm, and it had been their first time there. They'd spent the day running around the theme park like little kids. She smiled just thinking of it. But she had to remind herself this wasn't a date.

"You know, I've been loving those letters, and I was wondering if Grandma Ethel had any photos of the people in them—of Ellie and Clay. Or even old photos of Glacier Bay. It would be cool to see how things looked back then."

"I think she does somewhere, but you're not going to recognize anything from around this area. Everything's changed now."

"Changed? But there's still not too many houses or buildings."

He pulled onto the main road, keeping his speed limit to twenty-five miles per hour. "Oh, the buildings haven't changed much, it's the trees. Fifty years ago none of these trees were here. Well, not many. They've all sprouted up."

"No trees?" Ginny glanced around, trying to imagine that. Thick pine forests stretched in every direction.

"The glaciers came down the mountain and wiped everything out. I think it was about three hundred years ago. After the ice receded, things began to grow again and the land could be inhabited. I have Tlingit friends in Hoonah. The stories of when the big glaciers came down have been passed on for generations."

"But the trees, they're everywhere," she said again, still not able to believe it.

"That's how life is, don't you think? If given the chance, new life is born from what's once been stripped away."

Ginny turned to him, studying his profile. "Yeah." She crossed her arms over her chest. "I like that."

They'd driven past Four Corners when Brett pulled into a small lot on the left. A few other cars were parked there, in front of an old cabin that had seen better years.

"So…" She turned to him. "Is this a hot hangout spot in these parts?"

"You can say that." He slipped on a baseball cap and climbed from the truck.

She climbed out too, closed the door, and then followed him to the building. As they neared the steps, he paused.

"I have dinner reservations for us at the Glacier Bay Lodge, but today… well, the historical society is having a work day. You've been so interested in the letters, I thought this might be fun." He mounted the steps.

"Oh… Uh, that does sound fun." She hoped her words sounded convincing. Inside, her heart sank. She wanted time alone with Brett. She wanted to talk.

He opened the cabin door, and her gaze swept over half a dozen people to a pile of boxes stacked along the wall. She smiled as many turned and waved. The last thing she wanted was to spend all day talking with strangers and sorting through old boxes.

A middle-aged woman approached, and Ginny recognized Linda Parker from the Homeshore Café. Linda swept her up in a hug, and Ginny supposed she should get used to being treated like an old friend by everyone in Gustavus.

"There you are. Brett said he was bringing you by." Linda brushed her hand through her grayish-brown hair. You remember my husband, Lee?"

Ginny followed her gaze to a man wearing a cowboy hat and vest. His green eyes sparkled. Lee approached, stretching out his hand, and she shook it.

"Hi again, Ginny." Then Lee reached over and squeezed Brett's shoulder. "I hope you don't mind me stealing you away for a bit. There are a few boxes at the hangar I need help with."

"Sure, no problem." Brett glanced over at Ginny. "I'll be right back. Linda will take good care of you."

She reached out and took his hand, causing him to pause and turn back. His eyes widened.

"Hurry back," she whispered loud enough for only him to hear. "I came here to see *you* after all."

He nodded, and she released her grasp. Swallowing hard, she turned back to the other women. Linda motioned for Ginny to follow her to the boxes. "There is so much good stuff here."

A younger woman—not much older than Ginny—tucked her hands in her pockets. "I'm not sure if Brett told you, but we're setting up a museum of sorts. Today we're going through all the things to find the best of the best."

"He didn't tell me. But it sounds great." She heard a buzzing in her purse. She must be within reach of cell service. The temptation rose to check her messages, but that would be rude. Besides, at this moment she was tempted to text Danny to make arrangements to get her home. And while part of her wanted that, another part told her to wait, be patient.

Linda pulled a lid off one of the boxes. Inside were old photos, a wooden box, a harmonica, and some children's books that appeared to be at least fifty years old.

"When I look at these items, I don't see the rust and age," Linda said. "I imagine lantern light and guitar music, the community sharing fun and laughter in long-ago Strawberry Point."

Ginny's ears perked up. "Strawberry Point? Is it near here?"

"Ginny dear, you didn't know? Gustavus *is* Strawberry Point." Linda smiled. "That's what it was called all those years ago."

Excitement built in Ginny's chest. *This is the place. Ellie came here.* "I was wondering…." she began. "I've been reading letters about a young woman named Ellie and a man she came to be a governess for—Reverend Clay Parrish."

Linda's eyes sparkled, and she again brushed her hair back from her face. "Reverend Parrish has a wonderful history in these parts. I don't know about any letters—I'll have to ask Ethel about that. But you'll be very excited to learn that the cabin—this cabin—belonged to him."

"This is Clay's cabin?" Ginny glanced around, and suddenly the place took on new life. Her heart warmed as she noticed sunlight streaming through the front window and imagined Ellie standing at that very spot, looking out.

"Brett was the driving source behind moving it here," a woman with short red hair explained. "He did most of the work. When he heard of the historical society's dream for a museum, he went from house to house, asking for volunteers and donations."

Ginny picked up some type of metal contraption and turned it over in her hands. "He seems to love it here." She sighed as she placed it in back in the box.

The other women grew excited about a small locket found in one of the boxes. *He seems to love this place more than he cares for me. Not that I blame him.*

She sank down on the dusty floor and began to sort through some old records. The dust from the boxes filled the air, and she found herself sneezing every few minutes. Her head started to ache. She didn't know if it was from the dust or if she was coming down with something.

The women chattered on, and she was certain they'd forgotten she was there until one of them turned to her with bright eyes.

"Been out to the plane crash yet, Ginny?" an older women asked.

"You mean the one outside Juneau? Someone told me about it on my way here."

"No, that was a commercial jet crash. There was another plane that went down right here in Gustavus. Have you seen that hiking sign two miles out from Mountain View Road?"

"Oh, the one said that says TRAIL?"

"Yes, there is a trail there—or at least a worn spot. If you hike a quarter mile out, there's wreckage from a plane that crashed here back in the fifties."

"It was a National Guard plane," Linda explained. "They were on their way to Anchorage, but weather became a problem. High winds and turbulence prevented them from landing at Annette Island. They headed north to Gustavus, since we had good runway lights and equipment for night landings—even better than Juneau in those days."

"And they didn't make it?"

Linda shook her head. "The California pilot wasn't used to Alaskan conditions and the snow. He circled, missing the runway twice, and on his third attempt the plane went down."

"Was anyone hurt?"

"Everyone was hurt. Thankfully the passengers made it, but all the crew members were killed."

"That's so sad." Ginny placed a hand to her temple, realizing that the headache had grown into a pounding she couldn't ignore.

The women continued chatting about the plane wreck. Several of them had lived in the area at the time, and some of their friends and family members were the first to respond.

Ginny tried to listen, but the more she sat, the more her whole body ached. Finally one of the women paused and looked at her.

"Are you feeling all right?" the woman asked.

"Actually, I think I'm coming down with something. I'm going to ask Brett to take me back to Grandma Ethel's house when he gets back."

"Nonsense. That hangar is a mess. You should see all the stuff stored in there. I can't imagine it'll take them less than two hours. Thankfully Kelly was going to meet them and help sort through some things. Still, it might take a while. Why don't I take you home?"

Kelly. Of course. The pounding in Ginny's temples grew worse.

She didn't argue. She said good-bye to the others, and just ten minutes later, Linda was pulling her burgundy SUV into Grandma Ethel's driveway.

"I'm worried I wasn't more help," Ginny said. "But thanks for the ride. I appreciate it so much." She opened the door. The wind had picked up and the frigid air that blew in chilled her to the bone.

"One minute, dear." Linda reached out a hand, placing it on Ginny's arm. "Are you going to be around here long? Because I'd like to ask you about singing at the fund-raiser for Brett. It's this Saturday night. We're putting on a production—folks are reenacting scenes from our first settlers. I know you're not one of those types who shows off your fame, but I thought it might be nice for folks who enjoy your music."

Ginny was surprised this woman knew who she was—knew about her music—but that didn't surprise her the most. "Wait." She held up a hand. "What are you talking about? What is Brett raising funds for?"

"Don't you know, dear?" Linda patted Ginny's hand. "Brett's heading to Africa next month. We've been doing all we can to help him prepare."

* * * * *

Concern furrowed Grandma Ethel's brow as Ginny entered the front door. "What's wrong? Where's Brett? Are you coming down with something?"

Ginny nodded. "I think I am. My head hurts something terrible." She placed a hand on her forehead. It was the truth. What she didn't say was that her heart hurt something terrible too.

Why hadn't he mentioned Africa? Why hadn't he taken the time to talk to her? Maybe she should have left Alaska. She felt like a fool for coming at all.

"You better get a cup of cocoa and the warm quilt from my bed. In fact, why don't you nap in there for a while? And when you wake up, there are always more letters." Grandma Ethel winked.

"Thanks. That does sound nice. But I better call Brett and tell him I won't be able to make it to the lodge for dinner. He should cancel our reservations."

"No." The word shot from Grandma Ethel's mouth. "That's a few hours away. There's time to rest and still make it to dinner." She pattered to the kitchen and grabbed a big bottle from the cupboard. "Vitamin C." She shook a couple of tablets into her hand then brought them over.

"Uh, thanks." Ginny took them, then shook her head. "I really don't feel good, and I'm not sure these will work fast enough. Plus, it's so cold outside—"

"Which is a perfect opportunity for you to wear my fur. My sweet Harold trapped each one of those foxes himself. After we got rid of those pesky eagles, that is. For a while those birds nearly wiped out every fox in Strawberry Point."

Pesky eagles? Ginny sat in the armchair, and her fingers stroked the holes on the cribbage board on the side table, trying to imagine what some of her activist friends would think if she returned to LA and told them she'd worn a fox coat.

"Do you like cribbage, dear?" Grandma Ethel asked, interrupting Ginny's thoughts.

"I've never played."

"How about pinochle?" Grandma Ethel perked up.

Ginny shook her head. She used to play Battleship with a foster sister. She'd always lost, until one day she figured out that her sister could see the reflection of her pieces in the sliding glass door.

"We'll have to change that. Before you leave we'll have a pinochle night. I've been playing with my neighbors for longer than you've been alive. That's what we used to do around here for fun, you know. Play that and many other games."

Ginny nodded, quite sure she wouldn't be around for a pinochle night. She was also pretty certain that by the time Brett showed up, she wouldn't be feeling well enough to go out. Picturing Kelly's smiling face caused her gut to ache. It was hard to dislike a person like that. Hard to understand why Brett even humored her by asking her to dinner.

Ginny grabbed up a few more letters and hurried to Grandma Ethel's room. She sank onto the bed, noticing it smelled like Polident and talcum powder. The smells were yet another reminder of all she'd missed.

That was a hard thing about not growing up with a mom and dad. She missed having grandmas and grandpas too. Sure, she'd visited a dozen different homes of "relatives" growing up, but it never was the same. While the real grandkids got spoiled, she was given the obligatory doll and socks. Not that she should complain. She'd learned long ago that complaining never changed anything. She was just thankful for this time with Grandma Ethel now.

She leaned back into the soft pillows and slipped another letter from the envelope. For this moment, she could pretend that Ethel was her grandma. And that Ellie's heritage was hers too. Because deep down it felt exactly like it was.

Chapter Twenty-Four

....

January 11, 1929

Dear Clay and Ellie,

Nurse Schroeder again writes for me. I am blessed by her help. Even though she's a German, I think she's softening a little.

(Nurse S. here: Why he say things like this? To vex me. I know.)

How glad I was to get your letters. Amen and amen! They came in a big packet, which did my heart good to receive. It sounds like you two are getting along swimmingly.

I'm sorry, Ellie Bell, for those dark nights of the soul you've had. I trust our great Redeemer will bring you safely through till the light of His morning shines into your heart and lightens your face with His joy and peace. And you too, Clay.

Cheer up, my dears. He loves you!

Don't worry about me. I am safe and secure in my Savior's arms. I have many good friends here. They come in my room and we sing hymns. I've had wonderful conversations about all manner of things with the poor lost and lonely who spend their days in illness. Yet, despite their heartaches, they bring me joy. I'm honored to remember them in my prayers, as I do you both, as well as your ministry there.

I'm also lifting up your Joseph. Coming of age brings many challenges, even in the best of situations. He lost his mother, one who would guide him through these rocky paths. It may take longer than you like for him to come around. He may sink to greater depths before the Lord brings him home. But the Good Shepherd's loving hand will draw him back, perhaps not until His rod has given the loving discipline He reserves for His children. Amen and amen.

I'm told by a young woman standing by my bed with a silver tray that it's time for my medicine. I must say so long for now. I'm hoping for more and more letters from you, yet I know the mail boat doesn't come frequently.

My love to you both,
Grandfather

P.S. Please give the folded note to my friend Janey.
P.P.S. Nurse S. here: Since he did not mention. I will. That Felix, he come by. I do not trust that man. Another man come too. A younger, weak man with smooth hands. I do no like him either. I think you should know.

January 11, 1929

My dear Janey,

Stay steadfast, dear one. You have a very important job. You are my "eyes and ears," as they say. We must keep apprised of what's happening, in case the good Lord sees fit to use us in His great scheme. In the meantime, here are your assignments:

1. Encourage the others to give them time to talk without interruptions.

2. Make sure you and your brothers do your chores with a cheerful heart, so Miss Ellie and your papa have no reason to be anxious.

3. Pray!

Do those three things and all will be well, no matter what happens.

Your friend,

Mr. Barnett (or you can call me Grandfather, if you like)

P.S. I'm enclosing a penny for you. A small "thank you" for the information.

Ginny put down the letter, chuckling to herself. First because of the secret correspondence between Grandfather and Janey, and second because of the fact that Clay was in love with Ellie and didn't even know it. Yet the realization of their love made her keenly aware of what she'd lost—what she'd thrown away.

Ginny yawned. She needed to rest, but she had to find out…would Clay ever realize his love? Confess it?

March 12, 1929

Dear Grandfather,

How wonderful to receive your letter this morning! Clay and I didn't even know the mail boat had gone out. I'm glad you got my early letters. Many more wait for you at the mailbox. It's a good thing Clay didn't know about the mail boat's arrival; otherwise, he would've set me on it. He still talks about my going back in the spring. I go along with it, but in my heart I want to stay. Sometimes it seems as if he wants me to stay too.

One thing I know for certain: I love the children. What joy each brings to me. Even Joseph, although he's being more defiant each day, especially to me. He resents me simply for being here. I imagine that in his mind, his mother should be the one making supper, doing laundry, and kissing the little ones' boo boos. I try to respect her memory, not act too motherly with him. But it doesn't seem to matter what I do.

It's funny, all the other children long for their mama too, but they're willing to find some comfort in my care and love. While the others open to me, Joseph slams the door and locks it. He turns more and more to Tinle, the Tlingit girl who lives with the Curtises, and we see him less and less.

I know this is in the Lord's hands. Could He really be the rock, Grandfather? I still keep Mama's stone in my pocket, always reminding me of her and you, and now, the Lord. I try to trust in Him, but I don't know if I believe it deep down— can He really love me?

Later

So, may I tell you about our trip to Hoonah? So much to tell, it might take a few letters. The trip over was like nothing I've ever experienced. We took the kayak so Joseph and Linc would have the boat in case they needed supplies upriver.

I love adventure, you know I do, but carrying an eighteen-month-old baby in a cradleboard while being rowed in a kayak across frigid, whale-infested waters—well, that shook even adventurous me. Thankfully, Clay was absolutely confident, which calmed my nerves.

First, we made our way through the bay, so close to the jagged mountains with spiking turrets and gleaming white ice. Their majesty cast a fearful wonder over me. I hugged my arms, humbled by the glacier's danger and beauty. We are helpless in God's creation, aren't we, Grandfather?

Then as if to confirm my thoughts, a chunk of ice broke off an iceberg and crashed into the water. Clay yelled to hold on just before a huge wave rolled under us, almost capsizing our little vessel. My heart never pumped so fast in my life! I gripped the side of the kayak with one hand and reached back to Penny with the other. She giggled as if it were a pony ride. I love that sweet girl.

How grateful I am for Clay. That wave could've tipped us into the freezing water, but his focused hands steadied us through wave after wave until the water calmed again. I could do nothing but trust him.

In the quiet that followed, I touched his hand, to thank him. He instantly pulled it away, even though we both wore gloves!

He paddled us on and parked along the rocky shore of a small peninsula. My feet relished the feeling of solid ground again. Clay made a little campfire, and after gobbling her lunch of reindeer jerky and clams, which I had prepared and packed (I'm getting better at this!), sweet Penny fell asleep in the cozy bed I made for her in the kayak.

I think Clay craved the quiet more than the warmth and food. He surely doesn't strike up conversation too often— especially that day—but I like talking to him when he does. He's thoughtful about what he says; doesn't blurt things out. So I asked questions, tried to soften his resolve to close me out.

"Did you make the canoe?" I know it's called a kayak but wanted to taunt him.

"Yes."

That didn't work. So I tried again. "How?"

"Cut down the tree. Carved it. Burned out the inside."

I asked him how he learned, and he said Patricia's husband helped. The mention of Patricia renewed my chill.

He moved his gaze from the fire to my eyes. "Yes, Patricia." His voice was stern. He stood up. "I need to talk to you about what happened with the Tlingit ladies. You offended them."

A surge of guilt tightened my stomach. I confessed my bad behavior—even the way the rutabagas made me sick. Yet I couldn't help but mention that they took over my home without asking.

Clay eyed me. "Your *home?*"

The way he said it, accusing...I didn't know what to say. I felt his disapproval, the dislike I'd experienced in the first weeks I was there. I thought we'd gained ground.

Tears pressed to come out, but I held them back. I stood up, silently packed our things, threw snow onto the fire, and loaded Penny into the backpack. As Clay lifted her to my back, he was careful not to touch me, as if I was a diseased varmint or something. Then without warning, he grabbed my shoulder and threw Penny and me into the kayak. He shoved the kayak hard with his boot and scrambled in. I twisted back to see what the problem was. Then I screamed like a little girl and paddled like I never have before.

March 13, 1929

Dear Brother Peter,

Glad to get your letter. I know it did Ellie good. I'd like to tell you the events at Hoonah. Ellie said she told you about the bear.

After shooting (and missing) the ill-mannered grizzly who came after our lunch, I managed to take over and row fast enough (my muscles still ache) to escape her reach. Mind you, she splashed in after us, and they can swim.

Ellie had the good thought to throw the leftover salmon away from our boat. Thank God, the beast clambered after the fish's pink flesh instead of ours. We rowed to safety. Then after resting and breathing a spell, we found relief in a fit of nervous laughter.

Twice in two days I have laughed with that girl.

Hoonah takes many hours of slow rowing. Yet the journey's a mighty fine sight on a clear day, which we had. Bitter cold, but clear.

With Penny sleeping in her cradleboard, the hours passed right quick, and soon we spotted Hoonah. I venture to say the place surprised Ellie. She thought the Tlingit a primitive people, not the sophisticated society they are. Their large plank houses, from our view in the kayak, surely rival any in an American port settlement. I hate to say, but it's a good bit more established than Strawberry Point. The church and school have been there since 1881.

The church steeple's cross offered its familiar comfort, but I was still a mite anxious about meeting with Reverend Martin.

He's been patient with me, as all of you on the missions board have been, but this offense may affect his ministry as well as mine. One can't understate the damage an angry woman can have on ministry. Even the apostle Paul learned that lesson well. I warned Ellie that they might not go easy on her.

With the sunset at our backs, I paddled toward shore. Friends awaited our arrival, waving and smiling. A welcome sight—until I caught Rev. Martin's eye. And Chief Thomas's. No smiles there.

The womenfolk greeted Ellie with kindness, immediately unloading Penny and giving Ellie's back much-needed relief. My little angel found a Tlingit girl her age to giggle and toddle

*with. They held hands as the women hustled them off for an
eagle dinner.*

No dinner for me.

*Rev. Martin patted my back as I introduced Ellie. "We are
glad you've come to help our brother. Lord knows he needs it."
Then he laughed a mite too loud, and Ellie blushed.*

*Patricia greeted us with tight hugs and smiles. She took
Ellie's hands and offered to take her inside for a warm drink.*

*"Nothing with rutabagas, I promise," she said with a grin,
then put her arm around Ellie, and off they went.*

*Chief Thomas and Rev. Martin escorted me into the
reverend's office. Very Presbyterian, with white walls and dark
wood furniture. The chief leaned against the wall as Martin
and I took our seats. I felt like I was sitting right down into a
confessional, only without the screen of anonymity.*

*Brother Peter, I won't put you through the torture of the
whole meeting. Here is the sum:*

*First, the women were not offended by Ellie. They loved
her. Couldn't say enough about her sacrifices for me and the
children, how well she'd adjusted to life in Alaska. Not a word
of rutabagas.*

*Second, the Tlingits in Hoonah have had Christian
missionaries for over forty years. They know truth and won't
abide a preacher living with a single woman. The concept of
governess or maid or anything like that utterly escapes them.
They lay no blame on Ellie. Just me.*

Third, we must get married. We have a month.

*Fourth, I am not doing my job. There have been no new
converts since Adelaide died. Sadly, this is true. And what's
more, I have hardly even set out. My longing these days is for*

family. Afraid, I suppose, to lose a precious minute with them.

These were the "concerns" laid before me at the meeting. Afterward, Rev. Martin took me aside and prayed with me. He must've seen my pained expression, for he asked me if I still felt the call.

Yes, of course—that should've come from my lips, but I'm afraid it did not. Truth is, I'm not sure. I don't want to leave here, but the hurt hasn't healed. It keeps me down.

Rev. Martin rested his elbows on his knees and eyeballed me. "God can carry your pain. It's not too heavy for Him."

I will not soon forget those words.

He told me to start with Ellie. Open up to her. "She seems like a good woman. Possibly a good wife. Perhaps you could love her in time."

I already do.

I thought those words but didn't—couldn't—say them.

He said they needed to see a change, something to show them this call is for me; otherwise I will be sent back to the States.

I hear Patricia outside calling my name, something about Penny. I must say good-bye.

Clay

Chapter Twenty-Five
....

March 14, 1929

Grandfather,

We had a glorious trip to Hoonah. So majestic—made me feel that if God can create such immense beauty, He can take care of me too.

But then, our little Penny. She was so sick, Grandfather. While Clay sat in the meeting and I was busy learning to weave blankets with the women, Patricia's daughter Margaret watched the little ones. After our poor tired girl fell asleep, Margaret laid her back into the cradleboard and covered her with a blanket.

My weaving lesson done, I checked on her. At first she looked beautiful, snoring softly with her thumb just outside her mouth. When I fingered a stray curl from her forehead, my stomach dropped. She was so hot.

I felt her face, arms, hands. Everything emanated heat and she seemed listless. I felt her chest and it barely beat under my touch. She looked as if she might never wake up again. All I could think of was influenza, that great killer that took Clay's wife and so many others.

I kissed her forehead, then I went to work. One thing I knew, we had to cool her, break the fever. I sent Patricia to get Clay, and then I did the only thing I could think of. I lifted her weak body from the cradleboard and nestled her to my chest.

My pulse pounding, I hurried outside and knelt, then gently laid the sleeping girl in the snow. She wore her coonskin dress, no parka, no hood.

Jolted by the cold, she began to cry, and her cries ignited mine. I brushed them aside. Then with shaking hands, I wiped away hers too. "Just a minute more," I whispered.

I heard footsteps. Clay approached, his face tight, hands tightly fisted. He glared at me then grabbed her from the snow and held her tight to his chest.

I could barely speak, my throat felt thick with fear. "She must be cooled down, Clay." He swiveled away from me. I longed to hold her, touch her skin, make her better. I prayed, Grandfather. I prayed so hard. As if in answer, an arctic wind gushed up, blowing a waft of snow into our faces, on Penny's cheeks. Her fever-hot skin melted it immediately. Pulling a handkerchief from my pocket, I dried it, but Clay backed off. His eyes brimmed with pain.

I wouldn't step away, even though he obviously wanted me to. I loved this child as my own. And Clay. Clay couldn't lose another loved one. I placed my hand on Clay's back covered in a thick wool coat, rubbed the rough texture gently. His shoulders relaxed a tiny bit. He arched his head and looked at me, not angry this time. Just afraid.

"What do we do?" he asked.

I bent toward Penny, cupped her warm cheek. "She's cooler. The snow's making her a little cooler."

"Thank God."

I knew the sickness still held her, but I gave thanks to God for even a speck of hope. As we strode toward Patricia's house, the waiting crowd folded in upon us. Prayers, both silent and spoken, lifted from this strong Tlingit congregation to their Father in heaven, who holds the lambs in His arms.

She was sick for five days, there in Hoonah. The community rallied around, offering blankets, soup, and handmade sealskin dolls. When they weren't helping, they gathered in the church and prayed. Clay stayed next to Penny's bed in the small, white-washed bedroom in Patricia's house the whole time.

Clay wouldn't leave the room for but minutes. He sat on the sealskin stool, an Indian blanket around his shoulders, and held her little hand in his strong, reverend's grip. Like a shepherd, he wouldn't let her go. He didn't speak except to share calming, soothing words. Mostly he prayed.

I lingered in the tiny room, providing company, a loving touch. Sometimes I read the Bible to them, quoted his beloved catechism—that one Janey knows so well about God's providence. Did I bring comfort? He'd seen so many women in his life pass away, I know those thoughts rained down on his mind like the long Alaskan storms. Relentless.

Every day I carefully carried Penny's hot little body and placed it in the snow. I had to uncurl her fingers from my coat. Her blue eyes were pleading, confused. I sang to her. And it was good to hear her cry; she was so listless the rest of the time. After a few moments, I'd swaddle her nice and cozy, hold her to me, and feel her heart beating against my chest. I'd kiss her head, everywhere my lips could reach, until we laid her on the soft blankets for her papa to hold again.

Patricia agreed it was the right thing to do to cool her. Fortunately some snow piles still remained.

Patricia also helped me find analgesic roots. She does know everything. I can't help but be impressed by her. I may have misjudged her. At times when we searched for herbs in the hills *around Hoonah, a sob would unexpectedly overtake me. She'd stop, put her hand on my arm, and just wait. Not say a word.*

Most of those days and nights, I sat beside Clay. Sometimes when Penny woke up, her eyes would catch her daddy's, and a little girl's love for her papa would shine through. This happened in the dark of night after the second day, as rain hammered the plank roof and melted snow into the mud outside. The tender child's gaze broke through the strong front he'd built. He touched her face, tears streaming, until she closed her eyes again. Then he fell into a deep sob. Sliding to the floor, he knelt beside the crib and, like the torrential rain, poured out his heart to God.

His hands gripped Penny's bed, his knuckles white. "You are my God. You can save her. I give up. I couldn't protect the others. Adelaide. You are the only One who can."

Tears, hot and quick, ran down my cheeks, dripping onto my hands. As the moon's beams—clear and bright, almost carrying warmth like the sun's—shone through the window, I noticed a simple cross-stitch sampler on the wall. "On Christ the solid rock I stand. All other ground is sinking sand."

I whispered the words, speaking first, then singing. Clay turned toward me, then buried his head in my lap. "I'm sorry. I'm so sorry."

I wasn't sure if he was talking to me or to God. I stroked his hair as he lifted his chin. Though still mournful, his eyes held a new light as he reached his arms up and cradled my face in his hands. "Oh, Ellie. Ellie." He leaned in close....

You won't want to hear that part, Grandfather. Just know that God is healing all of us, and Clay likes me now.

I promise to finish later.

Your Ellie Bell

March 14, 1929

Father God,

 The darkness of the night matched my fear. Penny lay in her crib, blankets over her, sleeping in peace. I tried awful hard to keep my reins on my anger toward You. I couldn't— even when my own words to my children came back to me: "God is with us, even in the darkest night."

 But I'd already lost so many...Adelaide. How could You take Penny too? I yearned for that old anger to rise again and protect me from the pain coming back.

 Ellie was there that night. That second night of Penny's downturn. The medicine roots weren't working, cooling her only helped for a short spell. I thought my little girl would die. My girl.

 I broke, Lord. I crumbled to my knees and wept. I couldn't lose my girl. Not again, not again.

 And then, in the black, a light came. Somehow, I realized I wasn't trusting You. Not with everything. Not with my heart. I turned and fell into Ellie's waiting arms, collapsing in her lap. She touched my hair, and it was like a splash of water to my parched soul.

 I kissed her cheeks, her forehead, her lips. The love— desperation—was so strong. I was sure to die if my hands didn't touch her, if my face wasn't close to hers.

 The clouds moved, letting the moonlight break through, as she sang to me. I knew then that You had not left me when Adelaide died. I had a notion of that before, but I couldn't open to it. I aimed to keep out the pain and closed You out too, and Ellie.

 But You were with me all along. And so was Ellie. You didn't bring her to me as a temptation, to prove my disloyalty to Adelaide.

 Ellie is a gift.

This all rushed to me, Lord, as I held her soft frame in that room. Our tears blended as our faces touched. When I finally looked up, the love I saw in her eyes melted my hard heart. The wind opened the window a crack, and a flurry of snow blew in, white, pure. As I cupped her face in my hands I knew You gave her to me. Because You love me. And I wanted that love. Welcomed it.

Thank You, Father God, for my Ellie.

And beyond all hope, You gave us sweet Penny.

You are truly a good and faithful God.

Your servant,

Clay

A soft knock sounded at the door, and Ginny's eyes darted to the small turquoise alarm clock that looked as if it had been purchased in 1943.

She wiped her face, realizing she'd been crying. Really crying. Were the tears for little Penny? She wasn't sure. All her emotions were stirred up. Wave after wave hit her, as if a large chunk of ice had splashed into her soul.

Maybe it was the love of a biological parent that touched her so. Something she'd never known. She instinctively touched the back of her neck and her shoulder where scars lay hidden under her T-shirt. Or maybe it was the love of a woman for a child not her own. A love she'd experienced for such a short time…

"Ginny?" The door cracked open. "Are you decent?"

"Yes…" The word came out with a shuddering breath, and she pulled the quilt under her chin.

Brett stepped through the door, and Ginny let out a low moan.

"Is something wrong? Grandma said you looked a little pale when you came in earlier."

Ginny covered her face with her free hand. "No…yes."

"Did I do something?"

"Why would you say that? Didn't your grandma tell you I wasn't feeling well?"

"I can tell the difference when you're sick and when something's bothering you."

She swung up her head to glare at him. He wore new jeans and a black dress shirt that he'd rolled up at the elbows. It was open at the collar, and she focused on his neck. It was better than looking into his eyes. He'd read too much in her gaze, she was sure of it.

Anger surged through her at being left. She had wanted the day to be special without him taking off and leaving her to sift through dusty boxes with women she didn't know. *I could be in a studio right now, recording music. I'd be wined and dined, the envy of a thousand women. What am I doing here?*

She sat forlorn, staring at the seams of the quilt, running her finger across a checkered pattern, trying not to feel like a fool.

"It's hard being here. Harder than I thought," she finally admitted. "I assumed I knew you when we were in California, but now I wonder if I knew you at all."

He was quiet for a long moment. "I can understand. I'm sure it's a shock for you, trying to get used to this place—to get used to me here."

She looked up at him and read an apology in his eyes. Why didn't he say it? Why didn't he tell her that dropping her off to work with the historical society was a bad idea?

He ran a finger under his collar. "Since you're not feeling well, I've come up with an alternative idea. Stay home. Rest tonight, and tomorrow I'm going to take you on an adventure. A real adventure, out on the water. Lee said I could borrow his boat."

She sat up straighter. "Really?"

"Yes. I want to show you my world. The world not only here in Gustavus, but up the bay. I've told you a lot about this place, but now I want to show you."

"Are you sure? What will Kelly think about that?"

"Kelly?" His brow furrowed, and then he smacked his head with his palm. "You're right, I need to call her. Oh man, I told Jace I'd take him fishing tomorrow." He glanced at her sheepishly and then lowered his head. "How did you know?"

How did I know you care for each other? Ginny didn't ask the question out loud.

Instead, she cleared her throat, hoping to push down the emotion that rose up there. "I saw Kelly's drawing of you at the coffee house. It's pretty amazing."

"Yeah, she's a fantastic artist. Sometimes I feel bad she's stuck here in Glacier Bay."

"Stuck?"

"Not stuck in this town, but stuck working in a coffee shop to support herself. She could be doing so much more with her art if she wasn't worried about having to pay rent or buy wood to heat her place."

Ginny nodded, unsure of what to think. It was obvious he cared for Kelly, but if that was the case, why had he invited her out to the bay?

He's being kind to an old friend, that's all. She smiled up at him. Brett was that type of guy.

She blew out a breath, wiped her face, and pushed the quilt off of her legs. "I'm fine with staying in tonight, I really am. I was just wondering…"

She approached him and gazed up into his eyes.

"Yes?" he asked, his eyebrows lifting.

"Do you think your grandma would be willing to show me how to play cribbage? I'm sure if she did, I could beat you…hands down."

Chapter Twenty-Six

....

Brett's eyes were fixed on Glacier Bay Lodge as the fishing boat carried them out to the bay. Ginny sat beside him with her sweatshirt jacket on. She'd asked to borrow one of his caps, and she'd pulled her hair through the back of the cap in a ponytail. He blew out a breath. He'd never seen her with her hair like that before. Even in Africa she wore it down or in a low ponytail. She looked beautiful today. Then again, she always did.

Her eyes scanned the bay, her face bright like a child's at Disneyland for the first time. Yet even as her eyes glowed, her hand touched the back of her neck. Brett's gaze was drawn there, and he noticed small red marks. Scars from chickenpox maybe? Was that why she rarely wore her hair up?

He tried not to focus too much on this beautiful woman. Tried to look at the lodge instead. The more time he spent with her, the more he wanted to be with her...always. That was why he'd gone to the hangar with Lee. Once he'd walked into his great-grandfather's cabin and heard Ginny's reaction to Great-grandma Ellie's letters, he'd known he couldn't hide his emotions—his love for her. And if the women there noticed, his feelings would spread all over Gustavus in no time flat. *Poor Brett, getting his heart broken again...*

Brett cleared his throat. "I have lots of good memories of that lodge," he said, trying to focus his attention back to the world around him. "I'm not sure if Gustavus would have survived if they hadn't put that in. It made this beauty, this bay, accessible to outsiders."

"Isn't it hard sometimes, though, having all the tourists?" A strand of blond hair slipped from her ponytail and fluttered against her cheek. "Seems like it would complicate things."

He shrugged and continued to steer the boat. "Most of them are great. They're like extended family members who come to stay for a while. You can put up with them because you know they're leaving." He rubbed his chin. "Yeah, every once in a while there's a crazy aunt or an obnoxious uncle." He smiled. "But for the most part they're good folks who want to experience a bit of the real Alaskan wilderness before they have to get back to their busy lives."

The boat trolled down the bay, and a fine mist sprayed them. He was thankful Lee had let him borrow the boat. Brett could have bought two tickets on the day boat, but he wanted this to be special. He wanted time alone for them to talk. He still had no idea what to say to her.

The fact that Ginny came all this way told him she wanted to renew what they had, even if she didn't admit it—even if she didn't know it yet. But was he willing to take the risk of having his heart broken again? Was giving her a second chance still part of God's plan?

"Of course the tourists are here for only a short time," he said over the sounds of the motor and the water lapping against the boat. "The lodge closes to the public after Labor Day."

She turned, glancing up at him with her large blue eyes. "But… that's next week."

"Yes, and that's when all the extra summer help goes home. And then we get the lodge to ourselves."

"Really? They don't board it up?"

"Sort of, but they open it for special occasions—like Thanksgiving and Christmas. Everyone comes together to celebrate. I wouldn't know what to do without our 'family gatherings.' For Christmas we draw names, from the retirees to the newborn babies. At Thanksgiving we have quite the feast and..." A burst of laughter split his lips. Brett rubbed his forehead and then shook his head.

"What?"

"I was going to say, 'And you never know what's going to be served.' If it's been a hard winter and folks haven't been able to get to Juneau much, then all types of dishes show up. It's amazing what folks around here can scrape together from odds and ends in their cupboards. And the wildlife! You never know what type of meat you'll find in a dish. In the past, they used to serve bald eagle for dinner."

"No!" Ginny gasped. "You're making that up."

With one hand he reached out and brushed back the strand of blond hair that had escaped her ponytail. "Have you ever stopped to wonder why they're protected? When folks settled here, they were considered a nuisance. After World War I, food was hard to come by, and folks had a hard time supporting themselves.

"Here in these parts—and other areas of Alaska—fox farmers blamed the eagles. The birds would take their young blue foxes right after they left their dens, and fishermen complained the eagles killed large quantities of spawning salmon. The state was afraid the livelihood of their residents was in jeopardy. They paid fifty cents for every pair of bald eagle feet, and then upped it to one dollar. That was a lot of money back then, and they report that from the mid-1920s to 1940, some eighty thousand eagles were killed."

"Wow. I remember how Ellie mentions 'pesky eagles' in her letters and how the Tlingit people ate them."

"Ah, yes, Ellie's letters..." Brett narrowed his gaze. "How did my grandma talk you into reading them?" To tell the truth, his knees had grown weak when he'd walked into Grandma's house and discovered Ginny reading them.

Years ago he'd found his grandmother going through all her things to compile the letters in order. She'd received most of them from Ellie herself, but she had to track down some others, mostly the ones sent out. But she managed to gather almost all of them. Folks kept stuff like that back then.

"Are those for the historical society?" he'd asked Grandma. "I'm sure Linda would love to have them."

"Oh no." Grandma Ethel clicked her tongue. "They're for one person and one person only—your future bride."

He swallowed hard again as he remembered the conversation. What was Grandma thinking, giving Ginny the letters? Maybe she didn't understand that his path and Ginny's launch into stardom were heading two different directions. Or maybe she'd forgotten she'd said that.

"Your grandma didn't have to talk me into reading the letters." Ginny interrupted his thoughts. "Once I got started I couldn't stop. Ellie's life was fascinating. I can't imagine moving to Alaska like that. It's quite the wilderness." She glanced at the vast mountains and icebergs around her.

Brett's smile faded.

"I mean back then…." she quickly added. But it was too late.

"Yeah, it's never been easy living here." He steered the boat farther away from the shore, and while his mind was focused on that task, his heart did the only thing it could. Put up another brick of protection. The last thing he wanted was to be hurt again.

That strand of hair blew free again, and he couldn't help but reach out and tuck it behind her ear one more time, stroking her cheek with his finger.

Ginny gazed at him, cocking her eyebrow, curious.

Brett cleared his throat. "I want to hear about why you came in the first place. I mean after just getting that diamond necklace, what made you head up to these parts?"

Her head jerked back. "How do you know about that?"

"How could I not? We get the tabloids up here—or at least in Juneau—and People.com. As you may recall, if one person in Gustavus knows a bit of news, so does the whole town. They pretend they don't know who you are, but they all know about you, Ginny. About us." He held his breath and waited for her response. He longed for her to deny everything about the growing relationship between her and Danny Kingston—to say that the gossip columns had gotten it all wrong.

Instead, she lowered her head and let her eyelids droop.

"I did accept the necklace, but I don't want to keep it. In the world's eyes, a girl would be stupid to walk away from Danny Kingston, but I've been called worse." She glanced up at him. "I don't want to keep the necklace, because my heart keeps drawing me back to someone else...."

Brett's blood rushed. His heart pounded, and he felt as if liquid sunshine had been poured into his chest. *Stop it. Stop it...it's too late now to get your hopes up.*

She had chosen her way, and he had chosen his. There could be only one captain on each boat, and as far as he was concerned, Ginny still continued to steer in the opposite direction.

Chapter Twenty-Seven

....

Ginny was about to explain about Danny, but instead something ahead caught her eye. It—they—moved through the water beside the boat, gliding over the surface and then dipping back under again.

"What are those? Wow!"

"They're harbor porpoises. We have quite a few. Their favorite things are sending us out and then welcoming us back in."

"Porpoises, whales, moose, bears...is there ever a time when it simply becomes ordinary?"

"Not at all. Never. Not for me, anyway."

Ginny noticed that Brett steered their boat more to the left to create distance between them and their new friends. He looked handsome at the helm with the wind tousling his hair.

"Living here sort of reminds me of Africa." His voice carried over the wind. "All the times I've been, there isn't a day—an hour—that passes when I don't want to pinch myself. It seems the best type of life is one lived a bit untamed. And the best way to do that is with the creatures that man never can quite control."

Ginny turned her gaze back to the water, disappointed that the porpoises had turned around. She gave a sad smile, realizing they were most likely off to lead the next voyagers out to sea.

She considered asking Brett about his return to Africa, but she changed her mind. She didn't want to ruin this moment. Her attention turned to a large rock island ahead covered with sea lions. She sat straighter.

"This is amazing!" she called to Brett, but when she looked back at him, he was looking at her and not the animals.

As they continued on, the strangest thought hit her. Even as the raucous sea lions lifted their heads and barked—at the waves, the sky, and at them perhaps—there were people in morning rush hour traffic, breathing smog, with a sea of cars as their only view. Folks were listening to morning talk radio, their worried thoughts focused on their next meeting. Their next in-studio. Or their neighbor who kept them up half the night by shouting at his wife about racking up the credit card bill once again.

There were paparazzi racing around the city, checking out Rodeo Drive and the favorite parks that stars visited with their designer kids. For so long the media attention, and the mental list of her rising success that she'd check off in her mind, had seemed so important. But here? To see water as far as she could see, mountains rising from its grasp, and ice that appeared to be sculpted by a majestic hand—well, it made those things of last week, last month, last year seem like poorly written sitcoms put to life.

But even the feeling of gliding over the water and seeing the sea lions, the porpoises, and the various birds paled in comparison to the glacier.

Ginny had never felt anything like it. The fishing boat approached the base of the glacier, and she had never felt so small. Or so captured, as if the land, ocean, and ice had caged her in. The thing was, she never wanted to be released.

She thought of Ellie and Clay. Was this the glacier Ellie had written about? She understood the cresting of Ellie's emotions even more now.

She reached up and placed her hand on Brett's. "Thank you. This is amazing. I wouldn't want to experience this with anyone else—anyone but you."

His face softened, and she noticed a light in his eyes she hadn't seen since she'd arrived.

"You're welcome, Ginny. Thank you for coming—for finding me."

He slowed the boat and then turned off the engine so they were only trolling. The water was still, and there were only a few large cruise ships in the distance.

She stared up at the chunks of ice in awe. "The colors are so amazing. I never knew that ice could be that blue."

"If I was braver, I would have brought the kayaks," he commented.

She turned to him and smiled. "You mean you don't want to have to dive into this water to save me?"

"Actually, I think I'd be too distracted by you to get anywhere. See that puffin out there swimming in circles?" He pointed. "That would be me."

Ginny's chest grew warm at his words, but then she thought about Kelly in the coffee shop. The tension built until she couldn't hold back the question anymore.

"What about Kelly?" she dared to ask.

"What do you mean?"

"Kelly, Jace's mom, from Fireweed Coffee House."

"I know *who* you're talking about, but *what* are you talking about?"

"Kelly. You know. What would she think of you talking to me all sweet like that?"

"Why would she care?"

"Um, aren't you and she, you know, fancy on each other?"

"Who told you that?"

"No one had to tell me. I could tell by the way Kelly talked about you. And whenever you mentioned her...there's something special there. I could hear it in your voice."

"No one's told you yet?"

"Told me what?"

"Ginny, instead of a songwriter, you should become a novelist for all the fiction you come up with."

"You mean there's nothing going on between you and Kelly?"

"Smelly Kelly?" Brett laughed.

A gasp released from Ginny's lips.

"Yeah, there was something between us. In fifth grade. We 'dated' nearly the whole year. Everyone in class called her Smelly Kelly because her mom made candles. Every day she came to class smelling like a different fragrance. We'd always guess which one."

"But…she and Jace said they loved you."

"And I love them. But it's a friendship love. In fact, no one knows it yet, but she met someone on eHarmony. He's been up to Glacier Bay a couple of times. A few people who know Kelly best have met him…but for the most part she hasn't introduced him around to folks yet. Once you do that—let people know who you're keen on—it's over."

"Over? What's over?"

"Your privacy. Your right to your own opinion. Glacier Bay is a small place."

Laughter slipped from Ginny's lips, and she let herself relax. Worries lifted from her mind like the light fluffy clouds overhead.

She didn't have to worry about Kelly. And she didn't need to think about Danny and the studio. Not now. Not today. She blew out a soft breath and felt her heart beating in rhythm with the undercurrents.

When she was sure she'd never heard such quiet—felt such peace in all her life—Brett stood and moved to the front bench seat of the boat. He opened the seat and pulled out a picnic lunch.

Ah, perfect.

Then he reached inside again and pulled out a wooden box. Ginny's brow furrowed, recognizing it immediately. He couldn't be serious, could he?

"Is that your…chess set? Didn't you have enough beating me at cribbage last night?"

Laughter slipped from Brett's lips, and Ginny shook her head from side to side, her ponytail swishing as she did. Only Brett would think of bringing his chess set here, now.

He set it on the wooden floorboards of the fishing vessel and motioned for her to sit.

"I thought we'd finish our game."

"Our game?"

"Don't you remember? It was still set up. I was this close to beating you." He held up two fingers so they nearly touched.

Ginny's smile faded. She was glad he could joke about that. She didn't think it was as funny. She laid down the blanket and then sat on it.

He slipped a piece of paper out of his pocket and held it up for her to see. "I wrote down where the pieces were when…"

When I left. In her mind she finished his sentence.

She nodded dispassionately, but tension crept up her arms. Wind brushed against her cheek harsher than it had mere moments ago. She turned up her collar on the fleece jacket and then, restraining a sigh of sadness, let her chin drop to her chest.

The chessboard had been as much a part of their relationship as anything else. She couldn't believe she'd forgotten about it. Maybe it had helped her these past few years not remembering how fun Brett was to be around. And what a good, honorable man he was.

He had come up with the idea of their ongoing chess game after hearing their pastor talk about Psalm 1, about not walking, standing, or even sitting in places where they'd be tempted to compromise. Brett had taken that to heart and had set up a table, two chairs, and a chess set on his apartment balcony. It was there that they'd retreat whenever she visited his apartment, which was closer to campus than the house she'd shared with a few other girls. He'd insisted that they play at least one move, but most of the time that was as far as the game progressed.

It wasn't about the chess game. Not at all. It was about sitting in full view of their neighbors and those who hung out in the apartment pool below in order to resist temptation.

Sometimes he'd stretch his hand across the table to hold hers. Sometimes she'd even move her folding chair around to his side and lean against him as they'd watch the pink and orange sunset over the Pacific. But most of the time they'd just talk, words of future hopes, current struggles, and past pain crossing over the chess set, mingling with the sea breeze and filling each other's hearts.

The pieces made soft clicks as he set them up now. In the distance a birdsong carried through the air. She took a deep breath, noticing the salty air here too. Yet the air was different from in California. There was a wild crispness to it.

She glanced up and noticed the pieces were set in place, but she couldn't consider making a move. Instead her mind flitted back to Danny. Her fingers touched the bare spot on her neck where his diamond necklace had rested. Was it only a week ago? She tried to imagine him setting boundaries to honor her—honor their relationship.

No, that would never happen.

Danny would take everything if she let him—everything precious: her struggling faith, her body, her soul.

But as quickly as that thought entered her mind, new thoughts rose. *But I've worked so hard for my music. I can set my own pace. I can put up boundaries. I don't have to give all of myself....*

Besides, it was her parents'—Dale and Robyn's—dream too. They'd wanted this for her as much as she wanted it for herself. They'd paid for all those voice and guitar lessons. Robyn had driven her to countless auditions.

Giving up this dream was like saying their sacrifice didn't matter— that all they imparted into her life hadn't made a difference.

Ginny shook her head even as the breeze picked up. No, she couldn't let that happen. She couldn't give up so easily. She eyed the chess pieces. For Brett it would be an easy win, but Ginny didn't mind playing into his hand. She'd never lost—not really—with him by her side.

Chapter Twenty-Eight

....

After their boat ride up and down the bay, Brett had dropped off Ginny and told her to dress for dinner at the lodge. She put on a long coral skirt, white blouse, and green scarf, with jewelry to match. Her hair curled back down around her shoulders, just as she liked it.

Outside on the porch Grandma Ethel chatted with her friend Dove Fowler. Ginny knew she should be social and head out to talk to the women, but Penny had been on her mind all day.

From first glance, she knew the next letter was from Clay.

March 16, 1929

Dear Brother Peter,

I know Ellie wrote of our sweet Penny's ailment. Let me assure you she's mending. She's starting to eat and sit up in bed, even laughs a bit. I am truly grateful. We plan to head home tomorrow.

I need to ask your permission for a certain thing, but first, I owe you a load of thanks. Your faithful prayers and friendship—they saw me through a powerful hard time. You perceived my need more than I did, and I appreciate your tenacity to force your granddaughter on me against my will. It's done me some good, I'd say. So I gift you those words every man loves to hear, "You were right."

Adelaide's never out of my mind's reach. Her memory will always be close to me. But it's time for me to open up. She'd want me to, probably give me a world of discomfort if she knew my actions of late. I let my fear of another loss keep me from taking the risk, and that's wrong.

So I would like to request your Ellie's hand in marriage— if you find me worthy. I have a family ring, a simple diamond surrounded by littler ones. I'd like to slip it on her finger.

Seeing as we only have a week before I lose my call, and we're pretty sure you'd approve of the nuptials, we may just perform the ceremony before you receive this. Still, it's right and proper to ask, even if a person knows the answer. I plan to ask her all official-like, soon as we get to home and settle Penny. Have to say, in spite of all that took place, the journey to Hoonah was the most joyous I've had in over a year now.

Your future grandson-in-law,
Clay

March 30, 1929

Dear Grandfather Barnett (I like calling you that!),

My papa and Miss Ellie are home from Hoonah now. I missed them, a lot. Penny was sick but she's all right. Papa seemed so happy when he came home. Miss Ellie told me they even had a romantic picnic on the way home. Just as we hoped! Do you think he held her hand, Grandfather? Whispered sweet nothings like in the pictures? I do. I know that's what happened.

But then everything went bad.

I think Papa was going to tell us that they were getting married. I saw the happy looks on their faces, but then Joseph. He ruined it all.

I don't know what to do.
Janey

April 8, 1929

Dear Grandfather,

I have so much to tell you. When we got home, we were so excited to tell everyone about our time in Hoonah, about us. I imagined their cheeks rounded with joy, their squeals of laughter, their hugs.

What actually happened was a million miles from that. We strolled happily past the garden, saying hello to Mama Moose. Then I spied two little eyes peering out the window. I felt a pang of joyful anticipation as we trotted up the front steps.

As soon as my feet stepped onto the welcome rug inside the door, the tension in the room draped me like a smock, smothering my joy. No one greeted us, no one but sweet Zach. Thank goodness for one smiling face! The others stared at us, waiting.

Before I even had time to set down my satchel or let Penny out of the carrier, Joseph paced toward us. "Papa, Miss Ellie, we have something we want to talk to you about. Linc saw your kayak coming downriver and ran ahead to warn us you were coming."

My stomach sank like the Titanic. He eyed me with such disapproval, much like Clay did when I first came. Clay must not have noticed. He dropped his gear and pulled Joseph into an embrace.

"Good to see you, son," he said. He reached for Linc, who stood next to Joseph, a frown creasing his wide forehead. He put on a smile, though, when Clay held him.

"I'm glad you're home, Uncle Clay." He glared at Joseph, who shook his head as if in warning.

Next Clay went to Janey. She'd donned her best Sunday dress complete with a crooked pink ribbon in her hair. I fought the urge to fix it for her. Despite her fancy attire, her eyes were red, cheeks splotchy. Clay touched her chin. "Janey, aren't you quite the lady." She fell into his arms and cried.

"What's wrong?"

"Miss Ellie has to go."

He tossed me a smile. "I heard tell Miss Ellie's going to stay."

"That's not what Joseph said."

My hands moistened as I asked everyone to sit down, then I heated up water for blackberry tea.

Joseph relented, but his body was so stiff when he sat down on the wooden stool next to the table, I thought he would break it. Clay and the others settled in their spots.

"There's no use prolonging it." Joseph put his teacup on the table without taking a sip and stared at his father. "We've all decided Miss McKinley needs to go back where she came from." He shifted toward me for a swift second. "No offense to you, miss."

"Why? I thought you liked me." I knew that sounded ridiculous. "Did I offend you?"

Joseph pushed to the edge of the chair. "First, she don't fit here." He ignored my question. "She's a rich city girl. We've all had to do extra chores to make up for her...lack of ability."

He was chipping away at me. What would be next?

I glanced at Janey, Linc—surely one of them would contradict him.

"Second, she broke the outhouse."

Seemingly unable to keep his peace, Linc stood. "That was my fault, Joseph. And you know it."

"Hush. We decided I'd talk."

"I didn't decide anything. I don't think this is fair."

"Sit down, Linc, so I can tell Papa the third."

"There will be no third." Clay didn't move from his chair. He didn't raise his voice. He didn't pound his fist. But everyone knew—it was time to be quiet. "Son, I don't know what got you run so afoul, but this is going to stop. Now."

Joseph glared at his father. Then with a slow look at the others, he lifted a letter from his pocket. He flashed it in my direction first, as if accusing me. I recognized the handwriting at once.

It was from James.

Ginny scowled as she glanced down at the next letter and saw James's unfamiliar handwriting. She'd all but forgotten about Ellie's spineless former fiancé. Why did he have to come back? Why now of all times?

January 26, 1929

Ellie my love,

Whether at home in San Francisco or away, the sky is always gray as if the sun refuses to shine. How could it, when the only sunshine in my life has gone to the far-off regions of the Arctic? Why, after you accepted my offer of marriage, did I let you leave me?

Come back, my sweet Ellie. Come back today. There's nothing we can't overcome together. I'll work everything out with Mother. In fact, her opinion of you has changed of late. She only speaks with kindness. I knew she'd come around.

Most importantly, I'm sorry for how I treated you. Surely you can forgive me. After all, it wasn't you who called off the engagement, but me—silly, stupid me. I promise I will make you the happiest girl in the world. We'll buy that house, and your grandfather is welcome to stay. Yes, my dear, I'm asking you once again to marry me.

Come back to me, my love. Make me the happiest man in the world.

Yours,

James

* * * * *

A heaviness hung in the air even as Brett came to pick her up. Ginny tried to force a smile. She told herself it was the letters—that she was mad at that horrible James for butting in—but it was more than that.

The more time she spent with Brett, the more questions arose—where was this leading? Would she return to LA and would he go on to Africa?

She offered Brett a hug as he entered the front door, and as she stepped back, she noticed questions in his eyes too.

"Ready?" he asked.

"Yes, I'm starving. Let's go."

They waved to the two women sitting on the porch swing and had almost made it to Brett's truck when Dove Fowler rose, balancing on one foot and waving her hand. "Oh, Ginny, Ginny. I almost forgot. I have a message for you."

Ginny glanced back, brushing her hair back over her shoulder, the bracelets on her arm clinking as she did.

"A phone message?" Her brow furrowed. Who would have called?

Horror reflected on Grandma Ethel's face. Eyes wide, lips pressed tight, she tugged on Dove's arm. Dove brushed Ethel's hand away.

"Oh yes, dear, it was someone named Danny. He said he's been calling for days and leaving messages."

"Danny?" The name dropped from her lips. She looked at Brett, who climbed into the truck, pretending he didn't hear. Then she turned back to Dove.

"Thank you, Dove. I'll make sure to call him tomorrow." Then Ginny offered a smile to Grandma Ethel, wondering how many voice mail messages the sweet lady had deleted.

And also wondering whether she was mad or happy about that fact.

Chapter Twenty-Nine

....

Tucked into the wooded hillside, Glacier Bay Lodge was much bigger than it had looked from the boat. Two sets of stairs led Ginny and Brett from the gravel driveway to the front entrance. As they mounted the stairs, she noticed a network of wooden walkways leading out to guest cabins. More beauty greeted her when they walked inside and gazed across the seating and dining areas to a wall of windows looking out over the bay.

"Hey guys, welcome." A college-aged woman with light brown hair approached them. "Brett, Ginny, I've saved my best table for you."

"Thanks, Amy." Brett reached up and patted her shoulder. "Filling in for someone in the dining room today?" They followed Amy to the center table along the large glass window. The view took Ginny's breath away, and she could see why it was the best table in the house.

"Yeah." Amy handed them menus after they sat. "My friend Paulette is out on a date, and I'm filling in for her. She's been dating one of the local guys most of the summer and is leaving tomorrow." Amy released a breath. "I should be happy someone found love at Glacier Bay." The woman eyed Ginny curiously.

Ginny chuckled nervously. Would she ever get used to walking into a place and already being known—not for which producer she dated, but for her heart? Her friendship?

She'd miss that when she returned to LA…miss people talking to her instead of about her. Then again, maybe the people here just didn't speak what they thought.

She considered what Brett had said—that people in the historical society had pretended they didn't know who she was. What had they thought when they saw her? *Oh, there's that girl who dumped the most eligible bachelor in Gustavus....*

Thankfully, she didn't have to worry about that long. Within minutes Amy brought them salads and crab cakes.

"I hope you don't mind, but I called ahead and told them to prepare my favorites." He tilted his head, smiled. "Which I knew you would love."

"Are you kidding?" She took a big bite of the crab cake and smiled. "I was hoping we didn't have to wait too long for food."

They chatted about their trip up the bay, and Brett shared some of his adventures—confrontations with bears, the times he'd gotten lost hiking, and amazing whale sightings.

"I'm bummed you saw only one whale from a distance. Earlier this summer we had twenty-eight who were regular guests, feeding right here in the bay."

"I'll have to come earlier next summer. I'd love to see that."

Brett paused with his fork halfway to his mouth. "You're coming back?"

She winked at him. "Who knows, maybe I'll never leave..." Laughter spilled out. "Honestly, Brett, Glacier Bay isn't just a place you visit for a few days and never think about again."

Amy served grilled salmon next, but Ginny had a hard time eating. Even as they made small talk, she could see Brett had something more he wanted to discuss.

She leaned forward, lightly resting her arms on the table, and cocked her head. "You may be talented at many things, Mr. Wilderness, but hiding your feelings isn't one of them. Spill it."

Brett ran a hand down his face, apparently relieved. "I know why you're here, Ginny." His voice was barely above a whisper. Then he reached across the table and took her hand, running his thumb over her fingers.

"You do?" Her brow wrinkled and she cocked an eyebrow, waiting for him to elaborate.

"Wasn't last week the anniversary…of your parents' death?"

Her breath escaped unwillingly. "You remembered? I can't believe you remembered that."

"Of course I remembered. You were important to me."

"Were?"

"You still are, but I'm telling myself not to get my hopes up." He released her hand and took a roll from the bread basket, then buttered it. "You're heading back to LA soon…."

She nodded, agreeing with him, but then felt the pang of an early headache in her right temple. Traffic, the work schedule, the people… how could she return to all that after being here?

"I do have to go back," she said, for her own benefit as much as for his.

"Of course you do. Your music is important to you."

"You're important to me too, Brett. I hoped my coming here was enough to show you that."

"Ginny." He lowered his head and let out a sigh. Then he placed the bread on his plate and pushed the plate back slightly. "You came here because I'm the only one who truly understands about your parents. You were missing them, they weren't around, and so you came looking for me."

"Is that what you think? How do you know I haven't told other people about them? I mean, it's been a couple of years…"

"Do you remember how long it took you to tell me about them— about their deaths—about your siblings? Months. Maybe a year." His voice was soft, his eyes kind. "And perhaps it's a stereotype, but I have an idea of what LA is like. In my mind, people are too busy about making names for themselves to consider other people. They're too busy talking to listen."

She wanted to argue. To say he was wrong. The only problem was Brett wasn't wrong. Even her closest friends didn't know her deepest pain.

"Maybe you're right. Maybe that is why I came. Is there anything wrong with that?"

"Nope. None at all. But if that's the case then this has to stop."

"What?"

"You being so good to my grandma. Caring so much about Ellie's letters. Looking so beautiful. Getting my hopes up."

A rush of warmth hit her cheeks. She jutted out her chin. "What would you say if I claimed you were doing the same thing…getting my hopes up by being so kind, so handsome?"

Brett released a long sigh and focused on her eyes. "Is it really getting your hopes up, Ginny, when I've never backed away from my commitment of giving all of me—all my heart—to you?"

His dark eyes studied hers, and he waited. Hope widened his pupils, and she knew what he wanted her to say—that she wanted to try again. She knew now that her coming here had nothing to do with getting advice. Heck, she'd hardly mentioned the contract.

"I—I don't know what to say."

"You don't know, or you're afraid? Dale and Robyn left you, but not by their own choosing. You have to trust that someone, sometime, is going to stick around. You have to be willing to open your heart."

She nodded, but inside a thousand worries crashed through her head. She couldn't face giving him everything, just to be stripped bare.

"*The saddest part of a crumbling shack is the laughter that once held up the walls.*" The words emerged in a melody, and Brett's eyebrows rose. Two women from a neighboring table turned, and Ginny realized then that she'd sung it louder than she intended.

"But at least someone took the risk and opened the door." Brett's voice was sharp. "And opened it wider to let others step inside." He lifted his napkin from his lap, crumpled it, and placed it to the side of his plate. He looked at her, disappointed. The look was familiar. She'd seen it all her life.

"Excuse me." A middle-aged woman from the neighboring table leaned closer. She and her friend wore hiking clothes and looked as if they'd been out on some hiking trail for most of the day. "Are you Ginny Marshall? I love that song. I saw you perform it on the *Today* show. I can't believe you made Matt Lauer cry."

Ginny shrugged. "Everyone feels a loss when they think about the home that no longer is—realizing they didn't appreciate what they had when they had it." Her publicist had helped her come up with that line. It always made people cry. As if on cue, moisture filled the women's gazes.

Ginny brushed her hair back over her shoulder and flashed a smile. "But let's not let that song make us melancholy." She pointed to the woman's camera sitting on the tabletop. "Would you like a photo with the three of us?"

"Would you?" The woman's ponytail swished as she stood. She motioned to her friend, then handed her camera to Brett. "Would you mind?"

"Of course not."

Ginny stood, and the women huddled on each side of her as if they were close friends. She had no doubt it would be up on Facebook in less than an hour.

Brett held the camera out, focusing on the screen. "Say cheese."

"Cheese," rang out in unison.

Handing the camera back, he was polite, but as they sat she could read the thoughts behind his gaze.

He thinks I'm running...running from my feelings. Running from the truth.

Ginny took a sip of her water. The women thanked her again and then returned to their own table.

Yet she wasn't one to deny the truth. The truth was...Brett was right.

* * * * *

They finished dinner and dessert in near silence, storm clouds rolling in faster than she'd thought possible. The beautiful bay turned as dark as Ginny's thoughts. Brett wanted her to make the same commitment. For her to say that she *wasn't* getting his hopes up, that she *did* want to invest in their relationship. But something held her back. Maybe because of what awaited her in LA. Maybe because he was still planning to go to Africa, and that was no longer her heart's desire.

He hadn't even mentioned Africa—once their dream. He no doubt knew it would scare her off faster than a grizzly lumbering her direction. After living the life she'd been living, Glacier Bay was primitive enough.

Yet how could she voice her mixed emotions? Brett had accused her of coming to Glacier Bay because she missed her parents, and then he acted as if she didn't care for him at all, never cared. What could she say to help him understand?

"Do you know when you're heading back to LA?" His question was simple.

"Not exactly, although they are expecting me in a few days." She didn't tell him the 'they' was Danny. Brett's fist clenched on the tabletop, and she figured he already knew.

"But you *are* going back. I expected you would since your life is there—your fans. But do you want to?"

The question hung in the air. She opened her mouth and then closed it again. She wanted to tell him that her whole life everything had been decided for her. She'd been told where to live, whom to call Mom and Dad, what toys to like. It was easier to live that way still. To show up at the studio when she was told. To say what the publicist suggested. To wear the dress that arrived at her doorstep. To meet Danny at the restaurant of his choice at the correct time.

She wasn't Ellie. Wasn't brave. She couldn't open her heart to another and risk it. Didn't he realize only a thin sliver of her heart remained?

Brett cleared his throat. "I asked if you wanted to go back. Aren't you going to say anything?"

"What do you want me to say, Brett? I don't know what the future holds. I don't know…" She let her words trail off. *About us.*

He lowered his head. "I don't want you to say anything, Ginny. Don't know why I'd suspect you would."

On the two-mile drive home, the tension between them grew.

Outside, rain pelted the windshield. A storm raged and lightning zagged in the dark sky beyond the trees. She imagined it was on a night like this that the National Guard plane Linda had told her about went down.

Fear gripped her as the wind howled and rain seemed to come out of nowhere. She'd never been fearful of storms before, but this one caused her knees to quiver. Or maybe it was the storm raging in Brett's eyes.

"I don't know why you don't believe I care for you. I was ready to marry you." The words rushed from his mouth, pounding like the rain. "I don't know why you don't believe I'm certain of my commitment. You didn't then. You don't now." He reached up and turned on the defroster to keep the windshield from fogging up. "You want to be loved, Ginny, but anytime someone shows it to you, it bounces off like rain from this windshield."

Brett ran his fingers through his hair, then pounded a fist on the steering wheel. "I hoped you were coming to me, Ginny, but seeing the look in your eyes at dinner—I know the truth. You are running from Danny Kingston. Running from yet another person who tried to express his affection. You are running from the fans who love you, for fear that someday another pretty singer will take your place. I'm sorry to say I fell for it." Brett shrugged. "You're never going to find what you're looking for if you're not willing to open up...to crack open that hard shell."

His words stopped. She glanced over at him. His face was a gray shadow, his jaw tight.

"Go ahead. Continue. Put me in my place. A place that's well within your reach. You've always wanted to keep me under your thumb. To hold me back."

"That's not true."

"Yeah, you can say that, but you're the only one who told me not to go to LA. Everyone else believed in me." Ginny faced him while he drove. "There are people who *still* believe in me. Who think I can make something of myself. Something big."

The wipers squeaked against the glass, and Brett's fists gripped the steering wheel. She turned back to face straight ahead. And just when she was certain he wasn't going to respond, the truck jerked forward as he slammed on the brakes.

She stretched out her hands to brace herself, but there was no need. They'd only been going twenty-five miles per hour, the speed limit. She returned her hands to her lap, glancing in the side mirror. There weren't headlights for as far as she could see behind them, or in front of them. She supposed the middle of a dark road was as good a place as any to let it all out.

"Don't you understand? I wish you would listen to me. I wish you could take my words deep inside." His voice cracked, and he sounded as if his heart was broken into a thousand pieces. The emotion in his voice surprised her. A lump rose in her throat.

"What I had to tell you then is what I want to tell you now. You don't have to prove yourself. You don't have to make something of yourself." He looked away out the side window and then turned back to her. "You're amazing just as you are, Ginny. You don't need a big contract or a concert tour to prove that. God made something special when He made you."

Tears sprang to her eyes, and a memory came back to her. It was of Dale and Robyn the night they told her they wanted to give her a forever family.

The memory of that moment filled her mind.

"You're special, Ginny," Dale had said, taking her hands in his.

Robyn had placed her hands on Ginny's shoulders. "You may wonder why you've had to go through all the stuff you have, but we're confident that it happened so you can make your way to us. God's gonna use your story to inspire others someday, and we're going to be right there telling everyone that's our girl. That's Ginny Pierson."

"Pierson?"

Robyn had embraced her then. "If you'll accept us, we want to make you a part of our family—forever."

With the patter of the pounding rain stirring her soul, Ginny covered her face with her hands. The pain of the ache surprised her. Both the pain of what she had had and lost, and the realization of what she was on the verge of walking away from once again—someone who loved her just for her. Someone who wanted to protect and cherish her heart.

Tears welled up like the rain outside the windows, but none came. To cry over that memory would take her back to the darkness of losing the only parents who'd ever accepted her. Maybe the tears didn't come because tears meant sorrow, and as they sat on that empty stretch of road, it was hope that brightened in her heart.

Brett gripped her hands tight, as if he didn't want to let go. Maybe someone did want her. Maybe more than just one person…she'd just been too afraid to accept that.

Her brother's phone calls proved she was still part of the Pierson family, legal papers or not. And Brett…could she really believe what he was saying? If she did…well, that meant she needed to stay. But what did staying mean? Giving their relationship a chance? Staying in Gustavus? Going with him to Africa?

It also meant walking away from the limelight, didn't it? Walking away from the chance to prove that she wasn't a castoff. A reject. A charity case.

Ginny lowered her lashes. It was too much to think about now. She needed to make Brett know she believed him, but when she lifted her eyes and looked back into his, she realized he already knew.

His face had softened. Even in the darkened cab of the truck she could see that. He looked at her, searching her face. He looked at her lips, then his gaze moved to her neck, her hair, and back to her eyes, where he drank her in. The attraction between them was as palpable as the tension. She wanted to scoot closer. To be pulled into his embrace. But to accept his love meant she had to do something about it. And even though she'd come all the way to Gustavus to know this answer— the truth of their love—she had no idea what to do with the truth.

"I didn't want to believe it," she finally whispered. "Deep down I thought you were like my mom. Like Dale and Robyn in a way, too. I was afraid you would leave—would abandon me."

"Is that why you did the leaving first?"

She nodded. "I suppose so."

The glimmer of headlights turning the corner appeared ahead.

"I want to believe in you, Brett. I want to believe in us. I wouldn't be here if I didn't." She wasn't sure if he heard her or if her words were lost in the sound of the truck's engine.

"If they see us parked they're going to stop to make sure we're not in trouble. And if they stop they'll want to talk." She knew Brett had heard her when his voice was lighter than before. Much lighter.

Brett released her hands, put the truck into gear, and pressed on the gas, putting the truck in motion once again.

She nodded, even though his eyes were focused on the road and not her. She searched his face in the shadows. For a split second, the truck's interior was lit by the passing car, and Ginny was sure she saw a hint of a smile on his face.

When he finally parked in front of Grandma Ethel's house, she couldn't help but reach over and take his hand. "I want to believe you. I want to trust." Those were the only words that would come.

He didn't respond. Why should he? Did she really want him to explain his love? Wasn't it enough to accept it?

Chapter Thirty

....

April 12, 1929

Grandfather,

As I mentioned in my last missive, James wrote me a letter. It arrived when yours came but must have fallen between the cracks in the floor. Joseph found it.

His face serious, though not angry, Clay held out his hand, and Joseph gave him the letter. Clay read it, his face expressionless. It was James up to his old stunts again, saying he loves me and wants me back.

Oh, Grandfather, James and the life he represents—the dreams and hopes of being his wife, living in San Francisco's society—seem so far away from me now. I haven't thought of James for many weeks.

Then with a look, Clay summoned me to the porch.

A heaviness hung in the air, like a storm waiting to unburden itself. He handed me the smooth stationery. As I skimmed over James's words, I felt only sickness to know that Clay had read them. Yet I didn't see pain in his eyes, just patience as he waited for me to explain.

I simply told him James and I were once engaged, but he broke off the engagement before I came to Alaska.

Clay's chest rose and fell.

I longed to reach for his hand, but I refrained, waiting for

his reaction. "I did love him—at least, I thought I did, once.
But I don't anymore."

"You weren't attached when you came here?"

"No."

"You don't love him?"

I shook my head, smiling to reassure him.

He set the letter aside and wrapped me in his strong arms.

Thank you, Grandfather, for introducing me to this man.

I'll write more later,

Ellie Bell

April 17, 1929

Brother Peter,

*I aim to tell you what happened, so you'll see why I could
not ask your girl the question I long to ask—not yet.*

*I know Ellie told you about that foul letter and Joseph's
plot to send her home. What he has against her, I don't know,
except a fierce jealousy on behalf of his mama. And, well, he's
holding on to that grief, sort of like I was, letting it fester into
an unreasonable anger. He's chosen to direct it at my Ellie.
That's why I can rein in my frustration at him, hoping to steer
him back like a hurt dog, soft and careful.*

*After our talk on the porch, I took Ellie's hand and we
strode indoors. I eyed each one of the children, but especially
Joseph.*

*"I see no need to explain," I said, "except to say, no feelings
linger for this James. She loves us now. That's all." I hung up
my hat, picked up our bags, and peered at Ellie. "Where do
you want these?"*

"Papa, I don't think you read the letter."

"Yes, son, I did. Ellie is staying. For good. This is a conversation I won't be having again."

Janey jerked as if registering what I said. "Does that mean you're getting married?"

I couldn't help but shoot her a wink.

Janey rushed to Ellie and hugged her. Zach followed with a leap into her arms. They squealed to the detriment of a person's ears, and a grin spread over Linc's face. Probably thinking about some invention to make the wedding better...

In that moment I saw it. Our family, not the way it used to be, but different, new. A new life with a good woman, warm nights and happy days, like fresh growth in spring.

Finally, I caught Joseph's gaze.

He looked shocked, horrified. I suppose his rile got the best of him, for he forgot himself and let loose on me.

"What's wrong with you? I'd never forgive my woman if she betrayed me."

I stepped toward him, my hand reached out. He grabbed the chair, crashed it down. Broke its back. Both Zach and Penny started up crying.

I gripped his arm, hauled up the chair, and forced him down.

The bile in his glare ate through me.

"Go," I said. "Cool off."

A moment of quiet followed. His gaze met mine, and a speck of regret, the child hidden underneath, peered up. Ellie must've seen it too; she laid a hand on my arm, looked at him. But then he thundered out the door. Two days, I didn't see him. So I went looking. Found him, where else, at the Curtises' big house, living in their son's room. He barely said a word to me. Promised to come by to get his things.

Have I lost my son, Brother Peter? How can I find joy in my love for Ellie while my son turns his back on me? My heart suffers a mighty struggle over this. After Adelaide died, I promised myself to keep my sights on my children first. My own desires, they come last. Am I a fool to think I can be happy? Might my boy come around, accept her, be like sunlight to me again? I tell you, I want to hope for that. I do hope for it.

I know Ellie is a gift from God, not a test. And I accept that gift, gladly. But the Lord giveth and the Lord taketh away. What if Joseph makes camp in this rebellion? Do I marry Ellie anyway, knowing it'd mean losing my boy? He's my son.

Will you advise me, Brother Peter? I seek the Lord, but a fog spreads out before me. I can't see my way.

One thing I do know. In light of all this, I don't see how I can marry Ellie just yet. The month cut-off date has come and gone, so I mean to write Reverend Martin in Hoonah, seeking an extension of his deadline.

Ellie, kind and wise woman that she is, hasn't even mentioned the wedding to me. She supports me, wants to help with Joseph (not that she can), and cares for the children with a love as real as the dawn. How I love that girl! I never thought I could again, but she's gone and stolen my heart—which I gladly give. If only my boy would love her too.

What hopes we had when we got back from Hoonah!

Meanwhile, I've built an outbuilding for Linc and myself. With the new situation between Ellie and me, those Tlingit ladies are right. We shouldn't be cohabitating. Linc says he'll make a modern walkway to the house for me. I don't encourage it.

With Joseph gone, I'm appreciating my time with Linc. A comfort. Still not so fond of his inventions.

Yours,

Clay

July 9, 1929

Dear Grandfather,

How I miss you. I hope you are doing wonderfully, feeling healthy and happy. I've written my last dozen or so letters to you as if they were stories rather than letters. I think the writing itself helps me sort through it all. But hearing from you will be the greatest comfort.

It's been three months since Joseph moved out. Clay has tried to reach him, but he won't accept that his father is going to marry again. It seems the mere sight of me ignites his anger. Surely Joseph will learn to accept me. Clay and I pray to this end together and individually—we pray so hard! I know Clay would do anything for him.

Despite the worry over Joseph, Clay and I grow ever closer. Guitar lessons often fill our evenings, and I'm getting good enough to play "Sweet Betsy from Pike" along with our little family band.

I'm getting better at the chores, if you can believe that. Clay himself showed me how to can strawberries and even rutabagas (you really can't avoid them here). I'm smiling as I think about that day—a bright oasis of laughter.

Clay surprised himself by going on his circuit, preaching to the outlying settlements. He surmises the lost won't wait for his boy to turn around. He goes for only a few days at a time, never wanting to be too far away.

LOVE FINDS YOU IN GLACIER BAY, ALASKA

Our love has grown, not melodramatically as in those Saturday matinees, but gently, as we walk this road together.

Yet as time goes on, the burden of Joseph's ongoing estrangement sours our joy. I love Clay, Grandfather. But each day I worry. How can this work if his son won't accept me? Honestly—and it crumbles my heart into little bits to even think it—I don't know if I want to be a part of a family where I'm not welcome. I tried that before.

What does it say about me if I can't make my loved ones' families accept me? As I sit here on our recently painted porch, gazing at the fresh white, I wish I could paint myself into what others want. Make myself good enough for them. I've never been able to, though. I don't know if I ever will. At least I have you, Grandfather.

Oh my, you must be downcast, reading all my gloomy thoughts.

On a happier note, I've been teaching Janey to sew and design clothes. We've mastered fox fur shawls, by hand of course. I'd like to order a sewing machine from Sears and Roebuck come spring, a foot pump—not electric. I think the ladies around here would like it, maybe even over in Juneau. I never thought I'd get back to sewing. I was certainly naïve thinking I'd be able to start an Alaskan Wilderness Line and make lots of money. It makes me chuckle now. Janey has quite a gift for it.

You should see how big Penny is growing. She'll be two in October. The other day she called me Mama. I don't think she should, not until Clay and I get married. If we get married.

So much for the happier note.

I wish I knew how you were doing. I'm wondering about Felix and hoping he hasn't broken his promise to pay for your hospital bills. I know it's in the Lord's hands. Soon, I will hear from you. And you promised to come to the wedding, so maybe I'll see you then. Whenever that may be. I'm not even officially engaged.

I love you, Grandfather. I know you are praying for me.
Ellie

July 10, 1929

Dear Brother Clay,

Thank you for your message. Lester brought it yesterday. He's leaving this morning, so I'll write this in haste.

"A man's heart deviseth his way: but the LORD directeth his steps." Proverbs 16:9. We had it all planned out, didn't we? You were going to marry your Ellie, start up your circuit again, and all would be just fine. The fact that things have not worked out that way does not mean God has forgotten you, but that He has a better plan. Better than ours.

As for Joseph, lay down your life for him, brother. Do whatever you must do. If it means postponing your wedding, so be it. He's your son. God will use you in the life of your family—your first ministry. Always remember that.

Of course, I am glad you've been able to resume your circuit. Grateful to hear the positive reports of prospective converts, but your priority is Joseph. Seek him, as Christ sought you when you were lost.

Write again in a month if you're able.
In Christ,
Rev. Bruce Martin

P.S. Has Ellie learned to shoot the rifle yet?

Chapter Thirty-One

....

Ginny had woken up early with thoughts of Brett on her mind, read a few letters, and then made a breakfast quiche for herself and Grandma.

"Darling Ginny, this tastes wonderful," Grandma Ethel gushed.

Ginny agreed it did taste good; it was one of the few of Robyn's recipes she'd memorized. Still, Grandma didn't eat more than one small piece, and she looked a bit pale. Ginny was about to suggest that they have Jared come down and check her pulse—just to make sure everything was all right—when Grandma put down her fork and leveled her gaze at Ginny.

"So, did you and Brett finally get to talk yesterday?"

Her bluntness surprised Ginny.

"What do you mean?"

Grandma Ethel let out a heavy sigh. "Well, child, do you two love each other or not?"

Ginny lowered her head and couldn't help but smile. Her cheeks warmed. "To be perfectly honest, I think we do. We just don't know what to do about it."

Grandma Ethel stood and carried her plate to the sink. When she returned, she lowered her face closer to Ginny's. "You know I'm not one to butt my business into where it doesn't belong, but both of you are so concerned about what to *do*. I've been worried ever since you two talked about running off to be missionaries. Don't you realize it's the *doing* that often gets us into trouble? It's not the doing that makes

God happy. It's not about what *we've* done…it's about what's been done *for* us."

Ginny expected the lecture to continue, but instead Grandma Ethel pressed her lips tight, as if allowing the words to sink deep into Ginny's heart.

Yet instead of bringing peace, tension stirred within her. "I know you're talking about God, and I'm thankful for all He's done for me, but Grandma…" Ginny paused, trying to keep her voice steady. "It's all the stuff that's been done—*to* me mostly—that keeps holding me back."

"Have you ever read a biography worth reading? Seems like most of the book is all the stuff that goes wrong. It's only the last quarter or so when God starts making things right." Grandma Ethel pointed a finger into the air. "Think of Ellie's story. How interested would you have been if it was just one happy letter after another? If she'd married that James in San Francisco and lived a life of ease filled with rich folks and fine parties?"

Ginny rolled the sleeves down on her sweater in order to cover her hands. Hoping to hide their shaking. "I would have read it. I would have found it interesting—"

"For a while, maybe," Grandma Ethel interrupted. "But would you have been changed by Ellie's story then? Would anyone have? She'd be just like thousands of others who lived and died and are forgotten. Ellie, on the other hand, will never be forgotten. Not by me, not by the people of Gustavus and Glacier Bay, nor, I have a feeling, by you.

"It's hard to know, isn't it, whether the things we face are just because the world is full of sin and sinful people, or if God is working out a plan," Grandma continued. "I happen to think it's both. There's sin, but through it all, He takes the mess we make and paints a masterpiece. In fact, I'm quite certain that before God can ever bless a woman—and use her to impact many—He uses the hammer, the file, and the furnace to do a holy work."

Ginny frowned. "And what if that person doesn't want that? What if she just wants to be like everyone else and live an easy, successful life?" She thought of her apartment, her designer clothes, her things in LA... and so much more that could soon be hers.

"Depends what you consider easier." Grandma Ethel shifted in her chair. "Is it easier to live among rich and fancy folks and be a star—yet carry an emptiness inside? Or is it easier to just make ends meet, yet live in community, with someone you love—and who loves you—and feel God's pleasure?" Grandma Ethel let out a sigh. "It's up to you, dear girl."

Grandma pointed to the living room, her lips curling up in a smile. "Now go, wait for Brett. You might have time to read a few more of Ellie's letters. Maybe you'll be surprised by what she chose. There's only a few dishes. I'll take care of them."

Ginny nodded and put her own plate in the sink, then hurried to the sofa in the living room. She wrapped the quilt from Grandma's bed tighter around her shoulders.

She was almost afraid to read any more of Ellie's letters. Afraid they'd prove Grandma Ethel right. So instead she watched for Brett. After a few minutes, she spotted his white truck coming down the road. She was happy to see him, mostly because he'd distract her from his grandmother's words. Because to take them in—really take them in—would change everything.

* * * * *

Ginny waved at Brett as he parked. Today she'd worn her loosest jeans and had found one of his own shirts in Grandma's laundry room. She noticed Brett's eyes on her as he parked. He wore a red plaid shirt and looked as if he'd just stepped out of a Land's End commercial. She wanted to run to him, but instead waited for him to come to her.

"I want you to teach me to shoot," she said as he mounted the steps.

"Excuse me?"

"Clay wanted to teach Ellie. It's only fair I get to learn, too."

"Yes, but Ellie had to scare away bears."

Ginny crossed her arms over her chest. "Don't you remember some of the wild people who lived in California?" She laughed. "It'll be a useful skill for self-protection."

"Okay, but we'd need to go back to my place for a rifle."

"Is there a shooting range nearby?"

"A shooting range?" Brett shook his head. "Ginny, this is Gustavus. There's a dozen spots on my grandparents' property where we could shoot. But are you sure you want to do that? I had other plans."

He pointed up at the sky.

"We're going up in an airplane?"

Brett cocked his chin, and then he offered her his elbow. "No, Ginny. We're going up in *my* plane."

It didn't take them long to get to the airport. It didn't take long to get anywhere in Gustavus. Passengers from another flight were crossing the tarmac, and Ginny thought of the day she'd arrived, when she'd sported fancy clothes and hot-pink luggage. She'd come to talk to Brett, and discovered a community. She'd come to figure out her story, and found Ellie's. Maybe somehow her story would sort itself out through both these things.

The truck parked, Ginny walked by Brett's side to the hangar. He reached out his hand, and she gladly slid her smaller one inside his larger one. His thumb stroked the back of her hand, and tingles danced up her arm.

A group of guys were at the hangar, and they all called their greetings. Ginny recognized Mitch from Grandma's house.

Mitch playfully slugged Brett's shoulder. "What's this pretty woman doing with the likes of you?"

Brett shrugged. "Maybe I'm her muse. Heaven knows every hit song of hers has been about how I've dragged her heart through the dirt."

Ginny's eyes widened and she gasped, realizing how true that statement was. "Yes, but from here on out I'm hoping to write happier songs. Ones full of hope." She winked at him.

Brett squeezed her hand and leaned closer, speaking so only she heard. "Hearing that is just as good as a contract signed and sealed that declares your love."

Contract. Her shoulders straightened as the word replayed in her mind. She had to get back to Danny. Had to let him know that things would be different. How? She wasn't sure, but she couldn't imagine not having Brett in her life, even if that meant waiting for him to get Africa out of his system.

Like ants around an anthill, the other guys put aside their work and helped Brett ready his plane. They joked with him as they filled it up and performed a safety check. They respected Brett. That was evident. Not for his money or fame, but for who he was. Seeing that spoke to Ginny's soul more than anything had in a very long time.

Her stomach quivered as she climbed into the plane after Brett, sat in the passenger's seat, and buckled herself in. He gave her a quick safety talk, and then with his expert handling of the controls, they were soon roaring down the runway and lifting gracefully into the air.

Flying in the front of Brett's small plane was different from any commercial flight she'd ever taken. It was even different from the small plane she'd ridden in from Juneau. Pride puffed her chest to see Brett as a pilot. And when she pointed toward the bay, he turned the plane that direction.

With few words between them, they followed the same path they had taken a few days before, taking in the water, the cruise ships, the mountains, and the glaciers from a totally new angle. What she'd only seen in part down on the water, now she saw in whole. Beyond one mountain peak were a thousand. Beyond the inlet waves was an endless sea.

Brett was the only one in her life who, instead of setting her path for her, opened her up to possibilities. And hadn't Ellie's letters done the same? Hadn't they shown her that life could be—would be—hard and painful, but that it was faced most effectively, lived most beautifully, when surrounded by those you loved?

"Wow." Ginny's eyes peered into the expanse, wishing that they didn't have to stop or turn back. Brett cleared his throat and she looked at him. She realized then that his gaze wasn't on the view but on her.

"We can make this work." It was a simple statement, but her whole body warmed at those words. Ginny had no idea what "this" was or how in the world it would work, but she wanted nothing more than to agree.

"Yes, Brett," she said simply. "Yes, we can." A smile filled his face, bringing flutters to her heart. There'd be days and weeks to figure out the details, but for now she just wanted to soar with him. Soar and explore a world full of dreams. Full of possibilities.

* * * * *

On the way back to Grandma Ethel's house, Ginny asked Brett to pull over at Four Corners.

"I have a call to make. It'll only take one minute."

"How about I get us coffee then?" He parked by the Fireweed.

"Perfect." Ginny dialed a familiar number as she leaned against the wall by the bulletin board. She noticed a new posting. *Birthday party for Bill at Bud's place.* Ginny knew where Bud's place was. Would they mind if she dropped in? She chuckled, supposing they wouldn't.

"Hello?"

She smiled as she recognized her brother's voice on the phone.

"Hi, Drew, it's Ginny."

"Oh, hi. Is something wrong?"

"Why would you think something's wrong?"

"You don't call much, and your voice sounds different."

"Oh, it's just a good day." She shrugged. "I was just wondering how Cooper's birthday went."

"Great." She could hear the smile in his voice. "He got a bike. I taught him to ride last night." Drew laughed. "I think he's ridden two hundred laps around our cul-de-sac today."

"You're a good dad, Drew, teaching him to ride like that." She'd thought that every time she saw her brother with his kids, but she hadn't told him before. She didn't know why she hadn't.

"Thanks, Ginny. That means a lot."

She heard noises in the background, the sound of kids' voices.

"Hey, Cooper just ran in. You want to talk to him?"

Emotion rose in her throat. "Yes, of course."

"Hello? Who is this?" His voice was more grown up than the last time she'd talked to him. Fully boy.

"Hey, Coop. Aunt Ginny's on the phone." Tears filled her eyes, and she blinked them away.

"Aunt Ginny!" He laughed. "Will you sing to me, Aunt Ginny?"

"Do you want me to sing the birthday song?"

"No, silly." His chuckle lightened her heart even more—if that was possible. "My favorite song."

Hearing those words, Ginny's mind took her back to Christmas two years prior. She'd been talked into staying at Drew and Monica's house on Christmas Eve, and then when it was far past their bedtime, her two nieces and nephew had found their way into her room. They'd all circled around her on the floor, and she'd sung the only song she could remember from her childhood—one she'd learned in a Sunday school she'd only attended a few times. As Ginny sang the words over the phone now, she couldn't think of a better song for this moment.

"He's got the whole world in His hands. He's got the whole world in His hands. He's got the whole world in His hands—"

She was just about to sing that last line one more time when Dove Fowler came hobbling out of Fireweed on her crutches.

"Oh, Ginny, Ginny, there you are," Dove said, not even seeming to care that Ginny was on the phone. "I need to talk to you, dear. It's about singing tomorrow night. Remember we're raising funds for Brett's trip to Africa."

On the other end of the phone Cooper's laughter dulled to a low roar. The sunlight around her faded too. And as the last words of the song still hung on her lips, Ginny remembered anew—the whole world included Africa.

She bit her lower lip. She was warming up to the idea that she could move here. She was falling in love with the place. But there?

"Aunt Ginny, Aunt Ginny." She could barely make out his voice through the fog that filled her mind.

"Where are you, Aunt Ginny? Where you going next? Are you off on another plane? Another adventure?"

"I'm not sure, Coop," she said as she waved a hand at Dove Fowler. "I wish I knew."

Chapter Thirty-Two

....

August 4, 1929

Dear Grandfather,

My hands are shaking; I can barely write. I'm in the cabin, just me and the children. Clay and Linc have been hunting all day. It gets dark so late here. They can hunt all night, practically. I don't know when he'll be home.

A bear, Grandfather. It was Janey. She went to the outhouse and a bear... The gun. I couldn't...

I can't write. I'll tell you later.

Ellie

August 4, 1929

Dear Grandfather Barnett,

I asked Papa if I could write and tell what happened. I like putting my thoughts down on paper. I write a diary, you know. Like the princesses in books do. It makes me feel better, especially after Mama died. But this time, the diary wasn't enough. I wanted to tell you, because it was really scary, and I know you'll pray for me to not be afraid anymore. I'm glad you are my friend.

It was after bedtime, but still light. Did you know it stays light really late here? At ten o'clock it's sort of pink outside. You can still look around. I like it, except it's hard to fall asleep.

I went to the outhouse. I'm supposed to stay inside after

bedtime, or get a grown-up, but with it all nice and pink outside, I thought it would be okay. Miss Ellie was stitching up a fox shawl in her room and didn't see me sneak out.

When I was done, I opened the door a little, but I heard something breathing deep-like. Dark and scary. And footsteps, branches breaking, and such. I knew it wasn't Mama Moose because she's not dark and scary. I peeked out the door and saw him. The biggest, blackest, scariest bear I ever saw. I've seen bears before, but not so up close.

At first I couldn't move. I don't know. I was just so scared. My scream stayed in my throat. Has that ever happened to you? I watched it clomp around the garden. I was sore afraid he would eat my rutabagas, "Purple Top" and "Yellow Boy," but he didn't. He just walked on through, sniffing. I thought he might just pass through, not notice me.

Then, I don't know why, but that nasty bear turned and stared right at me. His eyes looked really mean, and his nose scrunched up. The rest was a big black shadow. He turned and started coming toward the outhouse.

I slammed the door shut, latched it, and held it tight with my hands. My heart raced so fast. I wanted to cry. Finally my scream came out, loudest in my life.

I couldn't see anything, because the little window's too high, but I could hear him stomping toward me. Then scratching on the wood. It was so awful! He pushed and pushed against the door. And I screamed and screamed! "Miss Ellie! Miss Ellie! Papa! Papa!" Even though I knew he wasn't home.

I thought sure the bear's claws would break through the wood. Then—oh, it was so scary—I saw his nose sniff the window. That's when he started growling, kind of low-like.

"Miss Ellie!!" I kept on screaming. Finally I heard the door to the house open. I heard Miss Ellie's scream, powerful loud, like mine was. The bear stopped scratching on the outhouse for a minute.

"Get out of here!" Miss Ellie yelled, but the bear went back to scratching. I could barely hear Miss Ellie, sort of talking to herself. "The gun. The gun." Her voice was all shaky.

"Shoot it, Miss Ellie!" I shouted.

Then, it felt like his whole body was leaning against the outhouse. It tipped a little. I thought for sure it was going to fall all the way over and that bear was going to eat me.

"Don't worry, Janey!" Miss Ellie yelled to me. "Get inside!" She must've been talking to Zach. "Take care of your sister." I heard the front door slam and Zach and Penny start crying.

Boy, was the outhouse tipping, almost as much as I was screaming. Through the cracks, the bear's fur touched my arm. That's when I started crying. He was so close. I thought sure I was gonna die. The outhouse just about tipped over, but then I heard a shot. Just one.

The bear let go of the outhouse and it tipped forward and back, finally ending up where it's supposed to stand. I was too afraid to open the door. After a couple of minutes, Miss Ellie came to get me. We hugged real big and cried.

I didn't see the bear. I thought maybe she'd shot it, but then she said no, she didn't. Just scared it off.

I won't go to the outhouse alone at all, ever, nighttime or day. Never ever again. Pray for me. I don't want to be a fraidy cat. Pray for Miss Ellie too. She feels really bad that she didn't kill the bear.

I love you.

Janey

August 4, 1929

Brother Peter,

I know Ellie mentioned the bear. Sleep's not having me tonight, so let me fill out the story. I've tried to teach Ellie to shoot, even though she's resisted. I give her credit for grabbing the gun. Not an easy thing when a person's as scared of guns as she is. She said she had a perfect shot, but her hands shook so much she couldn't pull the trigger. She dropped my father's Great War rifle into the slush and it went off.

I give thanks to the Lord the bullet didn't shoot her or one of the kids. Didn't shoot the bear either. Scared it away, for which I'm glad.

The bear gone, Ellie grabbed up Janey and ran to the house. When Linc and I got home a few minutes later, they were all hugs and tears. I held my Ellie till she stopped shaking. It's a kindness to be the one to comfort her. I want to take care of that girl all my days. Just thinking about her gives a warm feeling.

But I can't be home every moment. If a woman wants to live up here, she's got to shoot. For her own safety and my children's. I'd sure appreciate prayers, for I'm worried sick about their safety.

Clay

August 10, 1929

Dear Grandfather,

I think of you every day, almost every moment, during these trying days. I miss you and feel such a relief to write the events of my life to you, just as I always have.

Are you doing well? Is dear Nurse Schroeder taking good

care of you? I'm sure she is. How is your health? I trust you grow stronger each day. I trust Felix still covers your medical bills—I have no choice but to trust that. A letter would provide great comfort, Grandfather. I know you will write soon, or perhaps your letter was lost.

We are mourning here. The bear fiasco seems a trifle compared to what happened next. Part of me doesn't want to tell you, but I've always shared everything with you, so I will. I know you won't judge me. I'm already judging myself. Clay hasn't shown any sign of frustration with me, but how could he not feel it? I know he loves me, but I know how important his children are to him.

What I'm going to tell you happened over a week ago. With a laden heart—as if weighed down by ten of Christian's burdens—I will tell you.

It was that night, the same night I failed to kill the bear. A shuddering wind quaked the cabin, whispering in through the cracks. Clay and Linc returned soon after. We spewed out the story to their amazement. But then, with them home, our calm inched back. I made tea; Janey sat down to write you a letter; Zach "read" a book to Penny.

Soon Linc went off to the mansion to bed (that's what we call Clay and Linc's sleeping shack). Clay and I cozied onto the porch swing, nestled under a stack of fur pelts. My neck released its stiffness as I rested my head on his shoulder, felt his strong hand on my arm.

"Rough night."

Something about the way he said it, not cracking a smile, sent me into a giggle fit. Boy, was he proud to make me laugh. I smacked his arm.

"Oh yes," I said. "That's just the word I was looking for."

He smiled, and I snuggled closer. The moon, so sharp and clear, broke through the building clouds. He moved my hair behind my ear, then kissed my forehead. We sat like this for a few moments, taking in the stillness, the brisk Alaska air. Then I confessed that although I'd had a good shot, I'd missed the bear. He touched my hand and said, "Okay."

That's all. Not a sharp tone, not a hint of disappointment in me. But I know he was thinking about his little girl. And what might happen if that bear comes back when he's not home.

"I'm going to learn to shoot, Clay. I promise." My heart struck against my chest just saying it, but I knew it wasn't an option anymore. Janey could've been hurt or killed.

"That may be wise." Clay interlaced his fingers with mine. "I'll help you."

I leaned my head on his shoulder. "Thank you. I'm so sorry."

"Ginny dear, do you know if you're eating at home tonight?"

Grandma Ethel peeked out onto the porch. Ginny gently rocked on the swing. She paused, realizing she'd been holding her breath.

"You all right, dear?" Grandma Ethel drew near. "Are you upset that Brett had to run and help Lee? It was a horrible thing that he lost his glasses in that hangar. I hope they can find them."

"No, it's fine." Ginny placed the letter on the table, her eyes wide. Did the bear come back? "And I'm not sure about dinner. Maybe I'll cook. Would you like that?" She forced herself to look at Grandma Ethel. Forced herself to look away from the letter.

Grandma Ethel's eyes twinkled. "Little Janey doesn't get eaten by a bear."

"What?" Ginny jerked her head back. "I hope not." She placed a hand over her heart. "Well, I worried, but I was certain...almost certain...that wasn't the case."

"You sure about that?" Grandma Ethel winked. "You looked very concerned, dear. That ol' bear did scare me something fierce, though. The roar just outside the outhouse. On stormy days I'm reminded of it. And the feel of that fur through the cracks—"

"Wait." Ginny sat up straighter. She furrowed her brow. Had Brett's grandma read these letters so often that she thought she lived them? Or... "Grandma Ethel. You're not Janey, are you?"

Grandma Ethel grinned. "I was wondering if you were going to figure it out, but seeing you read...I couldn't keep it in any longer. My full name is Ethel Jane. My grandmother was Ethel, so they called me Janey. But after I married, Janey didn't seem like a grown woman's name, so I took on Ethel."

"So...you were there! Oh, I want to hear more about...everything! Could you tell they really loved each other, Ellie and Clay?"

Grandma Ethel didn't answer, but Ginny could see the answer in her eyes, in her smile. "I won't give you even a clue now, otherwise it'll ruin the rest of the letters, but I hope after reading them you'll understand even more what I was telling you this morning." She placed an open hand on Ginny's cheek, pressing it softly. "Dear child, don't try to figure out love, just embrace it...embrace it while you still have the chance."

Ginny nodded. What did that mean? She knew better than to press. Grandma Ethel—Janey—wouldn't give her any more answers.

With a smile, Grandma Ethel rose. "And don't worry about dinner, dear. There's some leftover meat loaf that Dove made. Just enjoy your time with Brett. Enjoy it while you have it. And until he comes, you better finish that letter. Otherwise you'll be just too distracted if you don't."

Clay stayed a bit. We sat out on the porch, playing guitar together. I like it now, even though my fingers were raw at first. It's comforting and a joy to share with him.

After Clay said good night, I settled the little ones back into bed, then wrote you that note. I have my own room, but with all of us—especially Janey—still distressed by our near escape, I slept on the rug in the living room with them. It had to be past midnight, the sun finally down. By the time I closed my eyes, it was dark.

Sleep didn't come, though, and about an hour later, I heard a woman's cries coming from the yard. Within moments, the door banged open, and Joseph ran inside the house, carrying Tinle. Her face contorted in pain, her body shivered, and she was bent double. Her long hair hung in soggy strands beneath Joseph's fingers.

I jumped to my feet and raced to them. "What happened, Joseph? What happened?"

"She's hurt. Help her." Joseph's gaze stayed trained on Tinle.

"Into my room." Somehow the children remained asleep as I quickly guided him. He laid her on the bed, and I covered her with blankets. "She's freezing. Go get some more blankets. Throw more wood in the stove. I'll tend to Tinle."

Those childish eyes of his, so full of rage of late, brimmed with a whirlpool of emotions I couldn't fathom. He gripped my hand. "Please help her."

"Get some blankets."

He raced out of the room, and I focused on Tinle, in so much pain. I didn't know what had happened, but she was obviously suffering from hypothermia. I've heard it feels like hands suffocating the air out of you. We had to get her warm.

I smoothed her hair, trying to calm her. After I removed the blankets, I changed her out of her wet clothes.

And saw bloodstains. Growing larger.

She saw that I saw. Her eyebrows gathered in the middle, her eyes tilted upward. Then she gripped my arm and cried out in Tlingit. I understood a little now. The word she said meant "baby."

How I prayed in that moment!

"Please, help!" Her hot tears lined her frigid cheeks, dripped down her neck. So young, she had to be no older than seventeen. She couldn't look at me, just grabbed her stomach and moaned. I got her out of her wet, bloodstained clothes and into a warm nightshirt, then covered her head with my wool hat.

Her moaning slowed down. Her breathing too.

"What happened, Tinle?"

Joseph came in, loaded with blankets. Tinle's eyes pierced mine. She shook her head sharply. "He go out!"

I grasped her icy cold hand. "I need to know what happened. Then I'll send him out."

He carefully layered each blanket over her.

"It'll be fine. You're going to be fine. I love you."

"Go out!" Tinle faced the wall, didn't look at him.

His eyes betrayed his hurt, but with trembling hands, Joseph rubbed her arm. "We were down by the brook, filling water buckets, when that bear... He charged down the stream like he was after something. The sound was so loud it startled both of us, but Tinle slipped on a log and fell in."

"The bear?" I asked, a dread building in my chest. "The big black one?" The one I should've killed only a couple hours earlier?

"It had to be the same one." He covered his mouth. "It splashed away from us after whatever it was chasing. Then I spotted Tinle holding on to a downed log in the river. Somehow I was able to get her out." He gazed into Tinle's eyes. "It's a miracle I was able to keep hold of her. Everything was a miracle."

I grabbed Joseph in a tight, quick hug. "You did so good, Joseph. I am so proud of you for saving her life." I felt his sob.

Jerking into a tight ball over her stomach, Tinle let out another gasp. "He go out!"

Ignoring Joseph's terrified look, I asked, "How long was she in the water?"

"Just a few moments. Everything happened really fast."

"Thank the Lord."

Joseph reached for her hand, but she ripped it away. "Go! Joseph!"

He shifted to me, searching my face for a clue. I wanted to tell him the truth, that she was pregnant, about to give birth, and the baby probably wouldn't live, but she obviously didn't want me to. I didn't know what to do, Grandfather.

"Go, Joseph," I said with as much compassion as I could. "Get changed. I'll let you know how she's doing in a little bit."

Clay, who'd come in as Joseph left, knelt next to me. "What can I do?"

Before I could answer, he noticed her holding her belly, the blood on the blankets. A breath escaped his lips. "She's not—?"

I touched Clay's hand. "Yes, she's with child, but it's early. I don't think—"

I'll never forget the pain in Clay's face.

More later.

Ellie Bell

Chapter Thirty-Three

....

Brett couldn't wipe the silly grin off his face, and Ginny had a hard time focusing on the meal. The meat loaf was good, but it tasted different from what Ginny was used to. She didn't ask what kind of meat was in it. Didn't want to know.

She was still trying to wrap her mind around the fact that Grandma Ethel was Janey. What had Ethel thought when Ellie had shown up? A stranger! How had she handled losing her mother? Did she remember her mother—Adelaide? Had she ever wished to live anywhere other than Glacier Bay?

The phone rang, and Grandma Ethel ignored it. She turned to Brett. "It's your mother, I'm certain. She's calling me back. We're planning a family reunion for next summer. Your great-uncle Elias and great-aunt Rose are coming all the way from San Francisco."

"Wait." Ginny ran down the names of Ethel's siblings. "Are those on your side?"

"They're my...." Grandma Ethel started, and then pinched her lips together and shook her head. She shook her finger Ginny's direction. "Silly girl, you're trying to get me to spill the beans, aren't you?"

Ginny was about to protest when the phone rang again. Grandma Ethel rose and wobbled toward it. "If your mother is anything, Brett, she's persistent." Grandma Ethel clicked her tongue.

"Now Judy, we're still—" Grandma Ethel answered. Then she paused, and her eyes widened. "Oh, excuse me." Grandma Ethel nodded. Then she turned and held out the phone to Ginny. "It's for you."

Ginny's fork slipped from her fingers, clattering onto her plate. The meat loaf she'd just eaten turned to cement in her stomach. She hurried to the phone, knowing who it was, knowing the last thing she wanted to do was talk to Danny in front of Brett.

"Hello?"

"Ginny, thank God you're alive." Danny's voice was so clear, goose bumps rose on her arms.

"Yeah, of course I am. I'm so sorry I didn't call—"

"Was that the old woman?" Danny interrupted.

"Excuse me?"

"The old woman you were helping to care for. It sounds like she's doing better."

"Um, yeah, she—"

"Then you can come home now, right? I can call the airline, set something up for you. I'm so sorry about this, babe, getting stuck up there like that, and all those old-people smells. I'd be sick, just sick to have to do it."

Ginny pressed the phone tighter to her ear. "Listen, can I call you later?" She walked toward the living room, pulling the cord taut.

"It's about your mother, isn't it? The reason you ran off to Alaska? Ginny, sweetheart, I paid off the photographer who had those photos."

"What photos…you mean the one at the lodge?" She thought about the photo she'd taken with those two women. She probably had looked a mess. Had he mistaken one of them for her mother? He didn't know much about her, did he?

"Lodge? No, when we were out." His usually loud tone softened. "Your back…when I put the necklace on you. Seriously, I had no idea about the scars. Thankfully the photographer came to me. He erased them right there in front of me—swore he didn't back them up."

Ginny covered her mouth with her hand. Her stomach lurched. "What do you know about my mother?" The words escaped through her fingers.

"Enough to hurt for you, babe. How someone could do that to another human being is beyond me. Your own mother. I'll look into it, see what I can find out—"

"No!" The word shot from her lips. "Don't look for her. I don't want to find her. Not now. Not ever."

How someone could do that... The words echoed through her mind. *Your own mother.*

"Are you sure? I thought it might help." Danny's voice softened. It seemed almost tender, and she felt bad for getting him in the middle of all of this.

"Listen, I really need to call you back later. But don't worry. I plan on coming home soon." That would get him off the phone.

"Good news, finally. I was about to come up and bring you home myself."

"No need." Ginny shook her head. She thought of Brett leaving—in a little over two weeks now. "I'll be back. And we can figure out what next steps I need to take then."

* * * * *

Brett was quiet for the rest of dinner. After dinner Grandma Ethel went straight to bed, even though it was only seven o'clock.

They sat on the couch, facing each other. Ginny knew what was coming.

"Ginny, we need to talk."

"About what?" she had to ask, even though she knew the answer.

"A few things, actually. They are things we should have talked about before I asked you to marry me all those years ago."

"Oh. Okay." Her brow furrowed. She thought for sure he'd want to talk about Danny.

"I want you to take my words and really pay attention to them, even if they make you mad."

She pulled up her bare feet and tucked them underneath her. "This doesn't sound good."

"Ginny, you're an amazing person. You're tender, gentle. Your eyes are open to those in need. I think that's what drew you to Africa in the first place."

Her heart dropped at the mention of Africa.

"I mean, you didn't need to stay around and care for my grandma as you did. I'm thankful you were there. And even Ellie's letters. I can see concern in your gaze as you read them."

Ginny forced a chuckle, trying to ignore the needle that pierced her heart again and again. "Yeah, I suppose I forget that she wrote those letters long ago. In a way it just seems like she's a dear friend I haven't heard from in a while…"

"But I also know that it's easier for you to turn your attention to others than to allow yourself to mourn what you've lost."

"I don't understand."

"Your mother. A happy childhood."

"I'm not concerned about her." Anger tinged her voice. "My biggest loss was the Piersons. They knew me. They loved me, unlike that woman who gave me life." She spit out the last words like nails.

Brett didn't say anything. He just scooted closer and waited.

The silence was heavy. She took his hand and patted it as if urging him to go on. He didn't.

She looked away, to the sky over the bay that glowed pink from the sunset. "Beautiful…" She was going to talk about the sunset, but doing so would prove his point.

He continued to look at her, studying her face as if he were an art critic and she was a canvas.

When she couldn't handle the silence any longer, she opened her mouth and the pent-up words exploded from her like a seething soda bottle.

"I don't understand it. Aren't mothers suppose to love their children? Protect their children? I'm not sure why she hated me so. I was just a baby. For her to do what she did." Ginny held her face in her hands. "Mothers are supposed to read stories to their kids, snuggle with them, tickle…" Her throat felt hot and thick, but no tears came. She'd cried about it for as long as she could remember. She'd longed for a mother's gentle touch—her mother's touch. She tossed her head from side to side, her long curls brushing her lap as she did. "You have no idea how she hurt me."

"You can tell me. I can share your pain." Brett cleared his throat, and when she looked over at him, tears rimmed his eyes. It was then that her vision blurred. A tear threatened to break through. She quickly wiped it away.

"I don't know how to put it into words. It's too hard."

He nodded. "Gentle whispers turn to rage. My heart cracks, spills on the stage."

Ginny's eyes widened. Her lips opened.

"Sad eyes, sad smile, lifted up to see. Why can't I see?"

She nodded. They were words to another one of her songs. "So you've been keeping track of me? Figuring out all the meanings behind the messages? Is that what you're trying to say, Brett?"

"No, what I'm trying to say is, you have been saying it all along, just in a different way. Most people might think it's just a song, but Ginny, I know it's more. It's what's on your heart."

"Do you really want to know everything?"

Brett nodded and squeezed her hand tighter.

Fine. I'll show him. Let him really know what he's getting himself into.

Ginny looked down at her light sweatshirt and slowly unzipped it, revealing the tank top underneath. Taking a deep breath, she placed the sweatshirt on the couch next to her and then turned her back to Brett. With trembling fingers she lifted up her hair.

A gasp escaped his lips. Then she felt his fingertips gently touching the spots. "Are those…"

"Cigarette burns. Or at least that's what the doctor told me." The trembling moved from her fingertips up her arms. Soon her shoulders trembled too.

His fingers touched each one. Fourteen spots. She'd counted them in her reflection more times than she knew, holding up a small hand mirror, pushing back her hair.

He scooted closer and leaned forward. "I can't believe I didn't know." His breath was warm on the back of her ear. "I mean, I guessed things had to be bad for you to be in foster care, but I never guessed this."

He wrapped an arm around her shoulder and neck, pulling her closer.

"You're beautiful, you know."

She nodded, knowing he meant it. Brett didn't lie. A sad smile emerged through the tears. Then Brett rose. He stood behind her.

Brett tapped her shoulder. He wanted her to rise, to turn. She slid her sweatshirt back on, stood, and turned to him, yet she couldn't look into his face. She couldn't let him see her tears. Not yet.

Instead, she stepped forward until their toes were only inches apart. He lifted his hand and wrapped it around the back of her head. She leaned forward until her forehead touched his chest.

"Oh, Ginny." Brett kissed the top of her head again and again and again. "I'm so sorry, Ginny. I want to have all the answers, but there is so much I don't understand. I want to make things easy, when they are anything but."

"I want to forgive my mother, but I don't know how."

"I agree, sweetheart. We need to forgive others as we've been forgiven. I think God will show you how to do that in His own way."

They stood there awhile longer. Ginny pressed her eyes tight. *Lord, help me. Show me how to let go so I can step forward to what You have for me.* Was it a future with Brett? Maybe.

She couldn't imagine stepping into the future with her past casting a dark shadow over every step. She needed to heal. She needed to turn to God for that healing. To become the woman Brett once knew. The one he deserved.

Ginny also couldn't wrap her heart around Africa. She couldn't go there, but Brett needed to. She needed Brett to follow God's call.

If the people of Gustavus needed someone like Brett, then Africa—and all the orphaned children like her, like Joseph—needed him more.

Chapter Thirty-Four

....

August 18, 1929

Dear Brother Peter,

Two weeks have passed since the events I intend to share with you. I don't care to admit how distressed I was then, but the height of the turmoil is over (though unrest lingers), so now I feel ready to tell you. You need to know.

I believe Ellie wrote you about the night Tinle fell in the river, how my boy Joseph saved her life, and that she was with child. That night, after I realized this fact, a dark trepidation fell over me. For my son to do that… It was "like another fall of man" (to quote old Shakespeare). Betrayed is how I felt. I trusted Joseph, gave him time, grace, again and again, and he stomped on me. The disrespect he showed to me, his mother, Tinle, and especially the Lord… Where was my kind, happy boy who wanted to be just like me? All I could see was the child. Memories, tainted with this grief, rolled over me.

I remember one night, when he was about seven, we sat by the campfire. It was just him and me. I took a bite of the roast salmon we'd caught together and spit out a bone. He did the same—spewed that bone out farther than mine. I watched to see if he'd keep on mimicking me. Sure enough. I slapped a mosquito on my neck. He did too. I sighed after a long swig from the canteen. He let out an even grander sigh. I started

humming "The Girl I Left Behind Me," and he hummed right
along as if he knew it.

That boy, my boy—gone—replaced by a rebellious
turncoat who thought nothing of breaking his father's heart.

All this rushed through my mind in seconds. My disquiet
must've shown, for Ellie, though occupied with helping Tinle,
took my hand with her warm, soft palm.

I didn't let her speak but stood up and left the room. This
burden must be borne by me alone.

I wish I'd stopped to pray, to think, but I went directly
after my boy. He was heating stones in the oven to put under
Tinle's blankets for warmth, though he was practically frozen
himself. The look of him sent a fierce anger through me.

"Joseph. Get up. Walk outside with me." My throat
clenched as I spoke. I doubt he'd ever heard that tone from me
before. He looked scared. As well he should.

We stood on the porch. So dark outside, the clouds blocked
the moon. I told him he had to marry that girl.

The lines in his forehead relaxed. "I want to, Papa. She's
going to be okay?"

"I think they are."

He stared at me, confused. "They?"

"You know that girl's with child." The words felt like gravel
choking my airway. I wanted to grasp his arms, shake him, but
I held back my rage. Thank God.

"That's ridiculous." He almost laughed. "She's not with child."

"Yes, son. She is."

He stared at me until he knew I was serious. Then his lips
tightened, and in a rush, his hands covered his face.

"She can't be."

"Well, she is."

He was crying now. "No, Papa. I never touched her. I swear."

"You lying to me?"

He flinched. "I swear, Papa! I swear I never touched her."
He collapsed to the porch swing behind him. Held his head in
his hands.

I sat next to him. The wind tossed the dire clouds aside,
revealing a slice of moon, and I remembered what Reverend
Martin had said. "Lay down your life for him." Finally, I
stopped to pray. Is he truthful, Lord?

I placed my hand on his quivering back and thought
about it.

A wind whistled though the cedars, swept against my face.
I believed my son.

I pulled him to me, and he collapsed in sobs.

Before we could breathe, take this all in, Ellie faltered out.
"The baby...it died," she said.

We stood still, motionless, gaping at each other. Numb,
I suppose.

Ellie graciously tended Tinle as best she could. After a few
days, Mrs. Curtis took her on home. Joseph made the mansion his
hiding place. Didn't even say good-bye to the girl who'd formerly
possessed his heart. Not a word. He told me he'd had a notion
to ask her to marry him. They'd planned a future together. But
apparently, she'd taken a shine to the Curtis boy too.

My son is broken—angry and buried in a sea of pain. For
a brief moment that night, I thought he'd finally accept Ellie,
but then this darkness over Tinle made his thinking run afoul.
He resents Ellie more than ever, but it's hard to get at why. He
says she betrayed me with that James, and if there's one thing

Joseph can't abide at this current occasion, it's betrayal. He also thinks I'm betraying Adelaide. And most, he's just plain jealous. Now he's back home, he wants me to himself—only intends to share me with "insiders." According to him, Ellie's not one.

Make no mistake, his reasons are rubbish. But what does it matter? They are real to him, and his pain is mighty real. What I'm afraid of are the permanent scars. Scars he'll carry a lifetime, keep him from joy, love, peace. I can't let my son sink. I won't.

He's right on one account. He needs me. No one else will do. No one else is his father. I mean to help my boy. If I spend sunup to sundown—or as much time as is possible— praying for him, listening, talking when he wants, waiting for opportunity, he will come around. He has to.

In light of my son's near desperation, one truth came home. All the months I've doubted whether I should marry, I've asked a million times, "Do I have a right to happiness when my boy's hurting?" Of course I don't. Don't know why I thought I did.

But God sent Ellie, despite my faults. Is He asking me to let her go for the sake of my son? The thought occurred to me. But no. He's not that kind of Father. I made a commitment to Ellie, and I intend to keep it.

I thank God for her. I don't know why He brought her here, to bind my heart with hers, but she's made me a better man. Let me open my heart again. Never thought I would. To revisit the love of a man and a woman—with beautiful Ellie.

And together we'll love my son back to us, if the Lord wills.

Clay

Dear Grandfather,

I tell you this because I dare not tell Clay. Joseph's treatment of me has worsened. He scowls at me and often belittles me. This morning he raised his hand to me. I was picking blackberries to put in our pancakes. I used an adorable bucket, carved from one piece of wood with berries painted on it as if by a child. As I walked back toward the cabin, Joseph stepped from the outhouse. He yelled at me to put down the bucket. I stared at him, confused.

His face turned so red, his jaw clenched. He said he had made that bucket for his mother. I imagined them together, picking berries. He probably imagined it too, because something about seeing me with that bucket sparked a rage in him. He told me again to put it down. I did, and stepped toward him.

"I'm sorry," I said. "I won't use it again. I don't want to replace Adelaide—"

That's when he raised his hand as if to strike me. "Don't say her name."

I winced, and he lowered his arm. Then I watched him storm off into the woods.

I felt all the more compassion for him, although I am bruised inwardly from his unkindness. I don't know if he'll ever accept me. And if he doesn't, how can I be part of this family?

For now, I'm going to persevere and pray. I know the Lord will guide me. Please pray for Clay. He's dreadfully worried about his son. He always shows great kindness to me, but I'm feeling him withdraw. I wish he would talk to me about this, but he only talks to God. He's been writing in his journal again.

Your Ellie Bell

Clay's Journal

My boy's behavior of late must stop. I want to serve him, love him, but he's not treating Ellie right. Lord, I may have to let him go in hopes he'll come back some day. To protect Ellie.

August 25, 1929

Dear Grandfather,

In my last letter, I only had time to share the incident with Joseph. Let me get you up to date. Much has happened.

The week I cared for Tinle after her accident was a mournful yet healing time—at least for Tinle. As I cared for her wounds, the Lord provided opportunities to share precious words of healing from the Scriptures. I even prayed with her. She's so sorry for the hurt she caused Joseph. She loved him—at least she thought she did—but she cared about the Curtis boy too. And she was tempted. I learned a lot about her during those days. Her father died when she was a baby. When she was five, her mother abandoned her. The Curtises took her in, raised her, but they didn't pay much attention to her (according to Tinle), so she virtually raised herself. The first time she ever heard of the Bible was when she came to the Sunday morning service at our place.

Two days ago, a week after Tinle left, I talked Clay into taking us for a picnic. Oh, Grandfather, it was a glorious day. Janey, Linc, and I packed the food, and then we filed into Clay's wooden fishing boat and traveled down the glassy Salmon River. The water was so clear I could see the salmon schooling beneath us.

After docking, we hiked to a perfect spot among the flats.

Clay and the little ones went ahead, but Joseph hung back, waiting. A nervous lump plunged into my stomach, but I offered a smile. His eyes narrowed, lips turned down, arms folded. "I wish you'd leave," he said. "You don't fit here."

Winter came early to my heart. "What?" I held up a hand. "Why?"

I saw the hate in his eyes, and I knew my concern from the morning he almost struck me was valid. A wind blew through, loosening a fir cone from the cedar. It dropped hard onto a stone, never to release its seeds, never to take root. Like me, of course.

In that moment, I knew. Joseph would never heal until I left. Clay would never marry me until his son accepted me. I should've seen it. All this time, I'd been hoping to win Joseph over, to be good enough that Clay wouldn't send me home. It was all useless. He'd already decided but was afraid to tell me.

I shouldn't have been surprised. I didn't deserve a wonderful life with Clay and the family. James's mother was right. I wasn't good enough, not for James or Clay or anyone.

As the falls crashed down, a sense of dread overcame me. I tried to banish it, or at least disguise it, until I could talk to Clay.

Descending the falls, we set up our luncheon in a field of swaying grass. The children played, pretending the blanket was a battleship and they were fighting pirates over the tall grass. I would've giggled, enjoyed them, if I hadn't known I would have to say good-bye soon.

After I cleaned up the picnic, I asked Clay if we could talk. He nodded. His brow was as taut as mine felt. Fear chased the edges of my heart as he stood. He held my hand and warm strength rippled through me. A strength I didn't want to lose. We strode in silence until we could not be overheard by the children. Fear ventured deeper.

"I'm grateful you suggested a walk," he said. "I needed to talk…." His voice faltered, the rims of his eyes moistened.

For an instant I imagined him dropping to his knees, producing a ring. But no.

"I love you, Ellie." His brow, so tightly wound of late, relaxed, as it had when he first mouthed those cherished words. He touched my cheek with the pads of his fingers, and I leaned into his touch. "Beautiful," he whispered.

I fell into his arms, my face against his broad chest, listening to his heartbeat. He kissed my head, lost his hands in my hair. I felt his heart race, his arms not wanting to let go.

"I'm sorry, Ellie."

I knew. I knew this was coming, but the pain stabbed my heart nonetheless.

"I love you," he said again, lifting my face, thumbing away my tears. "But my son…"

"I know. I know. You want me to leave. I understand. It's for Joseph."

He grasped my hands and shook his head. "No. I wasn't going to say that. It's Joseph who must go. I know you wanted to help him, but it's no use. He's a man now. He doesn't have to accept you, but I won't have him hurting you."

"You know about that? When he almost struck me?"

Clay's expression told me he hadn't known, Grandfather, and this made him all the more determined to send Joseph away. Clay had found a spot at the college in Juneau for him. He'd be leaving next week.

I admit a load lifted from my shoulders. I could create a home for us. We'd get married...

But I shook my head. "No, Clay. You can't send him away. Not when he's hurting like this."

"My door will always be open to the boy, when he's ready to come home, but you two can't coexist. It's not working."

A sob burned my throat. The words fought to stay back, but finally I won. "I'm going. I already decided."

"I won't let you."

"I don't have to leave. I know. But I'm going to...for Joseph. And you."

He tried to convince me to stay, but Grandfather, I knew in my heart it was the only way. We stood quietly, awkwardly for a moment. He finally conceded.

"When he comes around, perhaps we can..."

But I couldn't cling to an unknown hope. "No, Clay. Let's just say good-bye and leave it at that. Only God knows the future."

Tears didn't fall then, neither mine nor his.

We decided to tell the children the next day, after church. I would leave the following week, seven more days, and it would all be over.

But then the next morning, James came.

I'm exhausted, Grandfather, and the light is fading as sunset descends. I will finish telling more later.

All my love,

Ellie

Chapter Thirty-Five
....

The day of the program, Brett and Ginny spent the afternoon at the school gym helping Lee, Linda, and the other members of the Gustavus Historical Society.

She smiled as she organized the stage, set up chairs, and heard more about the earliest pioneers in Glacier Bay. Did Brett realize her smile wasn't real? What she hadn't told him yet was that her suitcase was already packed and in the back of the van. And she had just one final errand before she left—to pick up the refund Grandma Ethel had secured for her from Glacier Bay Lodge since she never did stay there.

Her ticket was booked, and the last few of Ellie's letters were tucked away in her purse. Grandma Ethel had made sure of that.

"I won't tell Brett of your going—I'll leave that to you, dear. I insist that you take the letters, finish the story."

Ginny had nodded and packed them, yet ever since Ellie had chosen to leave Strawberry Point, the letters had lost some of their glamour. There was a time for leaving for everyone, she supposed. And maybe that was the point. Maybe the mystery and wonder of Glacier Bay wasn't just for those who lived here year-round, but for those who changed in the coming...and who returned home a bit different than before.

And she had changed. She'd already sent Danny a string of text messages this morning, telling him she didn't want to sign that contract. She wanted to do things at a slower pace. She needed time to seek God and let Him—not a music studio—direct her paths. She hadn't heard back but figured it would give them a good starting place for their future working relationship.

That was something else she'd decided too. Danny wasn't for her. Brett was, even if she couldn't have him. What type of woman would she be to keep him from the mission field? She'd leave, and give him space to pursue God's call in Africa. And over the miles they could discuss whether God's plan included them being together at some time, some place.

It neared six o'clock, and she finished her slice of Thai pizza that Linda had ordered for the crew and then made her way out to the audience to watch the performance. She was thankful she hadn't agreed to sing. She didn't want this night to be about her and her fame. She wanted it to be about the stories they wanted to share. A retelling of the colorful residents of Strawberry Point. And then—after the curtain call—they'd take up a collection for Brett's journey to Africa.

She'd also slipped Linda a check to add to the funds for Brett. Ginny wished she had more to give and thought about the money wasted on shoes in her closet back home. That would change too.

The school gym was packed with folks seated in folding chairs, eager to see the show. A black curtain circled the room, hiding the gym walls. Only the basketball hoops overhead hinted of the building's true purpose.

Spotlights focused on a small stage. A small set had been made of a section of log cabin with an oar, a pick, and a washbasin hanging on the side of the wall. In the corner a pianist played old-fashioned music, getting everyone into the mood. A few video cameras were set up, and the crowd fidgeted in their seats with excitement.

Ginny found a seat near the back and felt strangely excited over this simple production. The performance mattered. People hadn't just come to be entertained. They'd come to hear *their* story. To hear about those who'd come before them and made their life here possible.

Just a few minutes after six o'clock, Lee strode onto the stage. "Good evening, everyone. Thank you for joining us tonight for *The Chronicles of Strawberry Point*. I want to tell you that the volunteers who have put this together are extremely appreciative of your coming, particularly on such a wonderful, sunny evening as tonight. I know it's a great sacrifice for you to be here. We have an exciting story to tell, and we're thankful that you're here. Without further ado, *The Chronicles of Strawberry Point*."

Two women, dressed in clothes popular seventy years ago, strode onto the stage. One woman cleared her throat and began.

"Where are the men and women, the children once young and then old, who lived in this place? Native families who came here each year to smoke fish up the Salmon River? Homesteaders and their families who arrived to begin a new life? Who smelled the fragrance of mud in low tide? Heard the call of the sandhill cranes? Tasted strawberries on the beach and felt—as we do—the power of the wind? The stories we tell you here come from women and men long gone. In their own words and word of mouth."

The two women's voices joined in unison. "The stories are here, although their bodies are gone."

"Some of their houses still stand," the other woman continued. "The home of May White and her children, now the Gustavus Inn. Glen and Nell's. Ruth and Fred Matson's house, still lovingly cared for by Amy Youmans. Reverend Parrish's cabin, soon to be a museum of our own."

Ginny smiled, feeling part of the story in a small way after reading Ellie's letters.

The women continued. Sharing about the music, the musicians, the roses planted by some of the first inhabitants that still bloomed, the drainage ditches still being used. The names were not forgotten. Their deeds were not forgotten either. Ginny's mind took her to the Hollywood

Walk of Fame. She'd walked the sidewalks of stars before, amazed by how few names she knew. Great performers whose names meant nothing anymore. Yet here…each memory was treasured, cherished.

"The stories are alive, the triumphs and trials," the women said together. "Accomplishment and failures, grief and laughter and fear. How they made do. The stories are here."

Then, dressed as their ancestors, folks from the community emerged from behind the curtain and paraded in front of the stage. Names were spoken—first names for the most part, since last names weren't needed.

Two rows up, Ginny spotted Gina with her family. A few seats down was Jared the EMT, with his wife and children. She recognized Mitch, Lori the librarian, and Lee and Linda, of course.

Ginny bit her lip. Her heart longed to be a part of this community, but if that happened, she'd have to give her whole self, her whole heart.

Standing on a stage in front of thousands or on a television performance in front of millions seemed less frightening. To be known in such a way—really known—seemed like giving a part of her protected heart away, not to one but to many.

The stories came next—of the three newlywed couples who'd first arrived to homestead. Ginny laughed as they shared about the first time the women homesteaders made bread. Thinking the dough didn't rise, the women dumped it out under the trees. It was only after they noticed a snowy pile of white under the trees that they realized the yeast had risen. They'd baked bread from the dough—after they'd picked out the pine needles and dirt.

Ginny learned about the Native American fishing camp up the river, and as they shared the stories she tried to imagine the gardening, the building, and the dancing to a gramophone.

Community had meant everything then, just as it did now. Ginny glanced around again, tears blurring her eyes this time. Kelly sat near the front, Jace on her lap. The reflection of the spotlight brightened his wide-eyed expression. Dove Fowler sat next to them. Bud stood in the back. He glanced as Ginny looked over and then waved. In a strange way she was going to miss that old van.

The actors continued, talking about Abraham Lincoln Parker, his wife, Edith, and their children and grandchildren. She heard about the ways the Parkers impacted the community, and then she heard the story she'd been waiting for.

"The end of the Roaring Twenties brought a gentle lamb to our community in Reverend Clay Parrish. With his wife, Adelaide, he shepherded the folks of Strawberry Point and the surrounding villages. Reverend Parrish lost his wife, but he didn't lose his heart. He continued to serve for many years to come."

As she listened, she was sad that Ellie's name wasn't spoken like the others. Ellie left and didn't become part of the community, yet God did a work in her—changed her, and changed those she knew for a time.

Ellie's letters also changed Ginny, reminded her what a relationship with God was all about. As she looked around, Ginny, too, felt a part of this place, and that was what hurt the worst perhaps. To get a glimpse of what could be, and know it would never happen.

Don't torture yourself, just leave. Drive out to the lodge, pick up your refund, and then go to the airport. It's no use longing for what'll never be.

Ginny rose, swung her purse over her shoulder, and headed out. She wanted to say good-bye to Brett, but she decided to call him tonight from Juneau instead. This was his night. His community was here to raise funds for his move to Africa. The last thing she wanted was to distract him from that.

A few people eyed her as she headed toward the back door, and Ginny pulled her cell phone from her purse and pretended to answer a call. She didn't want anyone to follow, to check on her, to try to help—which was exactly what the folks of Glacier Bay would do.

She hurried down the gravel road alongside the school, and the trees lining the road blurred. The wind picked up and she glanced up at the sky. The sun still shone, but a few clouds gathered in the distance.

She climbed into Bud's van and chuckled to herself as the seat tilted in. The window was cracked a few inches, letting in the breeze. She didn't bother to roll it up. She needed fresh air. Space to think.

She'd gotten down the road just a little when she saw the blue sign that read TRAIL. She had wanted to see the old plane wreck, but in just a few hours she'd be leaving for good. Now was her only chance.

She pulled the van over sharply, grabbed her purse and sweatshirt from the passenger's seat, and climbed out. The wind was still blowing, but it looked as if the forming clouds would hold back the rain, at least for a while. What had Linda said? It was only a quarter mile to the airplane. She could make it there and back in twenty minutes, before the clouds let loose.

Her tennis shoes sank down slightly as she moved toward the trail. The ground was spongy and green—a soft, bright green that covered everything she saw. Tiny ferns coated the ground, logs, and the base of the trees. It was as if a carpet of life had been laid over everything.

Only a tiny, muddy line marked the trail, and even as Ginny walked along, uncertainty joined her as a traveling companion. She'd heard about bears in the area, but surely not in this area...right? She thought about Janey's—Ethel's—fright.

More questions joined in. Was this the right direction? Shouldn't she be at the wreckage by now? What if it wasn't bears that she should be afraid of but people?

She continued on, questioning whether she was on the wrong trail, when suddenly a chunk of metal appeared on the forest floor. Hair rose on her arms and she slowed her pace. *Lives were lost in this crash.* More pieces of twisted metal came into view as she continued on. No moss grew on them. These scars refused to be hidden.

Ginny looked at the airplane pieces scattered over the forest floor. For so many years her life had seemed scattered like that. Her life had crashed before she could remember, and during the years that had followed, she lived among the wreckage. Yet maybe she wasn't the only one who'd had a hard life.

She'd never known people like she discovered here. Some grew up with outhouses, eating wild game for dinner, washing their clothes by hand. They were fiercely independent but just as fiercely loyal.

Maybe she should just tell Brett the truth—that she didn't want to go back to LA. Or at least not permanently. She wanted to settle down here. Wouldn't it be possible to sing, play, and then escape back to Glacier Bay for a while?

She could hear Danny now. "You're never going to be a great star unless you sacrifice everything to your career." Of course he would say it in a nicer way. But if she had to sacrifice for anything or anyone, it would be for God. Her soul told her that now was the time. This was the place.

After five more minutes of walking, the cabin of the plane came into view. It was larger than she thought. The nose was gone, and pieces of the tail and wings spread out in all directions. Names and quotes were spray-painted on its shell, and inside it looked as if at one time a campfire had been made there. She pictured teens sneaking out here to party. It was something she no doubt would have done—well, at least before she'd been part of Dale and Robyn's family. Being with them had given her a new idea of fun.

Her heart ached for the families of the men lost. And for her loss too. It was amazing how one event could change everything.

As she stood there, eyeing the wreckage, a sound broke the quiet of the forest. A lumbering of sorts, a movement from just beyond the trees where she stood. An image popped into her mind of a bear. She thought of Ethel as a child in the outhouse, and her heart leaped to her throat. Her eyes darted around her, and even though she didn't see anything, the noise grew.

Without hesitation, Ginny scurried into the hull of the wreckage. The metal was cold, and her jacket caught on shards of twisted frame. As she scurried on her hands and knees into the cold darkness, her knees crawled through pools of stagnant water from recent rain.

What was I doing coming out here alone?

"O God, please help me...." she whispered, sitting with her back against the metal and her legs curled up in front of her.

The noise sounded again, closer. Ginny was too afraid to look out. She balled her fist, closed her eyes, and held her breath, hoping whatever was out there didn't pick up her scent.

Ginny's insides twisted in fear. What was she doing, leaving like that? She should have just stayed and enjoyed the show even if it did break her heart that she was falling in love with these people and their community. Even though she didn't know whether she could be part of them.

After a few minutes the noises stopped, but Ginny was afraid to move. Afraid she'd come across a bear on the trail. Being this far north, the sun was still out. She had time to make it back to the van before it got dark, but she told herself to wait awhile—give the bear time to pass.

Ginny reached her hand inside her purse to pull out the small flashlight and get a better look at the inside of the cabin. As she did her hand brushed against the envelopes she'd placed there. *Ellie's letters.*

She pulled one out, eager to read it and pass the time until she felt safe enough to walk back to the van. Eager to get her mind off whatever creature roamed.

Chapter Thirty-Six

....

August 27, 1929

Dear Grandfather Barnett,

What happened? Miss Ellie just left! It's early. We haven't even had breakfast yet. Papa and Joseph are out fishing. A man came to the door, all skinny and clean, except for his shoes. They was all covered with mud. I tried not to giggle, but seeing his fancy shoes a mess made me happy. I didn't like the looks of that man.

Miss Ellie talked to him on the porch, then came in crying. Said she had to leave right now! And she just left, didn't even take anything with her. I thought she was going to come back, but now Papa says no, she's not coming back, but he's sure she'll write a letter to explain. It's been a week now. No letter. Why do letters take so long?

One more thing that will make you burn with anger like it did me. When they left, that man put his hand on Miss Ellie's back. I hate that man.

I wish you'd write. The mail boat is running, but we haven't got any mail yet.

I don't want to tell you how sad I am that Miss Ellie's gone. Linc says I'm too old to cry at night, but I'm not the only one. Even Papa seems real sad. Of course he doesn't cry, though. Men don't, I've heard.

Please get this all fixed for us. I want Papa to be happy

and marry Miss Ellie. I know you'd tell me to pray, so I'm praying real hard. I love you.

> *Janey*

August 28, 1929

Dear Clay,

I'm on an airplane! My hands are practically frozen solid as I try to write. James sits next to me, in his new flight jacket. He brought me a luscious black Lorna Dunn fur coat, but the opulence of it nearly turned my stomach. I much preferred my old Alaska coat that Edith brought over after I first arrived, so that's what I'm wearing.

You're probably wondering how I ended up riding the air currents. Well, that morning, my last morning, I was cooking up breakfast when James came to the door. Of all the strange things I've seen in the "land of midnight sun," James, dressed in a derby hat, beige coat, and slick shoes alighting on my doorstep was the most peculiar of all.

I thought of that horrid letter he wrote. Was he here to woo me? Oh, Clay. It made me ill. But the look on his face told me that wasn't his purpose. Something was wrong. Grandfather caught an infection—pneumonia—and the doctors think he's in his last days. James came to take me back to him. I would not have left with him for any other reason. I threw on my hat and coat, left the children with Linc, and we raced toward the boat dock.

Apparently Lester was over at the Juneau dock with the gas mail boat when James arrived there. James paid him for a round-trip ride in his boat. Every second seemed to matter.

We took the steamer from Juneau to Seattle and now, here

I sit on an airplane from Seattle to San Francisco. I can't seem to stop the tears, even in this icy-cold airplane soaring above the misty clouds.

Other thoughts also weigh heavy on my mind. I'm wishing I could've said good-bye—kissed Penny's sweet-pea cheeks, fought one last swordfight with Zach, admonished Janey to take care of everyone and not to fret. I'm imagining Linc showing me his latest invention. Did he finish that basket pulley for Falls Creek?

And Joseph. If only he'd listen, I would've gladly apologized for interrupting his life, layering pain upon pain. How I wish I could've shared my own losses with him, promised it would get easier as it did for me.

Yesterday on the steamer, a man sat by the railing with his little girl. The way he smoothed her hair, smiled, and laughed with her—it echoed of you. This morning I awoke in the Seattle Hotel. As I situated my hat and pinned my hair, I could almost feel your soft touch tucking that stray strand behind my ear.

Good-bye to you all. I'm sorry it's not in person.

Most of all to you, my dear Clay. As the years pass and shadows fall, perhaps the details of my time with you will fade, but your kind heart, wisdom, strength, and love will linger, always etched in my heart.

Ellie

Dear Janey,

I'm so sorry I had to leave you like that. I don't want you to worry. I can imagine what you thought when I left with James. You probably saw the way he acted toward me, like a beau and not a friend. I don't love him, Janey. He came to take me to my grandfather, who is very sick. Even though I'm grateful for that, I have no intention of marrying him. Please don't let a drop of anxiety cloud your sweet mind.

I love you very much. I don't know when I can get back to see you, but we can always write and be hopeful that Lester will not neglect to deliver our letters.
Miss Ellie

James,

I received your latest letter requesting I accept your marriage proposal.

My answer, James, is still no, as I told you on the steamer and on the airplane and in the taxi. I will not ever marry you.

Please be honest with yourself. Your improved zeal for me surely springs from the restoration of my grandfather's fortune. As you once wrote to me in a letter, I fear you wish to marry me "for my money."

If you truly cared for me, you would be more gratified, as I am, about the recovery of Grandfather's good name and the conviction of my distant cousin, Felix Cooney.

I feel sorry for you, actually. I hope this will help you transform your ways.

Elizabeth McKinley

September 27, 1929

Dear Reverend Martin,

I rightly appreciate your offer to come. You speak right. Every parishioner's due a pastoral visit at times. I suppose you're as much my reverend as can be found up here, but please don't trouble yourself. I know you want to help with

Joseph, everybody seems to, but I'm the one who must care
for him. Not that I've done much good so far. In fact, the dark
hold seems to tighten its grip every day. It's not improved since
Ellie left a month ago, either. A terrible anger hangs close to
the surface, but mostly now he seems to lack any life at all.
Blank, like a wandering sheep.

The one bright spot in all this happened two nights ago.
And I can tell you it surprised me. The Matsons invited us
to a get-together—card playing, dancing, and singing, with
Charles Parker playing the guitar. They invite us with great
frequency—two or three times a week, I'd say. But with Joseph
being so downcast, I usually say no.

This time the little ones asked with such earnestness, I felt
a need to say yes. As we put on clean clothes and Linc prepared
a salmonberry cake as an offering, I noticed Joseph combing
his shaggy blond hair. Did my eyes fool me, or was that a mite-
sized flicker in his eyes?

When we arrived at their large farmhouse, sure enough,
Joseph hung back, leaning against the whitewashed wall beside
their grandfather clock (I can only imagine the boat ride getting
that hulking thing over here). For quite a spell, he silently
watched the group laughing and singing. But then Mrs. Parker
sidled up next to him. I don't know what she said, but by the
end of their conversation his shoulders weren't so crouched
over. Then she grabbed his arm and demanded he dance.

One doesn't say no to Mrs. Parker.

So as Charles played "She'll Be Coming 'round the
Mountain," accompanied by Linc on a rigged-up drum set and
Janey on her harmonica, Joseph danced. I wish I could say he
smiled. He didn't, but from time to time he stopped frowning,

and that's a gift I gladly receive. Afterward, Mrs. Parker
handed him her violin, and he played the rest of the evening—
until it was time to eat. He can scarce resist Lester's goose and
turnip stew, much less Linc's cake.

I don't know what it was that lifted him that night. I'd
hoped his temperament would continue to lighten after we got
home, but it hasn't. Got worse, really. Dark, irritable, gloomy.
And most of all, apathetic. He won't talk about Tinle and what
happened. I encouraged him to write in a journal, or letters,
something to work through it, but he won't.

I thought if I could just love him enough, he'd get better.
I know that doesn't give me call to give up, but I confess I'm
tired, discouraged, especially now Ellie's gone.

I covet your continued prayers.

One more thing before I close. I got a letter from Ellie.
I told you in my last note how she left quickly and we didn't
know why. Well, her grandfather, Brother Peter, he's real sick.
I know he's a friend of yours too. Pray for him. And Ellie. I'm
sure she's heartsick over it.

Anyway, I thought you'd want to know about Brother
Peter and Joseph. Thank you again for your kind offer.

Clay

Chapter Thirty-Seven

....

Brett ran into the dark woods, brushing aside the tree limbs as he went. He moved in the direction of the aircraft, not caring about the rain that splashed against his face or that his jacket was already soaked and clung to him. The rain had been just a fine mist when he'd climbed from his truck, but by the time he was one hundred yards into the forest, it was already falling in big drops.

"Ginny!" He called her name to let her know he was coming. He hoped she made it to the broken-off shell before the rain came hard. Hoped she hadn't lost the trail in the darkening night. Hoped...

He didn't want to think about bears. They were thick this time of year, foraging to fill their stomachs before winter.

He'd walked this trail a hundred times. It seemed longer with her lost at the end of it.

Barely noticing the broken pieces of wreckage, he focused on the path ahead. He had to get to her. He couldn't lose her again without confessing his love. Tell her he'd never stopped loving.

As he neared the wreckage he saw her tennis-shoed footprints, and those of a big dog, but when he looked into the wreckage, she wasn't inside.

"Ginny!" he called.

"In here."

He heard the small squeak of her voice, and as Brett looked in, he saw a faint flashlight glow. Ginny sat—tucked way in the back—

wet and shivering, with a dimming flashlight and one of Ellie's letters in her hand.

He blew out a breath of relief.

"Did he go after her?" Her voice quivered as she spoke.

"What?" Brett climbed in.

"Did Clay go to California for Ellie?" Her voice spoke with urgency as if it was the most important thing.

Ginny's hair was limp and hanging around her face. Her eyes were red, as if she'd been crying. She was wet and muddy, and his heart doubled in his chest with care for her.

"I—I, uh, honestly can't remember, Ginny. I can tell you that—"

"No." Ginny held up a hand. "Don't tell me anything. I want to find out for myself. I'll read the rest of the letters later."

Brett climbed into the wreckage and scooted closer to her, placing a hand on her leg. "Are you okay? I was worried when I heard you left. Kelly saw you go. She came and alerted me. I drove around till I saw the van. I have never been so happy to see Bud's van." He smiled.

"I—I didn't want to ruin your night. If you found out I was leaving…"

She lowered her head, and her hair hung limp around her face. He reached up his hand, brushing it over her shoulder. He wished he could kiss her scars away. Wished he knew the right thing to say to keep her from running. *Will she ever stop running?*

"You're leaving?" He tried to keep his voice tender. Tried not to scare this timid fawn before him. "Why? We've come so far, Ginny. I thought we were just getting over those things that plagued our past."

"It's not the past I was thinking about, Brett. It's the future. I don't want to stop you from going to Africa. It's what you've always wanted. And as much as I love it here, I couldn't imagine staying in Glacier Bay without you."

Ginny's flashlight flickered and then went out.

"Dumb batteries," she whispered in the near darkness.

He pulled his own flashlight from his damp jacket pocket and turned it on. Light flooded the inside of the shell. He scooted closer so their knees touched and lifted her chin. *Look in my eyes, Ginny. See my love.*

"I'm flattered you don't want to be here without me," he finally said. "But it's only two weeks. Surely Grandma Ethel, Kelly, Linda, Dove, and everyone else could keep you occupied during that time."

"Excuse me?" Her eyes flashed with joy. Maybe the first glimmer of true joy he'd ever seen there.

"Two weeks." He took the dead flashlight from her hand and placed it on the cold metal. Then he took both of her hands, pressing them in between his, trying to warm them. "The mission trip. I'm not going to be gone that long, and while it's not the best timing, those kids need me. I'll be taking over supplies and roofing an orphanage."

"You're not moving there for good?" Ginny scooted closer to him. "And then what?" Alongside the joy, hope appeared in her eyes too.

Brett smiled and kissed her cold fingertips. "Ginny, I'm not going to assume anything. The first time we were together, I assumed that the best thing I could—*we* could—do with our lives was to serve as missionaries in Africa. After all, the need is so great. But now I know that although it could be that, it could be a million other things too. The best thing we can do for God is to grow closer to Jesus and follow Him day-by-day. All I know is I want that to be a 'we'—to experience life with you." He swallowed hard. Then he reached out and stroked her shoulder.

"I love you, Ginny. And I'm willing to support your dreams, even if that means living in LA." The words rushed out, full of emotion. "Even if it means coming to Glacier Bay only to visit. Last time I didn't follow you, but this time…I will. If it means we'll be together, I will."

There, I said it. A burden lifted from his shoulders as he spoke the words.

"Really?" She tilted her head. "You mean it?"

Brett nodded.

"I'm glad, really I am. But I want you to know that I have no plans to go back to LA. Long-term."

He opened his mouth to ask why, and she shushed him with one finger.

"Brett, I'm not sure what my future holds. I do know a few things. I know God will use my voice—my songs—for His glory. I know I need to open my heart to the family God gave me, and to these people here in Glacier Bay. God brought me here for a reason. I have something to learn from them, just like Ellie had something to learn. We're not made to live alone, or even live for ourselves. My heart is learning that."

"And?" Brett leaned closer.

"And to you, Brett," she said just above a whisper. "I'm supposed to open my heart to you. And I'm perfectly fine with that. I love you."

"Can you say that again?"

Ginny tilted her head. "I love you, Brett." Her lips curled up in a smile. "And after being here, I respect you more than ever before. A good man isn't good because he says so, but because the people around him say so. I don't know what I did to deserve—"

"Shh." He placed a finger over her lips. "My love, my commitment, is a gift. I know it won't be easy, but know I want to be by your side wherever your music takes us. I'll support your future, Ginny. And I'll hold you close and be with you until every past hurt is healed."

A single tear broke free and journeyed down her cheek. "You mean that?"

Brett wiped it away with his thumb. Outside, the rain picked up again, plunking on the metal like gravel dropped from the sky, but at this moment there was no place he'd rather be.

He leaned down and kissed her once, unhurried. Her lips were warm and tasted of salt from the inlet winds. He pulled back slightly only to have her reach her hand to the back of his neck and pull his lips closer.

He kissed her a second time. The kiss was long and sweet, and when she pulled away, her breath was so close it brushed his cheek.

"I suppose sometimes it takes getting lost to enjoy the joy of being found," she whispered. "I'm happier at this moment than I've ever been." She glanced around and then placed her hand on the cold metal wall of the wreckage. "New hope in shattered dreams."

"Sounds like a song," he said, bending down and kissing her forehead.

She scooted closer, and he wrapped his arms around her, pulling her tight.

"It just might be, Brett. It just might be." She snuggled against him—her cheek against his chest—and he wondered if she could hear the beating of his heart. Wondered if she knew it was beating for her.

"A wonderful love song," she whispered again, louder over the sound of the rain. "To be sung to an audience of glaciers and puffins and sunsets over northern waters. A song first hummed by the One who created our hearts."

* * * * *

They made their way to the van in the rain, and Ginny was thankful for Brett's jacket and flashlight. She blew out a breath as she climbed into the passenger's seat, sure the trail had to be more than a quarter of a mile long. She was spent physically and emotionally—but in a good way. Her heart warmed her even though a chill moved up her arms.

Brett climbed in Bud's van and started the engine, turning the heater on.

"It'll take a few minutes to heat up."

Ginny nodded, her teeth chattering. "What about your truck?"

"I'll get a ride back to get it. Don't you worry about that."

Ginny couldn't help but notice the smile on Brett's face. And liked the idea of seeing that smile every day of the rest of her life.

Brett put the van in gear and was preparing to pull out when she noticed his forehead furrow. He put the gearshift back into Park and then jumped out of the car.

A Jeep with its hazard lights on pulled up behind them. She watched as Brett talked to the driver. A minute later, he jogged back to Bud's van.

"What's wrong?" Ginny whispered as he climbed back into the car.

"We need to get back."

She placed her hand on her chest. Was it Grandma? Was it her heart? She leaned closer as Brett continued.

"We need to get back." He pulled onto the road and turned back the way they had come. "It seems someone with a video camera showed up at the school, and Dove Fowler gave them directions to Grandma Ethel's house."

"A video camera? I don't understand."

"They said it was some entertainment show." Brett glanced over for the briefest moment. "Danny Kingston was with them. They're looking for you."

In just a few minutes, they were parking at Grandma Ethel's house. Ginny touched her wet hair, looked down at her filthy clothes. What would Danny think of this? She didn't understand why he'd be here. She thought of Ellie's letters. Like James, had Danny come to take her back? Perhaps. But why would he bring someone with a camera?

She waited until Brett walked around the side of the truck and put her hand in his. Together they walked to the front door. Through the window she saw Danny seated on the sofa talking to Grandma Ethel. Her stomach knotted up, and she felt violated. How dare he follow her here? This was her place and hers alone. He wouldn't appreciate it—would have no understanding of this community.

Ginny stepped in front of Brett and opened the door, striding in. She no longer cared that she was a sloppy mess. She paid no mind to the video camera that rolled, taping her every move. She placed her purse on the kitchen counter and then strode up to Danny.

"What are you doing here?"

"Ginny, darling, did you get caught in the rain? You had these poor folks worried."

She jutted out her chin. "I went for a walk. I'm fine." She crossed her arms over her chest.

"It looks like your knight in shining armor rescued you," Danny commented, eyeing Brett.

Ginny nodded, refusing to start this conversation. Danny wouldn't understand that what she and Brett had was different, more special, than anything in Hollywood.

"What are you doing here?" she asked again, ignoring Danny's slight smile and his expensive pants and sweater. Ignoring how a part of her was still drawn to that.

Danny stood and took her hand. "I came because one of my producer friends heard your story—the abuse, the abandonment, and your life in foster care. It's something that needs to be talked about. Child abuse is happening every day, and most of us are unaware." He spoke as if he was reading a script.

Ginny squared her shoulders. "Yes, well, this is something we can talk about another time."

"I thought that too, Ginny, but then I found information. I know you. I didn't think you'd want to wait to hear about…your mother."

"My mother?"

The wind was knocked out of her. She sank onto the couch, and a thousand prayers replayed in her mind—prayers of a child who wanted to know *who* and *why*. Why had her mother done what she'd done?

Danny sat next to Ginny. "I know this isn't the best timing, but would you like to know?"

Ginny pushed her damp hair back from her face. The room faded. Grandma Ethel's and Brett's faces faded. She nodded. "Yes."

Danny picked up a manila envelope from the coffee table. "I have answers in here, but first, since you have the chance…do you have anything to say to her? I mean, after what happened?"

Ginny blew out a breath and put a hand over her stomach, willing its quivering to cease. "Yes." She turned and looked into the camera. "I don't understand all that happened. I don't understand why, but sometimes we find ourselves in dark, dark places. Sometimes we make mistakes, and I want you to know"—she looked at Brett and then back to the camera—"I want you to know I forgive you."

As she released the words, the trembling in her stomach turned to butterflies that rose and danced, carrying lightness to her chest.

She looked at Danny. He leaned back against the couch, then his eyes softened into a look she'd never seen from him before, one of respect.

"Yes, well," he fumbled for words. "If you were angry, then no one would have blamed you." He pulled a slip of paper out of the envelope. "The report from the social worker assigned to your case said you were thin, frail for a three-year-old. There were numerous bruises on your legs and cigarette burns on your back."

Ginny nodded. "Yes, I've heard that before."

Then he slipped out a photo of a young, pretty woman. She was standing on a stage singing. At first Ginny thought it was a photo of herself, but when she looked closer, she saw that the clothes were unfamiliar and the woman's hair was darker, though worn in the same way. *Mother.*

For some reason she was prettier than Ginny imagined. She looked more innocent too. The woman Ginny had carried around in her mind all these years was more like the wicked stepmother than this Cinderella.

"Do you want to know what happened to her?"

"What do you mean, what happened?"

"She's gone, Ginny." Danny's voice was tender. "She's been gone for a long time."

Ginny struggled for breath. In all the scenarios that had played in her mind, she'd never imagined this. Ginny'd always assumed that if she made something of herself—became someone important—then her mother would come to her. Was it true she was gone? If so... her plan wasn't possible.

Ginny looked to Danny, and her eyes widened as she waited for answers.

"She died over twenty years ago," he said simply. "She was in a car accident, and both she and her boyfriend—who was driving drunk—were killed. It was less than two weeks after she left you."

Ginny covered her mouth with a trembling hand.

"Your mother wasn't the one who abused you, Ginny. Her boyfriend was. He was a felon who'd been charged with child abuse before." Danny sighed. "How she got wrapped up with the likes of him, we'll never know." He patted the manila envelope. "It's all in here—your Child Protective Services records, his old police reports."

Ginny's breath escaped. She tried to comprehend what Danny was saying. She'd built walls around her heart on the assumption that her mother had been her abuser. She felt the walls sinking. She felt her heart softening.

"There's also information about the church where she left you."

"Church?" Ginny leaned forward. "Did I hear you right?"

"We found this information in their old archives." Danny pulled out another sheet of paper and cleared his throat. "A toddler was left inside a church. The pastor found her sitting on the front pew with a small suitcase, neatly packed. Her—your—wounds were fresh, and they'd been carefully bandaged. There was a note…"

He reached in and pulled out a slip of paper. Words were scribbled on the back of a Safeway receipt.

This is Virginia Rose, my song. My songbird. Keep her safe. Please do whatever you can. And when I find my own safety I will come. I

The words ended there. Ginny read the note again and again. It was a love song, written out of fear.

What was the last line supposed to say?

I love her.

I want to protect her.

I will miss her.

Ginny's shoulders shook. The air in the room seemed to thicken, making it hard to breathe. Sadness flooded over her. No longer for herself. No longer for the fact that she was abandoned. But because a mother had to do such a difficult thing to protect her child.

Tears filled Ginny's eyes, and gratitude warmed her chest. Her mother hadn't hated her. Instead, her love had hoped for a better way. *She had planned to come back for me.*

Ginny looked to Brett. He approached and knelt on the floor on one knee, taking her hands in his.

"She wanted God—His people—to watch over you, Ginny," Brett said.

She nodded and wrapped her arms around his shoulders, letting her forehead fall into the curve of his neck. "I know. And knowing this changes everything. She loved me, Brett. She loved me. And I think she'd want nothing more than for me to stay here, with the people of Glacier Bay. With you."

Chapter Thirty-Eight

....

September 13, 1929

Dear Clay,

    I have so much to tell you. This may be a long letter.

    After I wrote you on the airplane, I sat looking out the window. It was so cold, the blanket barely warmed me. I started thinking about Grandfather, and a panic came over me. He was spared last time, after his stroke. I couldn't imagine God restoring him to me a second time. I knew he was going to die, may already have passed, and I completely broke down.

    My whole life I depended on him, needed him. How could I live without him? I'd failed to make anyone else love me, Clay. Not James or his family, not Joseph… I know you loved me. But then I had to leave. I tried so hard to please everyone.

    All these thoughts, a year of trying and failing, and especially the fear of losing Grandfather, exploded over me. Through Tinle's recovery, the months Joseph rejected me, and even when I told you I would leave, I stayed strong. But I could hold that strength no longer.

    I sobbed, tears running through my fingers as I covered my face. I felt like I was in a kayak in the middle of Glacier Bay's vast openness. The stark mountains were hidden by a thick fog. Stuck, immobile, afraid to go any direction, I laid my oars down and leaned back. Around me a storm stirred, soon raging around my little kayak, filling it with icy waves, weighing it down. A dark terror encompassed me.

And then I heard James's voice as if from far away. "God is with you," he said. Not like him to speak of God, but he must've seen the intensity of my pain. To be honest, I ached for you, Clay. Longed for you to row up in your kayak and show me the way home. But you didn't come. I stayed in this place of morbid sadness until we landed. James gave up on trying to comfort me and led me off the plane in silence. I hardly noticed the scenery, so familiar, as the taxi took me to the hospital.

Ginny paused for a moment, glancing at the inlet outside Grandma Ethel's window. Her heart ached for Ellie, but not as it had before. Maybe because she had a sense that Ellie would find some hope to cling to. Even if her grandfather died. Even if she stayed in San Francisco, there was always hope.

Last night Ginny had stayed up late. After sending the cameraman on to the lodge, Danny had stayed to talk to her and Brett. He'd glanced at her time and time again with curiosity, but instead of asking about the changes in her, he had instead grilled Brett about the fishing, the tourists, the gold in the mountains.

Danny assumed she'd go back, of course, but she suspected he was giving her time to digest the new information about her mother. She knew she'd go back too. She wasn't going to give up music. She was her mother's songbird. She was just putting herself, and her music, into the place they needed to be from the beginning—into Jesus' hands.

She looked back at the letter, hoping Ellie made the same discovery.

I entered the hospital's lobby, and the first thing I heard was piano music. "The Maple Leaf Rag" by Scott Joplin.

Grandfather's favorite. I stifled a sob as I gazed at the grand piano gleaming in sunlight, which poured in through big windows. A troupe of patients stood around, clapping and humming, and an array of high-back velveteen chairs formed a half circle.

While wending our way to Grandfather's room, a woman grabbed my arm.

"You Ellie Bell?" She was short and sturdy, with arms like sausages.

"Yes. I mean, that's what my grandfather calls me. Do you know him?"

It was Nurse Schroeder! Relief loosened my muscles. I wanted to embrace her, but she didn't seem willing. She dragged me back the other direction, toward the piano.

I tried, but failed, to release myself from her grip and maneuver toward Grandfather's room. "I really want to see Grandfather."

"Ja, yes. I take you." She continued tromping ahead.

Reaching the piano, I yanked my arm from her grip and grabbed her shoulders. "Tell me! Where is my grandfather?"

The player suddenly stopped, and each set of eyes in the room turned to us.

She pointed to one of the high-backed chairs, and I spotted my favorite grin in the world. "Grandfather!" I rushed to him, knelt before him, and wept into his fragile hands.

"My Ellie Bell." He patted my head. "You see. Our God takes care of us. Doesn't He? I am well."

"Well?"

"Getting well, ja." Nurse Schroeder brushed lint from Grandfather's hospital gown. "The doctor say he respond

better than expected to treatment. Men his age usually do not recover from pneumonia, but God took care and he is okay. He still need time to recover."

I couldn't answer. No words. Every emotion of the last year—the good, the better-than-good, the heartbreaking—flowed out into Grandfather's arms. And, Clay, in that moment, I knew I wasn't alone. I grasped that God loved me even though I didn't deserve it. All my striving to make everyone love me—it was because I didn't really believe God loved me. But He did, He always did.

I was suddenly able to see everything that had happened to me as part of His providence—"His preserving and governing all His creatures and all their actions." All along, through the loss of my parents, my struggles with James and his mother, Grandfather's misfortune, the joys and heartbreaks in Alaska—through everything—God guided each of my steps. I didn't realize it, but that doesn't change the truth: He was there, loving me.

I finally understood what Grandfather had been trying to teach me all my life. Christ is my solid rock. Everything else can pass away, but He will never leave me. My hope is built on nothing less.

In that moment, my face must've shone with the joy of the Lord, because Grandfather kissed me and said, "Amen and amen!"

I pulled my half of the heart-shaped stone from my pocket, ran my fingers over the rough edges, and showed it to Grandfather. He smiled and pulled out his half.

"Christ da rock," Nurse S. said, quickly wiping a tear.

Grandfather and I held the broken rock, his hands lined

with years, mine rough with work. "Christ is my rock." I whispered. "No matter what."

That was three weeks ago now. A lot has happened. Grandfather's fortune having been restored, we got our house back. I never thought that would happen. James continues to come around. I think his mother pushes him. Imagine that! I heard an heiress from New York has been interested in him. Hopefully he'll look her direction soon.

And me, I'm content. Even if Grandfather died tomorrow, I'd be heartbroken but not destroyed. I don't need the approval of others to make me happy. I've got Christ, and He's enough. Well, at least that's what I'm trying to learn.

Of course I still love you, with all my heart, but I'm letting go of the hope I so wanted to cling to. I will miss you and the children. I wish you the happiest life possible.

Ellie

October 15, 1929

Dear Janey,

You must forgive me for not writing sooner. I have been very sick, my child, with something called pneumonia. Only our dear Lord could've saved me, and He did. Amen and amen! I'm grateful because it seems we have a great task ahead of us to forge a way for your papa and my Ellie Bell to head down the road to matrimony. Our plans are not as His, though. We must be prepared for a different outcome than we hope, but we can trust His ways are always the best. Right?

Having said that, cheer up, my girl! I still have one last strategy toward our great goal. I will write you again with more details. You must be patient, dear.

My dear Ellie is here, as you know. At first she slept right in my room all twisted and balled in a chair. Ridiculous! I made her go to the home where she grew up. (We need to sell that place, but I haven't told her that yet.)

   Grandfather

                             June 8, 1930

Dear Janey,

   Hello, my dear! Yes, thank you for your last letter. Our plan is going wonderfully, don't you think?

   As the months have passed, I'm gaining strength. I think I'll soon be able to come to Glacier Bay! Now, to convince Ellie to come with me. I've got an idea to make it happen. Keep praying and keep the letters coming. How I enjoy them.

   Grandfather

                             August 15, 1930

Dear Janey,

   It worked! Ellie has agreed to take me to Glacier Bay. Let me tell you how it happened.

   Every day I asked her to tell me more stories about her time in Alaska. What a magnificent place you live in, little one. Such a kind and loving community. She showed me how well your papa taught her to play guitar—she's quite good!

   Well, after she told me about little Penny's illness and how the Tlingits at Hoonah cared for her so compassionately (do you know that word? It means kindly), I told her I was sold! I had to go see it for myself.

   She patted my hand and said, "Oh, Grandfather, wouldn't that be wonderful? I miss it so. I wish you could."

*But I was serious, of course. It took a lot of convincing!
Even with the doctor's approval, I had to promise to take Nurse
Schroeder along. (She's the one who writes the letters for me.)*

*(Nurse S. here. Guten Tag, Janey. This is the daftest idea
Herr Barnett has had so far.)*

Don't mind her. She's German, but we like her anyway.

*Ellie finally agreed to come! Just so she can show me
around, share her memories with me. She doesn't want
to bother your papa or brother. Over the past year, she's
missed you all very much, but she doesn't want to cause any
problems with Joseph. I think she's a bit afraid too. Don't
you? But we know she needn't be. Your father still loves her.
Am I right?*

*Now, don't forget, Miss Janey. She and your papa believe
it's not right for them to be together. If that's the case, then we
must accept it. This could all end with their being apart. That
happens sometimes, my dear. But we'll have a great adventure
trying to work it all out!*

*We'll keep it a secret, yes? Just between the two of us.
A surprise! I'm so excited. Not just that maybe, if the Lord
so wills, He could bring them back together, but to see your
beautiful home, and especially to meet you, my little one.*

I'll see you soon,
Grandfather

*P.S. I almost sent this, but I must tell you one more
thing that happened. Ellie is so strong and confident; she
has decided to move back up to Alaska permanently! Not
to marry your papa, but because she fell in love with the
place and feels like it's "calling" her. I've heard of the "call*

of the North." Isn't that wonderful? It'll make our job that much easier.

She plans to homestead her own place and find a way to fit into the community, maybe by making fur shawls. She's even taking shooting lessons. She's not doing that great at it, however, but at least she can hold it steady now.

Chapter Thirty-Nine

Ginny dressed in her dirty jeans and one of Brett's old flannels shirts that Grandma Ethel had been using as a dust rag. It had one hole near the shirt's tail, but it didn't matter. They were going on a walk—or so she'd been told—and none of her things were appropriate.

On their next trip to Juneau, she'd have to fix that. She was sure she could find some casual clothes there. And when she was a little stronger, she'd return to LA—to record a few songs, pack some things, sell even more, and say good-bye to the life she thought she wanted but that no longer fit.

The house seemed empty without Grandma Ethel there. She and Dove Fowler were holding a pinochle game day at Dove's place. It seemed the folks around Glacier Bay knew how to have fun—and they enjoyed having fun together.

As she waited, Ginny looked in the box. There was only one letter left. The address on the envelope was marked out, and next to it the words: *This letter never made it to Grandfather. It was "Returned to Sender" because we had already left.*

We? Was that "we" Ellie and Grandfather Peter?

As eager as she was to see Brett, Ginny hoped she still had a few more minutes before he got there. She opened the letter to find out if the "we" was who she thought.

August 28, 1930

Dear Brother Peter,

I feel a conviction to finish the story of my hurting boy, Joseph. It has come to an end, for he's leaving Glacier Bay.

The last few months have had me scratching my thick head over and over. Each time the Parkers or others invited us to a shindig at their homes, I'd ask Joseph if he wanted to go. He always shrugged, saying he'd go.

Every night, just about, a different friend from the community took time to talk to my boy. Showed an interest, listened, enjoyed him. Slowly, his eyes perked up, even at home.

I remember the first real smile. It's spring, you know, and Linc's throwing himself into making a way to get across the river. It all started at Falls Creek, but now he wants to make a pulley to get across our own Salmon River. Well, the three of us were outside, working together on it. Janey was watching the children.

Yeah, I know. I usually discourage his inventions, but some of them have actually turned out all right, so I figured I could offer a hand. We rigged up a rope to hold a person in the pulley. I thought I should be the first to try it, since it could be unsafe.

Well, Joseph was sour as usual until that rope snapped and I fell into the water. When I sludged back, shivering, soaked like a seal, he smiled and sniffed a little chuckle. Then he put his arm around Linc, who was laughing his fool head off.

Brother Peter, that spark in his eyes, smile on his lips, it undid me. Made me think for the first time, he may be okay.

But there's more, because just at that moment, we had a visitor.

Tinle.

I heard a crack, like someone treading over a branch, and

*when I turned, there she stood. A shy smile, a humble dress, a
basket in her hands. She said hello as I slogged toward her.*

*My shoulders tightened underneath my drenched work
shirt. This girl, she could destroy all Joseph's progress.*

*Her eyes flashed toward Joseph, whose back was turned as
he worked on the pulley. Then it looked as if she thought better.
Lifted the basket. "I brought you a strawberry pie."*

*I heard Joseph from behind me say her name. He jogged
past me, toward her, then stopped short.*

*She drew in a breath, lifted her chin. "I wanted to talk to
you, if I could." She dropped her gaze.*

Joseph glanced at me.

*"I don't think it's a good idea...." I started, but stopped.
Joseph's look told me to let him, to trust him. I nodded.*

*He led her to the talking porch, where it seems all
important conversations take place.*

*That was the first of many encounters between them, all
here at our home, with me in close proximity. (I am still a
worried father.) Then one night, we invited her to sup with us.*

*In the summers we do our eating outside on our picnic table,
even cook over the campfire. The late light makes for good long
outdoor enjoyment. Linc and Janey cooked up a real nice meal of
roast duck and potatoes, the scent of which stirred our stomachs.*

*When Tinle strolled into our yard, I tell you, a light
shone in that girl's eyes I never saw before. Joseph gasped a
little. I heard him.*

*He strolled to her, offered his hand. I noticed his hair
was combed, his clothes clean. He led her to our table, topped
with the checkerboard tablecloth Ellie made. (She may have
struggled with many of the other chores, but sewing she knew.)*

We all sat down, and the conversation had an easy feel. I hadn't realized how heavy a burden this mess with Joseph was until it started to lift. Then Tinle shifted to me, put a hand on my arm. She asked me if she could write to Ellie. I asked her why. Here's the gist of what she said:

"I want to thank her. She prayed with me, when I was sick. And it gave me hope. I was ashamed of everything." Here she eyed Joseph. "Ellie told me I could be forgiven. That Jesus, He took my punishment." Her lips formed a tight smile. "I never thought someone else could be in trouble for me. But once, my auntie told me a story of an old Tlingit who sat in the forest, waiting for a friend. When his friend came, he was attacked by a bear. His friend, he laid down so the bear would attack him and not his friend. Miss Ellie said it was like that—except Jesus would protect me not just from a bear, but from my own shame. I don't know why, but I believed her." She closed her eyes, let the sunlight soak in. "Now everything is different."

The longing I kept locked away for Ellie came back so strong. She did my job for me. I was too busy being worried about my own pain to reach out to anyone, but she poured her heart out for Tinle.

Now Joseph spoke up. "I want to talk to Miss Ellie too. I've been worse than terrible to her." And will you believe, he confessed his selfishness and jealousy. How she didn't deserve one bit of the anger he directed toward her. How he resented my being happy when he was so miserable. His eyes glistened, as did mine, I expect. "But Mama wouldn't want you to be unhappy," he told me.

I clutched his arm, couldn't believe his words.

Then Zach crawled on my lap and Janey crept close, holding Penny. "We want you to marry Miss Ellie."

I studied Joseph's face. "I can't. What about all of you? I need to take care of you."

"You can't do it alone, Papa." Joseph tightened his grip on Tinle's hand. "That's what I had to learn. I thought I had to struggle through it all alone. Thought I couldn't let anyone in or I'd get hurt again. But all those nights at the Parkers, each one who talked to me helped me some. Then when Tinle came, she talked to me about Christ, and His love. And…" He gently let go of Tinle's hand and leaned toward me. "Most of all, you, Papa. You showed me a love I'll never forget. You sacrificed your own happiness for a rebellious child who took you for granted and gave you nothing but disrespect." Moisture welled in his eyes. "Thank you, Papa. How can I ever thank you?"

By now I couldn't hold back the tears, even though I'm supposed to be a tough Alaska man. I tugged him to me. My son who was lost was found. He was dead and was now alive. Praise God! Praise God!

So you can see, Brother Peter, God healed my son, but He used many, not just me.

I wanted you to know, my Joseph is doing well. He's decided to go to college in Juneau after all and has already left for his first quarter. He and Tinle are writing letters, perhaps to wed someday. We'll see.

As for me. Well, sir, I'd sure like to marry your granddaughter. I don't know if she'll have me. Truth is, I've been offered a position as a missionary in Africa. As much as I love Glacier Bay, I intend to take it. That is, unless Ellie would be willing to come on back to us.

*I don't want to pressure her. It's been a year, and she may
have moved on. But if you think there is a hope, would you be so
kind as to let me know? In that case I'll come chasing after her
to the ends of the earth. If not, Africa will be a new life for us.*

*I need to know soon, seeing as the last ship's going to be
leaving out of here in a month.*

*I thank you, Brother Peter, for everything. It's all in God's
hands, and I trust that with all my heart.*

Clay

Ginny turned the letter over in her hand. "What?" she mumbled
out loud. "That was it?"

There were no more letters.

She put the envelope in the box and slammed the lid shut. What
was the point of that? How could Grandma Ethel just leave things
hanging like that? Did Ellie ever return? Did Clay find her? Did they
marry? And what *was* it with Africa?

Ten minutes later, Brett pulled up, and she called to him through
the open window. "You have to tell me, where's the last letter?"

He stepped out of the truck, pulled her into his arms, and kissed
the top of her head. "I have no idea what you're talking about...but
you're sure cute when you're anxious."

Ginny stepped back and playfully slugged his arm. "Brett, I'm serious here." She crossed her arms over her chest. "I called your grandma
at Dove's house, interrupting her pinochle game and everything. I
could hear the smile in her voice when she told me that you held the
answer—that I'd never be able to read the rest of Ellie's story without your help...and without being in Glacier Bay." Ginny laughed. The
humor of Grandma Ethel's plan was striking her, even in her anxiety.
"She knew all along I'd have to come back and get your help."

Brett scratched the top of his head. "What does that mean? Did she say anything else?"

Ginny closed her eyes, trying to remember. Then she opened them and focused on him once again. "She said there was a secret hiding spot. She'd hide treats there for you as a boy."

Laughter poured from Brett's lips. "Yes, I remember now." He motioned for her to get in the truck. "It's at Great-grandpa Clay's cabin. Get in my truck, Ginny. I know what she's talking about."

It only took a few minutes to get to the cabin. When they entered, Clay eyed the pile of boxes stacked against the wall. "It's back there—where the woodstove used to be. One of the stones behind the stove was loose. Grandma said her father used to hide matches there to keep them out of the hands of the little ones, but she'd always hide treats for me there."

They moved the boxes out of the way, and Ginny held her breath as Brett reached for the stone. Sure enough, it came out easily. And inside there wasn't only another letter, but something else that caused Ginny's heart to jump in her chest.

Brett pulled out two pieces of rock and placed them in Ginny's hand. A smile filled her face. They were the two parts of the stone heart. "Grandfather Peter's heart—Ellie's too. They had to have come back here, to Clay's home."

Brett brushed his thumb on her cheek, wiping away a stray tear. "Why don't you read the rest, Ginny. I think you'll like how Ellie's story ends."

Chapter Forty

....

December 24, 1933

Dear Janey,

How many times have I seen you rummage through the letter box, piecing together the story of your parents' romance? Don't think I haven't noticed your frustration over the missing last episode, but you were there, dear! Doesn't your young memory serve you?

In answer to your requests to explain, "for future generations," how everything worked out, I am writing this letter...to you. Consider it your Christmas gift. You've heard this story a million times, as I've told it to you, Zach, Penny, Elias, and Rose, but regardless, here it is.

How clearly I remember that journey back to Alaska! Grandfather, Nurse Schroeder, and I had traveled from San Francisco to Juneau. We took the same route James and I had, but backward this time— airplane to Seattle, then steamer. You should've seen Grandfather on the airplane. He pestered the flight crew with question after question, translated by Nurse S., who had gotten used to his garbled speech. Sometimes they couldn't understand her strong German accent either, so I had to step in. What an adventure!

I loved how his frail body didn't slow him down. He kept looking out the window at icy mountains, lush forests, the white-capped ocean, and saying, "Amen and amen!"

When we got to Juneau, Grandfather was so excited to be

out of the hospital, he kept wheeling his chair away from us, like a child wanting to see everything.

"It's my first trip to Alaska, ladies," he said. "Give a man a second to look!"

I was back on our Yosemite explorations again, experiencing the world through his wonder-filled eyes. What a gift he gave me, to perceive the glories of creation.

We arrived in Juneau, exhausted, and spent the night at The Alaskan. There weren't many inns to choose from. What a night! When Nurse S. realized the nature of the place, she nearly packed us up and marched us out into the cold night, but knowing Grandfather wasn't as strong as he let on, she settled for second best.

With a steely jaw and a steady brow, she stomped downstairs and told the proprietor that no "business" would be done while Herr Barnett was on the premises. I watched from the balcony as the man, his slight build camouflaged by the best suit I'd ever seen in the Territory of Alaska, glared at Nurse S. I thought he was going to give her a knuckle sandwich, but her iron gaze must've done him in, because he backed down. In minutes, "customers" were shooed out the door, and only we and the ladies were left.

If it had been up to Grandfather, he'd have set up a pulpit, unpacked his hymnal, and held a church service right there, but instead, he vowed to get his friends at the Gideons to place Bibles in every room. And as you, know, Janey, the next summer we all journeyed over and assisted with just that.

The next morning, a stellar pink sky dappled with swashes of white greeted us, but my stomach roiled. I longed to move back to Glacier Bay, to embrace Edith, Nell, and the others, to claim my homestead and create a life for the three of us, but I didn't want to see your father. I still loved him, but I had no reason to hope for reconciliation. I couldn't bear the thought of being near him, his strong eyes, his handsome build.

I wandered into Grandfather's room. He still slept, and Nurse S. was out making sure this place was "up to snuff." I stood next to his window, its coolness fresh against my cheeks, and watched the birds along the shoreline. Such a variety, I didn't know all their names back then. Soon, a bald eagle caught my eye, its majestic wingspan cutting through the air as it dove for fish.

"An amazing bird God made, isn't it?" Grandfather said.

I pivoted around to see his crooked smile, his hand reaching out to me.

"What brings you in here? Have I overslept? You can blame that on Nurse S. She's supposed to wake me." He chuckled.

I shook my head. "Grandfather. Be nice to her. She takes wonderful care of you."

"You're no fun." He mocked a frown.

What comfort just being in his presence gave to me, but still my fears grappled in my stomach, like an otter playing with a ball. Grandfather must've seen angst reflected in my face. He rubbed my hand with his wrinkled one.

"Tell me, dear. Are you afraid?"

I sank onto the side of his bed, tried to smile. "I'm trying not to be, Grandfather. But what was I thinking? How can I possibly live out at Strawberry Point and not be with Clay?"

The Alaskan wildlife, even here in the state capital, brought back a familiarity I longed for but had no right to. I felt more out of place in that moment than I ever had before. I glanced back out the window at the ferry being loaded. I needed to get on it. Go far, far away from here.

I grasped Grandfather's arm. "I can't go back there, as

LOVE FINDS YOU IN GLACIER BAY, ALASKA

....

*much as I love it. I'm so sorry to have brought you this far, but
I think we should go back. I can't stay."*

"Yes, perhaps you're right."

*He caught me off guard. I certainly didn't expect him to
agree. "What?"*

*"If that's what you want, dear." His twinkling eyes grew
serious, compassionate. "Is it?"*

*The sunrise tinted the sky from pink to orange, brightening
with day's awakening. God's grandeur dripped from the
scenery there like nowhere else, I was sure. I relished it, yet it
wasn't mine.*

"No, Grandfather, I don't want to turn back, but..."

"You don't want the life you've been planning, either."

*"I do want to live in Strawberry Point." I couldn't say the
rest. That I only wanted it if I could be with Clay.*

Ginny paused and looked up at Brett. This was his family, his
heritage. It still did something to her to realize that. He'd gone to
the truck while she'd been reading and returned holding something
behind his back.

"Does she end up with him? Did Ellie marry your great-
grandfather?"

"Why don't you keep reading and find out?"

She tilted her head and brushed her hair over her shoulder. "What's
behind your back?"

"I'll tell you, beautiful girl, but when the time is right." He pointed
to the letter. "Keep reading."

"And you'll know the right time?"

Brett nodded. "Yes, I'll know."

After breakfast, we set out to the ferry dock. We would go home, back to San Francisco. It was the only decision. I knew Grandfather was disappointed not to see Glacier Bay, but he and Nurse S. showed abundant kindness for my last-minute reversal. I hated myself for giving up, but life at Glacier Bay without Clay crystallized each moment. I wasn't strong enough to live with that heartache every day.

The ferry dock sat aside the one for smaller boats, like those to Strawberry Point. How odd I felt, following that same path I'd traveled two years before, by myself, not knowing what the future held. I wasn't alone this time, but I still had no idea how my future life would unfold.

When I approached the ticket counter, a woman in a short-sleeved cotton dress (it was sixty degrees after all) informed me they were sold out to Seattle, the last boat of the season! She suggested I charter a smaller boat and pick up the ferry at Sitka where they'd drop some travelers. Grandfather was overjoyed by this. An adventure!

Well, I knew the drill. I had Grandfather and Nurse S. hang back while I traipsed down the wobbly dock as before, seeking a charter—this time to Sitka. Gratefully, I wore more appropriate shoes and didn't have to lug a huge chest.

About six boats were moored there. None heading to Sitka. We'd have to check back tomorrow, see if anyone else showed up. My stomach clenched even tighter than it had all morning. Would we be stuck here till spring? Discouraged, I was heading back to Grandfather and Nurse S. when I noticed a boat creeping toward the dock. My heart pumped. Please, Lord, let this one be going to Sitka today.

The small, white fishing boat easily jumped over the waves. Crates lined the deck. Children perched on them, watching the dock come into view. My eyes focused on the boat, still small in the distance.

"Hey, lady?" a mate on the boat next to me asked. "You the one going to Sitka?"

I pulled my gaze away from that boat and looked at the scruffy sailor. "Yes. I thought you said you weren't going."

"Well, I was thinkin'. How much you payin'?"

"We have three passengers and a bit of luggage. How much would you charge?"

"You real desperate to make tracks outta here, aren't ya? Winter comin'."

Before I answered, the sounds of children laughing rolled along the wind from the distant fishing boat, snatching my attention. I could hear their voices, but they seemed to be gathering their things for mooring. I couldn't see them. The white boat looked familiar, but then they all seemed the same to me.

"Lady? Whaddya say? I'll give you a real good deal."

"Of course." I gave the man a smile. I learned to never judge folks by their appearances here. Great men live beneath the rugged Alaska persona. "I'd appreciate it."

He reached out to shake my hand, but I heard a squeal as that white boat approached. I stepped toward where it would dock. *That looks a lot like Clay's*, I thought. *But it can't be.*

It was you, Janey, who saw me first. You were standing next to a mound of crates marked To Uganda, gripping your satchel. "Miss Ellie!"

How my pulse beat, slammed against my chest. My palms started to drip an icy-cold sweat. I didn't know what to do.

Should I just wait there? Should I get Grandfather? Should I be afraid? Excited? Everything swirled in me until I almost fell over.

The sailor was persistent, eager as he was to be on his way, but he finally agreed to give me "just a few minutes."

A huge smile took over my face, despite my fear. My eyes fought back tears. "Janey!" I called.

Soon Zach spotted me, Linc, and even little Penny, whom you held in your arms. You all raced to the railing, waving at me, calling my name.

Within minutes, the boat slid up next to the dock. You all stayed back, waiting for your papa. Then Joseph came out of the engine room, his blond hair cut neatly though tousled by the wind. A knot formed in my chest. I feared catching his gaze. Feared the dark glare, the disappointment at seeing me. But no. His eyes sparkled, and he smiled!

"Miss Ellie?" Joseph quickly tied the boat to the dock and jumped off. "Is that you?" He ran to me and grabbed me in a two-armed hug. "I'm so sorry," he blurted out. "I was so wrong."

I didn't understand where this change sprang from, but how it filled me with joy. "Joseph. I forgive you. Of course." I soaked up that hug.

"I'm better now," he said, as we parted. "Working on getting better."

"That's wonderful. I know how hard it is."

And then I saw your father.

Clay strode onto the boat deck, halting my words, but he hadn't seen me yet. Zach raced to him. "Miss Ellie! Miss Ellie's here."

Then you grabbed his hand and led him to the railing, so he could see me. He stared my direction, confused. I knew the *moment he saw me, because his eyes widened and his hand flew to his chest. "Ellie?"*

Oh, Janey, I didn't know if he was happy to see me or not. In fact, his lips drooped downward, like a frown. I wanted to run back to the hotel, hide away and never return. But I didn't. I had to face him now, even if it meant another rejection.

He slowly (far too slowly) sauntered off the boat, telling Joseph to tend the children, and then stepped up to me.

"Ellie."

"We want to see her, Papa!" Zach blurted out.

You shushed him.

"C'mon." Clay placed his hand on my back and led me to the end of the dock. A chill bounced through every ounce of my body.

The water lapped against the wooden planks that jutted out, making me feel like we were suspended out there, together.

We stood, silently sizing each other up.

"Ellie? What are you doing here?"

"I was going to move back, but then..." I tried to explain but fumbled over my words.

"It doesn't matter. You're here now. But you—you didn't write back. I thought you—"

"Write?"

"I sent a letter to Brother Peter, saying... Didn't he get it?"

I shook my head. "I've seen all his mail. I would've noticed something from you." I gave a smile. I wanted to give so much more. "What did it say?"

"Well, it said, uh, Joseph's doing well."

"I see! I'm so happy to hear that."

"He's going to college in Juneau. Came to Strawberry Point to help us move."

"Move?"

"I'm taking a call to Africa. Uganda."

"You are?" My heart plummeted to my shoes. "You want to leave Alaska?"

"No." He took a step closer. "I want you."

I gasped out loud when he said that. "You want…me?"

He touched my cheek with the back of his fingers.

"Clay." I closed my eyes, relishing his touch.

"That's what the letter said." His voice was soft, close. "That I was wrong to shut you out, and that if you'll have me, I'd sure like to marry you." His strong hands cupped my chin, then moved to my hair. "I love you, Ellie."

My hands slid to his hips.

He leaned close, and I waited for a kiss, but he stopped. I almost fainted.

"I've a notion to kiss you," he said. "That all right?"

I didn't answer, and we… Well, Janey, you know the rest. You were watching!

After, he held me to his broad chest. "I'll never let you go again."

"I won't let you."

Then you children, having waited long enough apparently, rushed to us.

Nurse Schroeder and Grandfather, in his wheelchair, arrived next.

"We can't wait forever," Nurse S. said.

"Does this mean you're getting married?" Janey, you asked, unfazed by the new arrivals.

"Yes, I'd like to know that too!" Grandfather piped in.

Your papa rustled your hair. "Well, she hasn't answered

that yet." He cupped my cheek in his hand. "Will you marry me, Miss Ellie McKinley?"

"Of course I will." He kissed me again, and you all howled and hooted.

"Are we still going to Africa, Uncle Clay?" Linc asked after he received an embrace from me.

"Yes, I'd like to know that too," I said.

Clay eyed me. "Do you want to?"

"I'll go anywhere with you."

He gazed at each one of our loved ones, standing there, then shook his head. "Nah. Glacier Bay is our home. I'd never want to live anywhere else."

"Neither would I."

The letter gently slipped from Ginny's grasp. Brett took it and set it on top of one of the boxes.

"But I'm, uh, not finished yet...." She tried to hide her smile and glanced up under her lashes to see the adoration in his gaze.

"I thought you wanted to see what I'd gotten out of my truck. It's really important, Ginny. It could change everything."

"Is it now?"

He moved his hands down her arms and then grabbed her left hand, pulling her palm to his face. He kissed it, and she couldn't help but notice the twinkle in his eyes. "There's a problem. A big problem, you see."

"What are you talking about?" she asked.

"With your hand. Don't you realize it?"

Ginny looked at her hand, opening and closing her fingers. "I never realized. I mean my fingertips are a little calloused from the guitar, but nothing too unusual."

"I'm not talking about that. There's something missing." He glanced at her ring finger, and suddenly she understood.

"Oh there is, is there?" She smirked.

"Bare naked. You should be ashamed to be walking around like that."

She took his free hand and spread his palm on her face, drinking in his gaze. "Oh, Brett, what are you saying?"

"I'm saying that I have a ring that needs a finger to go on."

"What a coincidence. I have a ring finger ready and willing."

He reached into his back pocket and pulled out the priority envelope. It was the one she'd mailed back to him nearly two years ago. His grandma's address was written on the front in her handwriting, yet it wasn't open.

Brett ripped it open, and then a small wad of white tissue paper fell out. Bret opened the tissue and then held up the ring. "This is the first time I've touched this ring since it was on your finger, Ginny. I told myself I wouldn't until I was putting it back where it belonged."

"Did you know, Brett—" Her words caught in her throat. "Did you know we'd end up together?"

"I was praying, Ginny." He offered her a wink. "Was praying it would be God's will in the end."

Then with a smile as big as Glacier Bay, Brett dropped to one knee. "Ginny, I know I've already asked you this, but you can't take back your answer this time." He breathed deep. "Ginny, will you marry me?"

"Yes, Brett. A thousand sunsets over this beautiful bay, yes."

Brett's hand trembled slightly as he slid it on her finger.

"Ellie's ring," she said with a smile.

"Ginny's ring." He rose and pulled her into his arms, tucking his face into her neck. "I'll love you forever, Ginny. You can count on that."

He pulled back slightly so their faces were only inches apart, then ever so gently Brett offered her a kiss. His lips were warm and sweet.

They were a fulfillment of God's plan to her. They were home.

It took a minute for Ginny to calm down—for her heart to stop racing and for the kisses to slow—but she had to finish the letter.

Brett released her, stepped back, and handed her the last page with a smile. Whatever words were to come, deep down, Ginny had peace. Peace that her and Brett's story—while not always happy or free from pain—would end as beautifully as Ellie's. As long as they looked to Jesus, trusted Jesus, it would.

> And so, Janey, we all grabbed the gear and headed back across the inlet to our cabin.
>
> We were married the next week at the schoolhouse. Reverend Martin performed the ceremony. Grandfather and Nurse S. lived with us until Grandfather died two years later. What a joy it was to spend those years with him in Alaska. Wasn't he a hoot? It was like he was born to live here. After that, Nurse S. talked of returning to San Francisco, but then she met Lester, and they bickered enough that they decided it would be better to bicker as married folk.
>
> That's our story, Janey.
>
> Perhaps you're right, maybe future generations will find the simple tale of our love a blessing, not because it's the grandest, but because throughout, God's love shone through ever greater. From beginning to end, He was—and still is—the Rock on which we stand.
>
> All my love to you and anyone who may read this,
> Ellie
>
> P.S. In case you're wondering about James. He ended up marrying Lavinia Doodle, an heiress from New York. I've heard she's a terrible gossip who drives both James and his mother quite mad.

Authors' Note

....

Two excited authors, one husband, one adorable little girl, all on a whirlwind trip to Alaska. Sounds like fun to me! In September of 2011, Tricia, her husband, John, and their sweet little girl met me, Ocieanna, in the Juneau airport to launch our adventure. We had the same reaction as our character, Ginny. Is this the airport in their capital city? It was small and friendly—not what we're used to. But we soon fell in love with Alaska.

Our next experience reaffirmed Alaska's uniqueness—the little incident of the bear. Tricia and I were shopping for books (what else?) in the gift shop at the Mendenhall Glacier, when John came in and told

us a bear just crossed the walkway. The ranger was pretty ho-hum about it. "Yeah, she'll wander down to the meadow if you want to see her."

What a once-in-a-lifetime experience. As we stood

watching on a footbridge, the black bear hunted salmon mere feet away from us.

Not quite as harrowing an experience, but just as spectacular, was traveling in a tiny aircraft from the Juneau airport to an even smaller destination, Gustavus—the entryway to Glacier Bay. A gorgeous blue sky greeted us as we wove between high peaks toward our destination. I got to sit in the front!

The tour of Glacier Bay—amazing!

Throughout our stay, we caught a glimpse of the tiny town of Gustavus. Trust us, all the quirky facts in *Love Finds You in Glacier Bay, Alaska* are true—Bud's Rental Car, the lack of license plates, the community bulletin board, the unsecured ATM, the absence of doctors nearby, and more. Also true are the warmth of the people and sense of community. I can see why people return year after year. It's a special place.

About the Authors

....

TRICIA GOYER is the best-selling author of more than thirty novels, including *Night Song*, which won a Carol Award in 2005, and *Dawn of a Thousand Nights*, which won the same award in 2006. Her co-authored novel *The Swiss Courier* was a Christy Award nominee. She has also authored nine nonfiction books and more than three hundred articles for national publications. In 2003, Tricia was one of two authors named "Writer of the Year" at the Mount Hermon Christian Writers' Conference, and she has been interviewed by *Focus on the Family*, *Moody Midday Connection*, *The Harvest Show*, *NBC's Monday Today*, *Aspiring Women*, and hundreds of other radio and television stations. Tricia and her husband, John, have four children and one grandchild and live in Arkansas.

OCIEANNA FLEISS has cowritten two historical novels with Tricia Goyer: *Love Finds You in Lonesome Prairie, Montana* and *Love Finds You in Victory Heights, Washington*. She has written for several publications, including CBA *Marketplace* and *Guideposts*, and contributes a bi-monthly column to the *Northwest Christian Author*. Ocieanna has edited many of Tricia Goyer's novels and nonfiction titles. An avid historian, she teaches home-schooled junior high students intense history classes involving considerable research and creative methods of bringing history to life. She lives in the Seattle area with her husband and their four children.

POST CARD
CARTE POSTALE
Love Finds You

**Want a peek into local American life—past and present?
The *Love Finds You*™ series published by Summerside Press
features real towns and combines travel, romance,
and faith in one irresistible package!**

The novels in the series—uniquely titled after American towns with romantic or intriguing names—inspire romance and fun. Each fictional story draws on the compelling history or the unique character of a real place. Stories center on romances kindled in small towns, old loves lost and found again on the high plains, and new loves discovered at exciting vacation getaways. Summerside Press plans to publish at least one novel set in each of the fifty states. Be sure to catch them all!

Now Available

Love Finds You in
Martha's Vineyard, Massachusetts
by Melody Carlson
ISBN: 978-1-60936-110-5

Love Finds You in
Prince Edward Island, Canada
by Susan Page Davis
ISBN: 978-1-60936-109-9

Love Finds You in Groom, Texas
by Janice Hanna
ISBN: 978-1-60936-006-1

Love Finds You in Amana, Iowa
by Melanie Dobson
ISBN: 978-1-60936-135-8

Love Finds You in
Lancaster County, Pennsylvania
by Annalisa Daughety
ISBN: 97-8-160936-212-6

Love Finds You in Branson, Missouri
by Gwen Ford Faulkenberry
ISBN: 978-1-60936-191-4

Love Finds You in Sundance, Wyoming
by Miralee Ferrell
ISBN: 978-1-60936-277-5

Love Finds You on Christmas Morning
by Debby Mayne and Trish Perry
ISBN: 978-1-60936-193-8

Love Finds You in Sunset Beach, Hawaii
by Robin Jones Gunn
ISBN: 978-1-60936-028-3

Love Finds You in
Nazareth, Pennsylvania
by Melanie Dobson
ISBN: 97-8-160936-194-5

Love Finds You in Annapolis, Maryland
by Roseanna M. White
ISBN: 978-1-60936-313-0

Love Finds You in
Folly Beach, South Carolina
by Loree Lough
ISBN: 97-8-160936-214-0

Love Finds You in
New Orleans, Louisiana
by Christa Allan
ISBN: 978-1-60936-591-2

Love Finds You in
Wildrose, North Dakota
by Tracey Bateman
ISBN: 978-1-60936-592-9

Love Finds You in Daisy, Oklahoma
by Janice Hanna
ISBN: 978-1-60936-593-6

Love Finds You in Sunflower, Kansas
by Pamela Tracy
ISBN: 978-1-60936-594-3

Love Finds You in Mackinac
Island, Michigan
by Melanie Dobson
ISBN: 978-1-60936-640-7

Love Finds You
at Home for Christmas
by Annalisa Daughety and
Gwen Ford Faulkenberry
ISBN: 978-1-60936-687-2

COMING SOON

Love Finds You in
Lake Geneva, Wisconsin
by Pamela S. Meyers
ISBN: 978-1-60936-769-5

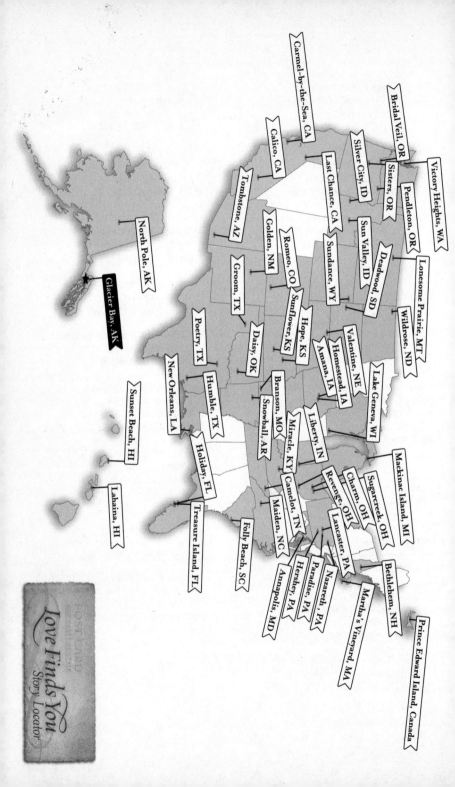